THE TROJAN
BROTHERHOOD

Berwick Coates

Published by Berwick Coates

Publishing partner: Paragon Publishing, Rothersthorpe

ISBN 978-1-78222-791-5

Cover design < acapellabookcoverdesign.com >

Book design, layout and production management by Into Print
www.intoprint.net
+44 (0)1604 832149

To

My son Stephen,

whose idea this was

Acknowledgments

The same team has helped me so many times now that these acknowledgments practically write themselves.

Mark Webb at Paragon Publishing has delivered goods with the physical production of the book, and with the necessary administration concerning all matters of layout, copyright, presentation, and protocol. He has listened patiently, as before, to my concerns and suggestions. Yvonne Reed, as usual, has brought her authoritative eye to bear on the search for wayward misprints, inconsistencies, and infelicitous aberrations of style. My son Stephen has made his regular contribution with frank comments, criticisms, and general watchful eye. And this time he has gone further: the whole idea for the book came from him. He offered a blueprint; I simply built the device.

Finally, we have an extra member. Jennifer Givner of ‹acapellabookcoverdesign› has produced an eye-catching, optimistic cover, most promptly and efficiently, and so made all our work that much easier and more rewarding.

I am grateful to all of them.

Prologue

1.

The Italian Riviera, 1968.

'SHERMAN, WILL YOU put down those goddam glasses?'

Sherman Foster twiddled the focus knobs again and shifted his buttocks on the wicker chair.

'Sure, honey.'

Bette Foster poured herself another drink and stared at her husband's taut shoulders. Evening sunlight streamed through the open window. The gold watch gleamed on his sunburned wrist. Fair hairs shone on his thick, freckled arms.

Bette fidgeted.

'Sherman, we'll lose our place at the table. Those damned Germans will take it again.'

'Aw, come on, honey, it's only a few minutes. The sun's nearly round. Gino said it would be an unforgettable view when the light flooded on to those cliffs, and I don't want to miss it.'

Bette grimaced over the whisky; she did not really like it.

'Gino this and Gino that. Two days' hire of an open boat and suddenly some unemployed fisherman is a one-man travel bureau and walking encyclopaedia.'

Sherman grunted without turning his ample back.

'I noticed you were sitting doe-eyed at his feet till you discovered he was married with a baby.'

Bette flared.

'If I had a husband who took some notice of me instead of starting up aimless conversations with every beach bum we came across – '

'Aw, Bette – '

' – and going on route marches round every classical ruin and shrine on the whole damned coast.'

'We're on holiday, aren't we? In Italy? What chance will we ever have to see all this again?'

'My feet ache, for Chrissake! I get tired.'

'Jesus, Bette, you're only thirty-two.'

Bette's face twisted.

'Thanks.'

She took another sip, grimaced again, and put the drink on the table. She cupped her hands on her elbows and walked up and down.

Sherman heard her heels clacking on the tiled floor. Reluctantly he lay down the binoculars and turned round.

'Come on, Bette. Remember why we came, huh? A fresh start. That's why I do all those ruins; that's what the Doc said.'

'What – go round ruins?'

Sherman tossed his head.

'You know what I mean. A new interest, he said. Something new, anything to begin with, so long as it's different. Accepting the truth isn't enough.'

Bette opened and shut her eyes as if they were pricking. Sherman leaned forward with his elbows on his knees.

'Bette, we have to do something, start something, build something, to take the place of – ' he hesitated ' – to take the place.'

'Ruins.'

'Bette, you're not being fair. You liked the idea back home.'

'That was back home. Right now, I hate ruins, and I want dinner.'

Sherman lifted his shoulders.

'Okay, okay, anything you say.'

He looked at her and smiled pacifically.

'Tell you what – anything you want to do tomorrow – anything you like. Just say it, and we'll do it.'

Bette stopped pacing.

'I'm sorry, Sherm.'

Sherman stood up and put a large arm round her shoulders.

'That's my girl.'

He kissed her hair.

'But before we go – '

She simpered.

'Yes?'

He dashed to the window and seized the binoculars.

'C'mon, Bette – look at this. Right now – look at it.'

He held them out, and pointed with his other hand.

'Honest to God, Bette, have you ever seen anything like it?'

Bette looked, and gasped. It was a staggering sight. No one would ever believe such colours. She twiddled the knobs to focus. Sherman stood behind her and pointed.

'See the road? Gino says – '

' "Gino says," ' she mimicked, grinning.

He punched her playfully.

'Yeah, Gino says the sun hits the bend in the road almost exactly as the bus comes round the corner. Set your watch by it, he says.'

'He knows, of course.'

'He should do; his wife comes back on it from work three times a week. See? Here it comes.'

'What does she do with the baby? Does she take it with – '

Bette stiffened.

'My God!'

She felt Sherman's hand tighten on her shoulder, and knew he had seen too.

It was all the more sickening because it was silent and in slow motion. Even the noise of the explosion as it hit the rocks below and burst into flames was muffled and delayed by distance.

Bette laid down the glasses and looked up at her husband, her face haggard.

'My God!' she said again.

They both had the same thought.

'Gino!'

*   *   *   *   *   *

'D'you think they'll ever know?'

Sherman gazed out of the window.

'I doubt it. Not for sure. There were only two eyewitnesses. Both said the vehicle just swerved suddenly and went off the edge. You know what those corniche roads are like – straight up a cliff one side, and straight down the other.'

'What about the wreckage?'

'Aw, hell, Bette, we've been through this before.'

'Tell me again.'

Sherman looked searchingly at his wife, but did as she asked.

'From what I could gather, they failed to find most of it. What they did find was bent and burnt, consistent with the explosion it made hitting the rocks.'

'Nothing suspicious.'

'Nothing whatsoever. The driver either had a fit or a heart attack, or he was blinded suddenly by the sun. Other drivers have complained of it before, appearing low and quickly like that, at that place, at that time of day. The company said it was even considering changing the timetable.'

'And they never found the driver's body.'

'Never found the driver's body. They never found ten or twelve others either. I shouldn't think there was much of what they did find.'

Sherman stared moodily out at the billowing banks of cloud below them.

He could still see Gino's stricken face.

'When the police tell me they find Peppina, I shake with fear. I cannot do what they want. My brother Marco – he go there for me – and he – he tell them what – what they need to know.'

Strange how hard it was to shake off a feeling of guilt, yet Sherman's intellect told him there was absolutely no reason for it.

Bette felt it too, even more strongly. He was sure this was why she went over it again and again, asking the same questions to which she already knew the answers.

But there was nothing else to know.

There had been a terrible tragedy, and it had been a million-to-one accident. The evidence, both human and mechanical, was largely buried in the Mediterranean; and even if it were to be recovered, it was most unlikely that the slightest scrap of extra knowledge would be added to what was already established.

True, true, true. Yet an obstinate tremor of conscience, an unreasoning streak of puritanism, told them that they should not be so happy now.

Not that they had been short of reassurance.

Firstly from Gino's brother, Marco.

'Believe me, we are saving Gino. He is mad with grief. He will kill the child and then himself. He has sworn to. It is I who have heard him.'

He had gone out of his way to settle Bette's mind.

'Signora, you can do this much better than I.'

A succession of officials and public servants said substantially the same, especially when faced with a whole file of affidavits and disclaimers and guarantees from Marco and his next of kin.

Sherman, who had usually found trouble doing nothing more complicated than getting through the customs, was amazed at the speed with which foreign red tape could be cut.

Had it not been for that lawyer, they could have become almost suspicious, if only because of his expensive cufflinks and the cut glass decanters in his office.

'Who's paying for all this?' said Bette, her eyes narrowing.

The lawyer smiled and spread his manicured hands.

'Do not disturb yourself, Signora. It is not I, nor you, nor Marco. I represent the insurance company. Believe me, they can well afford it. And believe me too when I tell you that it is not often that a man with my sad duties at such a time can also perform a service which will bring such relief to some and such happiness to others.'

Every brush with officialdom was equally swift and painless – registrars, immigration, customs, police, embassy staff, passport control, doctors, security, welfare. It was all too good to be true.

Bette said so in as many words.

Sherman put an arm round her shoulders.

'Honey, we've seen just about everyone except the Secretary-General of the United Nations. It couldn't be more legal.'

'I know, but – '

'And it's what you've always wanted. What we've both always wanted. It's just that we never expected it to come this way.'

'And so fast.'

Sherman gave her a squeeze.

'Fast, slow, or medium – honey, I don't care how it comes; I've never seen you so happy.'

Bette smiled radiantly.

Sherman leaned across and gazed into his wife's lap. He poked a finger into the white bundle and peered.

'Hi, Gina Foster.'

2.

The Home Counties, 1973.

'HELLO, AUDREY? ROSEMARY here. . . . What? . . . Oh – fine, fine, thank you. Look, I'm sorry, Audrey, but I won't be able to get over for coffee this morning. Peter's car is in dock and he's taken the Escort. . . . What? . . . I know, it is rather tiresome, but – well, he is the bread-winner, poor dear. . . . y – y – yes. . . . well, actually, it's probably a blessing in disguise because I've a million things to do this morning; John and Esther are coming with the children, and you know what a. . . . What? . . . Is she? Again? . . . My! It can't be more than a year since she. . . . yes, yes, I know. . . it is the fashion these days. Gets it over with quickly, I suppose. . . . Yes. . . . yes. . . . yes. . . . look. . . . y – yes. . . . Look, Audrey, I'd really better be. . . . What? . . . Already? . . . But they only bought it in the spring. . . . Did they? . . . I always maintain that. . . . Y – yes. . . . It's a funny thing you should say that, because the Russells have done it again. . . Yes. . . . Of course I'm sure. I have it from Polly Bevan, and she. . . . Yes. . . . Well, I mean! . . . Just what I say. The Russell household must be like the United Nations by now. God knows, Audrey, I'm as broadminded as the next person, but it's the *way* they get them. I know it must make you pretty bohemian, being globetrotting journalists and all that, but really – first there was the Cambodian child – you know, the cross-eyed one. Then they came back from Chungking with that little yellow goblin. Oh, and the boy from one of those awful banana republics. God knows which side he was on. Thank Heaven they didn't christen him "Fidel".

'But they've surpassed themselves this time. D'you know where they've got this one from? A refugee camp in the Middle East. . . . What? . . . Oh, I don't know – Arab, Jewish, Palestinian – they're all refugees, aren't they, more or less. All pretty much the same colour anyway. Peter says they haven't had a stable political situation there since the Crusades.

'Anyway, it seems there was a bomb or something – bits of corrugated iron scattered for miles. . . . What? . . . Oh, some Liberation Front or other rang up the *Daily Mirror*, I think, and said they'd done it. The Russells went in with their notebooks and their cameras, and came out with another infant – swaddling clothes and all. . . . Mmmm?. . . . Less than three months, I'm told.

'Pardon?. . . . I've no idea. . . . "Ali Baba" or "Jesus", I should think. They've no regard for convention. . . . That's just what I say. . . . I shouldn't call myself prejudiced, but I do think there's a limit to the extent to which one can flout the feelings of one's neighbours. I was saying to Polly only the other day. . . . What? . . . Oh. Yes. . . . Yes, of course. I understand. . . I'll pass on your good wishes to John and Esther, shall I? . . . Yes, and to the children. . . . Yes, it was just that. . . . Y – yes. . . . No, no. Not at all. . . . Goodbye, Audrey.'

My word – Audrey could certainly talk.

3.

Normandy, 1981.

'A STORY, PAPA.'

Armand Sainval smiled at the freshly-scrubbed, shining cheeks.

'What is it to be?'

'My story. How you found me.'

'Again?'

'Again.'

Armand tucked the blankets round the pulled-up knees.

'Well, it was like this. Mummy and I were on holiday – '

'In Yugalsovia!'

Armand nodded solemnly.

'In Yugalsovia. We had lots of nice times by the seaside – '

'And you got sunburned.'

'I got sunburned.'

'And Mummy said you looked like a lobster.'

Armand frowned severely.

'Who is telling this story?'

'Sorry, Papa.'

Pink hands locked themselves round blanketed knees.

Armand coughed importantly.

'Now – where was I?'

'Sunburned.'

'Ah, yes.'

'Like a lobster.'

'Hmmm. Well – just to make a change, we borrowed a motor car and went for a drive away from the seaside, and we stayed at a very nice village up in the hills.

'We drank lots of wine and had some lovely dinners. Many people there were very kind to us. We were sad to leave. We went back to the seaside again – '

' – and two days later – '

'Ah, ah, ah!'

Armand held up a warning finger.

Pixie eyes gleamed above a gummy gap in front teeth.

'Sorry, Papa.'

'Two days later we heard on the radio, and we saw on the television, that there had been a terrible earthquake. The ground rumbled and roared and shook, and houses came tumbling down.

'Luckily it was a bright, sunny day, and most people were outdoors at the time, so not many were hurt. Still, some unlucky ones were buried in the ruins, and Mummy and I were worried. We had been so happy in this village that we thought we had to go back and help.

'When we got there we found nearly all the houses were down, except for a few outside the village up the valley.'

'What about the crash?'

'I'm coming to that. While Mummy and I were helping to clear away the bricks and the stones, we heard a crash from higher up the valley. And we looked up, and those other houses I told you about – remember?'

An eager nod.

'They had fallen down too. The policeman said there

must have been another small rumble in the earth.

'They sent firemen and scientists and doctors and nurses and special men from the president's palace to see that everything was all right. Everyone worked very hard right through the night.

'Mummy and I were having breakfast in the morning when one of the special men came to see us. He said he had been to the houses up the valley and had found a gentleman and a lady dead – a very handsome young gentleman and a very beautiful lady. He said it was very sad. But he was pleased too because he had found a small baby, still alive, and fast asleep.'

Another broad, gappy grin.

'Yes, there you were, in a great pile of bricks and dust, with a big, big beam just above your nose holding up everything else, and your cradle and your clothes were covered in dust, and you were fast asleep.'

'Was I covered all over?'

'All over. At least that's what the special man said. He was the one who found you.

'He showed you to us. Of course you had been cleaned up a bit by that time and you were wide awake.'

'Was I crying?'

'No, you were gurgling.'

Giggles were so violent that knees and bottom wriggled.

'Then the special man said that there was nobody to look after you because nobody knew the young lady and gentleman in the house; they had only just come to the valley. And did we know anyone who wanted a little baby.

'And we said that was very easy because we did, because Mummy had been very ill and couldn't have

16

babies, and it was very lucky you coming along because that way everyone was happy.

'The special man was very kind and helped us, because you know it is difficult taking babies out of one country into another. We had to see lots of people – '

'Who?'

'Oh – people like – um – doctors and agents and special men – in big offices – who gave us very expensive drinks, and they took us to see more people in more offices. We had to answer lots of questions and sign lots of papers.

'But in the end the special man in the biggest office said everything was fine and we could bring you home.'

Armand unwound the blanket from the knees.

'And here you are, and it is time for little girls in dusty cradles to go to sleep.'

'Yes.'

'Goodnight, my pet.'

'Papa!'

'You forgot something.'

'What was that?'

'The special man, in the big office.'

'What about him?'

'You forgot the gold buttons on his shirt.'

'Ah, yes, so I did. I'll put them in next time. Remind me.'

'Yes.'

'Goodnight now.'

'Goodnight, Papa.

Chapter One

London, 1984.

ICE CUBES CLATTERED into cavernous tumblers of Dartington glass that must have weighed a ton.

A beautifully-manicured hand held the whisky bottle poised in mid-air.

'I'm afraid we have only *Glenmorangie*, Mr. Bliss. Will that do?'

Yes, that would do very well. Rather a lot of water followed, but Bliss made no demur.

For *Glenmorangie* he was prepared to tolerate the dilution. It was so long since he had tasted malt whisky that he was almost prepared to accept lemonade with it.

The lights from the cocktail cabinet threw flashes from the whisky on to immaculate white cuffs in which gleamed solid gold cufflinks.

'There. You will forgive me if I do not join you. Business habits of a lifetime, you understand. Cheers.'

The cufflinks flickered to and fro over a buff file spread open on a sumptuous leather-topped desk. Discreet lights shone everywhere with never a hint of anything so tasteless as a glare or an exposed bulb.

Expensively-capped teeth flashed a smile.

'Now, Mr. Bliss. Mr. – ' a slight hesitation over the file ' – Mr. Hector Bliss. Yes?'

'Yes.'

'My employer has instructed me to ascertain your suitability for the position, though I hasten to reassure you that there is to be nothing said or done that might be construed as mere formula or routine. This is to be an informal meeting, and you are to feel as free to ask questions of me as I do of you.'

The neatly-turned phrases, just the merest trifle ornate, spoke of fine command of the language; they also spoke of a certain lack of genuineness. There was too the faintest vestige of an accent that was difficult to place.

Bliss found himself thinking that it would be a good idea to be well on his guard. He sipped his whisky and watched the white hand turn a page.

Rimless glasses were adjusted on a pale, ascetic nose.

'Your letter was most informative.'

'Were there many?'

Light blue eyes flashed up.

'I beg your pardon?'

'Did you get many applications?'

Bliss had decided that the best form of defence was attack. He had no intention of giving the impression of a nervous, out-of-work ex-schoolmaster sitting on the end of a stool and twiddling his cap.

The eyes dropped to the page.

'A gratifying number.'

A courteous, uninflected reply, which told him nothing, and was intended to tell him nothing. *Touché*!

'In case it should be a source of gratification to you, I can reveal that you are on a short list. A very short list.'

Which could also mean more than one thing. Humouring him, and at the same time telling him, perhaps, to mind his own damn business. *Touché* again.

'Now, Mr. Bliss, your background. You say your father

is American?'

'Yes, but he came over here long before the War. He took up a lecturing post at an English university.'

'Ah, yes – I have it. Homer Bliss.'

He raised his head and pretended to search his memory.

'I seem to recollect the name. Was he not at one time a classical scholar of some repute?'

'Not "was" – "is". He is very much alive. He has retired now, but still contributes regularly to the learned journals.'

You insinuating bugger, thought Bliss. You pretended to think that Dad was dead and contrived to imply that Dad was past it, all at one go. And you didn't have to rack your brains. I'll bet a pound to penny you knew all the time.

'Ah, yes, of course,' came the smooth answer. 'I beg your pardon. Pre-classical Greece was – is his speciality, I believe.'

'Yes.'

Well, you've done *some* homework, at least. Dad is well known in scholarly circles, but his name is not exactly a household word. Still, I'm not going to let you get away with it that easily. Let's see how much you really know.

Bliss raised innocent eyebrows.

'Certain features of pre-classical Aegean civilisation, actually – Achaean and Dorian invasions, the Mycenean settlements, and economic and military rivalry with Asia Minor. Dad is a world expert on the Trojans too.'

The blue eyes were glazing slightly.

'Yes, yes.'

Bliss pushed him further back.

'That's why Dad had me christened "Hector". I have

two brothers called "Priam" and "Paris".'

'Yes, yes, of course.'

That'll teach you!

The eyes went back to the buff file.

'If I may run through your career, Mr. Bliss. Oh – your mother is in good health, I trust?'

You dare; you just dare.

'Yes, she is very well, thank you.'

'Good, good. Now, it says here – public school. Which one?'

Bliss told him.

'And preparatory school before that, presumably?'

'No. Common old council school. My father, being American, had a lot of pretty democratic ideas about education. Mother is solid bourgeois stock and agreed with him.'

Bliss found himself chuckling.

'No airs and graces for her sons. But when the chance of a scholarship came along, of course we were encouraged to aim high.'

'The best of both worlds, in fact.'

'I like to think so, yes. The experience from each has served me very well since.'

'In the Army.'

'In the Army and in my teaching career.'

He winced inwardly at the use of the word 'career' to describe the last dozen years or so.

'Let us take things in order.'

Bliss was not sure whether the remark was a piece of self-discipline or a reproof. However, having put himself level by means of the Achaeans and Dorians, he was content to let it go.

'You say here – "history degree" – and you give the

university. May I ask what class of degree?'

'I scraped a third.'

No sense in being coy. He had never been truly academic, as Pri and Parry had been. He had gone to university because it had never really occurred to him not to. Mum was proud, and Dad of course was delighted. Classics was out. No matter how much he worshipped Dad and loved listening to him talk, he could never see himself putting up with three solid years of undiluted Plautus and Pindar. After considering, and rejecting, most of the other 'normal' subjects, he settled for History, because he adored the military side of it. His excellent memory allowed him to retain with ease endless details of dates and battles and foreign names and casualty figures.

University had turned out to be a most enjoyable place, and he had never been short of sporting fixtures and entertainment rendezvous. Hence the 'scraped' third-class degree.

He found himself not caring about the impression this made. The more the interview went on, the more the suspicion grew that his success or failure would not depend on the quality of his degree or the brilliance of his record.

'And then National Service.'

'Yes. I was lucky enough to get a commission. I found I liked it, converted it to a Short Service Commission, and later to a Regular one.'

'Any active service?'

'Yes, if you count anti-terrorist campaigns and police actions in civil wars. I can supply details if you wish, or alternatively you can check with War Office records.'

In other words, if you know about Dad, you already know about me. And I know you know. And now you know that I know you know. So let's get on, shall we?

'No, no further enquiries will be necessary in that quarter. You left the Army with the rank of Major, I see.'

The thin eyebrows lifted the smallest trifle necessary to indicate that comment was being invited.

'Yes. I couldn't see myself making it to half-colonel, and, looking around me, the Army suddenly seemed full of majors who weren't going to make it to half-colonel. I had the chance to re-train, and the time seemed ripe to – er – '

'To step out.'

'Yes.'

'Into schoolteaching.'

'Schoolmastering, yes.'

Try as he would, he could never come to terms with being called a 'school*teacher*'. It was difficult to analyse why . . . something condemnatory about it, perhaps, as if he were being labelled for life, like being called a Mormon. Or maybe it savoured too much of shiny suits and chalk dust, of crocodiles of noisy kids in crowded streets, or mountainous piles of unmarked yellow exercise books. 'Schoolmaster' was not ideal, but it was an improvement; it suggested, for some reason he couldn't fathom, a more dignified, academic atmosphere, with obviously a greater air of command. Schoolteachers were harassed; schoolmasters were in control. Schoolteachers walked, or at best proceeded; schoolmasters strolled or strode.

But he never really got to the bottom of it.

'You taught History?'

'Yes. I'd kept up my interest in military history, and my own Army experience naturally reinforced it. I had found in the Army that I enjoyed lecturing, so it seemed a natural progression. I had a good knowledge of games, and of course of various other outdoor pursuits. A lot of my teaching time was spent out of the classroom.'

He smiled.

'It's surprising how much more notice boys take of you the minute they see you in a track suit or a combat smock.'

The capped teeth flashed, but the pale eyes remained dead.

'Yes, I'm sure.'

The cufflinks flickered again over the file.

'You left your post only recently.'

'I resigned, yes.'

'May I ask why?'

'Combination of things, really. Ours was a grammar school which had gone comprehensive. Well, I had survived that. Thanks to my mother and father, I had roughed it as a lad, and I was able to relate to our new children more easily than many men with better degrees than me. But I did value my sixth-form work. Last year our local authority reorganised everything and took away our sixth form. So that was that.'

'Could you not have applied to other schools?'

'Not at my age. I don't know how familiar you are with our educational system, but I'm afraid you're over the hill at thirty-eight, never mind forty-eight.'

'But all your experience. . . . '

'Doesn't count these days, I'm afraid. They're not interested in experience. What impresses them is fancy terms and fashionable philosophy. You must learn to use the right words like "rationale" and "subsume" and "holistic". That's a very good one – "holistic"; they like that. But you try filling in application forms and writing words like "example" and "leadership" and "discipline" and "specialist knowledge" and "excellence" and you're immediately in the leper colony.'

He hadn't meant to say all that. It made him look a bit obsessional, at the very least as if he was suffering from a bad attack of sour grapes.

What the Hell – the damage was done now. Bliss made a dismissive gesture.

'There were other things too. Our only daughter died, then our marriage broke up. Everything seemed to have come to a full stop.'

God – it was getting worse. Not only was he up to his ears in sour grapes; he was steeped in self-pity as well.

'What made you apply for this post?'

'It was unusual; it was different; it was abroad. I like the idea of a one-to-one situation. It takes in other subjects besides my own, which will be good for me; I shall have to do some fresh learning. Who knows – perhaps I was getting stale.'

'Nothing else?'

The eyes gazed unblinking.

'You will lose nothing by being frank.'

Bliss sighed.

'Well, if you must know, the wording of the advertisement. I nearly missed it, by the way. It was only a chance meeting that brought it to my notice. You know those things I was talking about just now – about "leadership" and "discipline" and "excellence" and so on? Well, I got the impression that whoever wrote that advert might for once be interested in someone who believed in them. I felt I had something to offer the boy.'

A very pretty speech. Even so, it was partly true. Something in him did genuinely respond when he read the tiny print in the 'Personal' column. Funny how stray remarks in chance conversations can lead you to strange places. Funny too how that chap had only just finished glancing down the 'Personal' column when they started talking.

What was even more true, though – and Bliss had no intention of admitting this bit – was that he badly needed somewhere to run to.

The Army had proved a dead end. Teaching was now a dead end. Thanks to Joy going off, his marriage was a dead end, though he couldn't in honesty say it was all grief. And Sarah was dead – and, if he were totally honest, he couldn't say that was all grief either. Relief intruded often enough to make him feel guilty.

Still, there was a yawning gap.

Mum and Dad had been wonderful, but wouldn't spoil him much longer. Mum's Yorkshire grit would come to the surface sooner or later.

'You'd best get on, son.'

He could hear her saying it.

Pri had helped him sell the house and arrange the sharing of assets with Joy. He had also advised him on the best way to invest his remaining funds. What with that and his Army money, he wasn't short of a pound or two, but it wouldn't last for ever. And now that the house had gone, he had no home, no base. Parry had offered him a job, but he knew it was charity, and turned it down.

No – he needed time and space to – well – he needed time and space.

The cufflinks closed the file.

'Now, it's your turn, Mr. Bliss. I'm sure you must have questions you wish to ask me.'

The ball had been tossed at his feet. Time for some practical demonstrations then. No fancy dribbling, but enough moves to show that he knew his way round the field.

'May I ask about the boy?'

'Certainly.'

The file was pushed aside. Elbows leaned. Cuffs shot further. Blue veins stood out against white flesh as fingers clasped under the desk light.

'His name is Alan. He is eleven years old. He is fond of school, and enjoys most outdoor sports. He is a bright, lively lad, and gets on well with people.'

One hand was held up to forestall the next question.

'In case you should think that such a terse summary should reflect the naturally biased views of an indulgent parent, I have, at my employer's behest, prepared a file on the boy's record to date. You can judge for yourself.'

A second, much thicker, buff file came across the desk.

My word, they were thorough. Besides the school reports, there were photostats of every feature of the child's life – medical certificates, inoculation records, dental appointment cards, routine intelligence tests, receipts for purchase of clothing (he was certainly a much-dressed young man); there were copies of his attempts at writing, drawing, and calculation at every age from five onwards; there were group photographs of diminutive teams and Nativity play casts and museum outings (clipboards clutched uniformly to chests). The reports spoke inevitably of Alan's 'steady progress' and 'sound achievement' and 'general all-round capability', though Bliss noted that more 'C' and 'B' grades appeared than 'A's. But that was not necessarily significant; he had long ago lost count of the number of occasions on which a primary school's judgment of a child and a secondary school's judgment of him differed so widely that you kept looking back at the name to make sure they were discussing the same one.

So far as he could tell, Master Alan Sherrif, with his healthy outdoor tan, his dark eyes, and his wayward curls, looked a pretty ordinary, lively, likely lad.

'Thank you.'

Bliss passed back the file.

'You said abroad, I believe, in southern France.'

'The advert said southern Europe, but you are correct in deducing that it is in France.'

Elementary, my dear Watson. You're not going to put me down now that I've got this far.

'You did also specify that fluent French would be an advantage.'

Another surgical flash of the teeth.

'So we did, so we did. Where did you pick up your French, Mr. Bliss?'

Parry and thrust, eh? 'Pick up', not 'learn' – as if he'd found it lying around with wet cigarette ends.

'I was well taught at school. My father is an excellent linguist; he doesn't spend all his time in the first and second millennia BC. And we boys had dozens of holidays in France – most Easter holidays and nearly every summer. I have been told by Frenchmen that my accent is good.'

Pick the bones out of that.

The stance was deftly changed.

'You will doubtless wish to know more about the domestic background. The main family home is on the Côte d'Azur, near Cannes. It is set in its own estate behind one of the lesser-known resorts on the coast – Ste. Sophie. Perhaps you have heard of it.'

Bliss had, just. He inclined his head the smallest casual

fraction to indicate that ex-Army, ex-teacher has-beens were not all totally untravelled bumpkins.

'Ah, good. Well, there is a smaller village higher up, called, naturally, Ste. Sophie-en-haut. The house is a kilo-metre or two away from this village – "Ste. Sophie-les-Mimosas". '

There was the briefest of pauses.

I know just what you're thinking, you supercilious blighter. You're thinking – shall I tell him that the area is famous for its mimosa. If you tell me and I don't know, you're one up. If you tell me and I do know, you've been caught out underestimating me.

Caution prevailed.

'There are other homes in London and Switzerland, and business flats in Sydney, New York, Buenos Aires, Johannesburg, and Hong Kong.'

Diamond league stuff, obviously, unless His Nibs was merely the front man for big corporations. And brass didn't necessarily mean class, as his mother was fond of saying. However, this was clearly the build-up; the man himself was due to be announced any minute.

Cuffs shot and fingers folded again. Out came the veins.

'It is only fair at this juncture that I reveal to you details of your prospective employer.'

It was like the last chapter of a cheap thriller – 'and, thanks to my detailed analysis of the beerstains found on the milkman's thermal underwear, I can now reveal to you that the murderer's name is . . . . '

Bliss composed his features into an attitude of respectful attention.

'Alan's father is Sir Alec Sherrif, Chairman of . . . . '

Oh, *that* Sherrif! Of course. Stupid of me.

'President of . . . . Other business interests in . . . . ' The recital ground on.

Sir Alec Sherrif, eh? 'K.B.E.', and God knows what else. My word, we have landed up with the first eleven, haven't we? When the financial press wasn't listing yet another take-over, the tabloids were carrying double-page spreads of his wife, dripping more diamonds to the square inch than Elizabeth Taylor and Zsa Zsa Gabor put together, cutting a silk ribbon in front of a cancer hospital or a transplant research clinic. Failing that, he was always coming to the eleventh-hour rescue of struggling opera companies or beleaguered archaeological foundations.

No wonder the boy went to that expensive prep. school. But that raised another question, and, since the recital of Sir Alec's multifarious activities had at last subsided, he asked it.

'What is the point of a private tutor at this stage? Surely the boy will proceed to Common Entrance and then public school?'

'Not necessarily. Sir Alec enjoys experimentation, and feels that a spell of private tuition would help to develop the boy's knowledge and skills in those subjects he will need to study if and when he does proceed to public school.'

'You mean, put him ahead in the game?'

An austere nod.

'If you choose to express it in those terms, yes.'

So Sir Alec wasn't taken in either by all those reports about 'good progress' and 'excellent development'. Bully for him.

'Sir Alec would also like to see more of his son, and inclines to the view that the boy might benefit from more regular contact with his home and family on a long-term basis. Even if he does go on to public school at thirteen, he will have had two years at home to strengthen and develop family ties.'

'But why now? The summer holidays are coming up soon.'

How long would it take him, he wondered, to stop dividing the year automatically into 'terms'?

'Sir Alec, no doubt like yourself, is wary of the dangers of excessive haste or extremes of practice in educational experiments, and therefore proposes a trial period for the duration of the summer holidays. If it proves successful, the boy will be withdrawn from his school at the commencement of the autumn term.'

'So I'd be on probation, as you might say?'

Well, you said I'd lose nothing by being frank.

'In a sense, yes. But I should stress that the scheme is intended to be experimental in more than one direction. Not only would we require to be satisfied with your performance, Mr. Bliss; you would need to feel happy and fulfilled in your work with us. Sir Alec would need to be assured that the new arrangement was proving beneficial, and of course the boy's own feelings would be consulted.'

Lips were pursed.

'I need hardly point out that, in the event of Sir Alec instructing me to terminate your contract prematurely, you would be reimbursed to the full extent of your original contracted time, and would receive moreover an *ex gratia* payment to cover travel, inconvenience, and re-settlement.'

'Very handsome.'

Another nod.

'I can assure you that my employer's terms are most generous.'

I'll bet!

'But won't the boy object to doing lessons right through the summer holidays? I know when we went to France as lads, we practically lived outdoors.'

'Since it is to be a trial period, Sir Alec sees no advantage to be gained by insisting on a full timetable which may make too many demands on the boy's willingness. Moreover, he is anxious to develop his son's outdoor interests, an area in which your own experience may be particularly relevant. He would be prepared to leave the arrangement of the day's time very much to the boy's inclinations and to your own discretion and judgment.

'If, by the end of the summer holiday, the experiment has been deemed a success, you will be offered a more permanent, and, quite probably, a more remunerative contract.'

Before Bliss could even raise his eyebrows, more gilt was carefully laid on the gingerbread.

'If the succeeding two years or so prove satisfactory, there is always the possibility that Sir Alec, and his son, may wish to continue the arrangement.'

'What, right up to "O" Level?'

All those bunsen burners and balances and isosceles triangles, which he had said goodbye to so happily after his own 'O' Levels, now suddenly loomed larger and more frightening than ghosts into King Richard's tent before Bosworth. 'O' Level History and English, even Geography and French, were one thing; Maths and the sciences were quite another.

Fingers smoothed out an imaginary wrinkle in the virginal blotting pad.

'It is not beyond the bounds of likelihood.'

'I see.'

'There is plenty of time for you to consider all the implications, Mr. Bliss. No long-term assurances will be required from you at this stage.'

A typewritten sheet was passed across.

'Those are my employer's financial terms. As you can see, they compare very favourably with those offered by your Burnham Committee.'

Favourably! They dwarfed them.

'You will also notice a separate grant for periodic travel to and from England by mutual agreement. If you so desire, facilities can be arranged for you to continue pension payments. You may retain that sheet, by the way.'

Not 'keep it', but 'retain that sheet'. The English was so – well, so shiny. And where the Devil did he come from?

'Subject to our acceptance of each other, Sir Alec envisages your commencing your duties some time in late May or June. Alan will still be at school, of course, but it will enable you to become acquainted with the household and its staff, and to assess the potentialities of the surrounding area for any outdoor education schemes that you find coming to mind. You will also have the opportunity to arrange what orders and purchases you require of text-books and teaching materials. You will have *carte blanche*.'

– I need hardly point out!

It was too smooth for words. The job had not been offered to him, but the interview was proceeding as if it had. Everything, absolutely everything, had been thought of.

More wrinkles were ironed out of the blotting pad.

'We do not require a considered reaction immediately, Mr. Bliss, and we need time ourselves to assess what has transpired today.'

And time to see the rest of that 'very short list' – if it existed. So no offer was forthcoming just yet. That could be simply in order to keep him in his place. The conviction was growing that, short list or no short list, this job was his as soon as he gave the word. All the more reason, then, to keep *them* in *their* place.

'I should like a day or two to think it over.'

'Of course, of course. Shall we say by Monday next? Good. And, should any queries arise in your mind in the meantime, I am at your disposal at this number, or in this office. Do feel free to ring at any time, or fix an appointment with my secretary.'

An embossed card appeared as if by sleight of hand between two pale, veined fingers.

Bliss gulped the last of his *Glenmorangie*, leaned forward, and took it.

'Thank you.'

'And now, if you have no further questions, Mr. Bliss . . . .'

The eyebrows were raised in interrogation, but this was clearly the regal dismissal.

'No, no. That's fine, thank you. You will be hearing from me.'

'Or you will be hearing from us.'

Capped teeth paraded in rows again. The remark was dressed up as a joke, but the thrust was obvious.

Touché again, you swine.

*   *   *   *   *   *

'Well, what do you think, Aunt Jane?'

'Pass me those number tens.'

'Here.'

A wrist flicked in impatience.

'No, no – the number tens – there.'

'Oh. Sorry.'

The fingers began their rhythmic movements, persistent yet unobtrusive, active yet restful and reassuring, like the pendulum of a long-standing grandfather clock. One of the many things Bliss admired about Aunt Jane was her ability to combine knitting with total concentration on a conversation.

'More to the point, Hector, what do *you* think?' The eyes were down over the needles.

Bliss scratched his cheek.

'On the face of it, it's impossible to fault it. I'm being offered easy, congenial work, which I can arrange entirely as I please, in a superb part of the world, at a salary far higher than I've ever earned in my life.'

'Then why are you hesitating?'

Eyes looked up now. Over heavy-rimmed spectacles. Very direct. Bliss fidgeted

'I feel a bit like a chap meeting a barrow-boy in the street who is giving away five-pound notes to one and all. Why? Why?'

'Well?'

'Well, what's the catch?'

'Does there have to be one? This Mr. Sherrif, you say, is very rich, and very powerful. So he is used to getting his own way. And he is accustomed to paying well for what he wants.'

'But why me? Why am I so special?'

'Who says you are? You haven't been offered it yet.'

'No, but I'm going to be.'

'Any why not? If I were your cufflink man, I'd think you were just what the doctor ordered.'

Bliss grinned.

'You're biased, Aunt Jane.'

The steady eyes blinked.

'Biased, maybe, but not blind. You were a good officer, Hector, and a good teacher, and you have a lot to offer that boy.'

Bliss grimaced.

Aunt Jane switched needles at the end of a row.

'It'll do you good to be at close quarters to a young person again.'

Bliss shook his head. Only somebody close and honest like Aunt Jane would have referred to Sarah. Not even Pri or Parry had dared to do that.

'I'm not so sure. It's not the same. He won't be entirely mine.'

'Neither was Sarah.'

God – that hurt!

It was not until Sarah had died that he had asked himself that question: had he tried too hard to make her his own blood daughter? While she was alive there had been no time, no resources left; he and Joy had been too busy puzzling over her moods, her hatreds, her callous outbursts; too busy with injured feelings over her constant rejection of their love; too busy with shame over dealings with angry teachers and doctors and policemen and court officials and probation officers. During her lifetime it had been pain and rage and bafflement and despair. With her death had come relief – but guilt too. Not only guilt at the relief, but guilt about the whole tragic, short life. How much had it been their fault?

Aunt Jane had snapped him out of that too.

'You *learn* from the past, Hector; you don't live in it.'

Bliss poured another cup of tea. The needles clicked away. One of Aunt Jane's priceless gifts was to know when to stop persuading.

'He certainly looked a pleasant enough lad,' said Bliss half to himself. 'From his record.'

Aunt Jane sipped her tea and offered another biscuit. Bliss put up a hand.

'And I could drop in and see Joseph on the way.'

'You could indeed.'

'And it would be a way of finding out whether I want to continue with teaching in any way, or whether it's time to strike out in a completely new direction.'

'That's right.'

Bliss smiled.

'I'm persuading myself, aren't I?'

'Much better than having me to do it.'

'I don't see what I have to lose.'

'Only a little time, at the very worst, and you are, if anything, slightly over-endowed with that at the moment.'

Bliss got up and kissed her.

'Aunt Jane, where would we all be without you?'

Aunt Jane waved a knitting needle in the air.

'Stuff and nonsense. Now – I have some news for you too. Get me my handbag over there.'

The needle pointed imperiously.

Aunt Jane found what she wanted at once. Unlike most other women Bliss knew, she never used large handbags and she never rummaged in them; hers was more like a miniature, highly-efficient filing system, in which anything from a lipstick to an unpaid gas bill could be found at a moment's notice. The legacy, probably, of a lifetime of regular travel.

'There. Read that.'

Bliss did so. He looked up, incredulous.

'Are you going to accept?'

'Of course.'

'But how old is she, for Heaven's sake?'

'She is not tottering on the edge of the grave, if that's what you mean. And before you get around to it, neither am I.'

'But she must be older than you.'

A fierce gleam appeared in the eyes.

'Oh? Why? And don't talk as if such an idea is impossible. I'm not Methuselah.'

'Sorry.'

'And who says that ladies' companions must always be younger than their employers? You must have led a very sheltered life in the Army; you don't know anything.'

'But she may need looking after.'

'I am a nurse. And I do know when to send for a doctor.'

As so often when discussions with his favourite aunt became heated, Bliss was beginning to feel about seven years old.

Aunt Jane was the one member that most families have – the one over whose decisions the other members shook their heads and smiled wryly. To them her actions and motives seemed at best unusual, at worst, eccentric, even outrageous. To her they sprang from the most obvious and transparent common sense.

'When do you start?'

'Next month.'

'Where?'

Aunt Jane pretended innocently to count stitches.

'London, then the Riviera.'

'You're kidding.'

'I wouldn't kid you about the Carlton Hotel in Cannes, my dear boy. Or the Dorchester. I believe there was some talk of a yacht too, at la Napoule.'

'Where's that?'

'There's a marina there a few miles along from Cannes.'

Aunt Jane almost wriggled with mirth.

'Hector, they're just dripping with dollars. I told them about our early days in the States, and about the War. Then I told them some of Grandpa's stories about the frontier and all the rest, and they bought it all. They're crazy about me.'

She lifted her shoulders and raised her eyebrows in an attitude of mischief. She looked like the cat who had eaten the canary; Bliss could almost see the feathers sticking out of her mouth.

'Aunt Jane, you're impossible.'

'Pretty damn smart, though, don't you think?'

'You'll be out there when I shall.'

'It looks like it, doesn't it?'

'Why didn't you tell me?'

'I wanted your decision to be your idea, not mine.'

'That was very good of you.'

Aunt Jane shrugged.

'Pretty simple stuff for a genius. Anyway, when you get out there, you can play hookey once in a while from your Sherrif's posse and take me out to dinner.'

'Are you joking? I expect you to entertain me – with the best the Carlton has to offer.'

Aunt Jane sighed.

'No gallantry, the younger generation.'

*   *   *   *   *   *

'Hallo, Parry? . . . . How's Thelma? . . . . Good . . . . And the kids? . . . . Ah!. Well, you tell him from me to stick to the leg-breaks; far too many boys fancy themselves as fast bowlers, but true leg-spinners are rare . . . . No, I mean it; he really can turn the ball, you know. If he keeps . . . . What? . . . . Ah, yes . . . . Well, I've decided . . . . I'm going to take it . . . . No, she didn't! I made up my own mind. Just bounced a few ideas off her, that's all . . . . Here, and d'you know what? . . . . Oh, she told you . . . . I'm not surprised. She's like a dog with two tails at the moment . . . . Yes, I expect she will; I've told her to take me to dinner at the Carlton . . . . Oh, no, they've offered it all right; I said they would. I had another session with Mr. Smoothie yesterday . . . . No, I don't. And I wish I could place his accent. He's certainly not English, though he speaks it better than you or me. I don't think he's from one of the Latin countries either, yet I wouldn't mind betting he's good at their languages too . . . . I noticed some books on his office shelves in Spanish . . . . Oh, I wouldn't like to say; the best I could manage would be mid-European. That could make him anybody from Hans Christian Andersen to Count Dracula . . . . Oh, no, I shall find out soon enough . . . . I daresay we shall meet again . . . . About mid-May, I should think. I'm going to drop in on Joseph and Sylvie first . . . . Yes, I've no doubt we shall – several! Thirsty work, travelling . . . . Of course I will . . . . And let me have those snaps soon . . . . Sylvie says she hasn't seen a decent picture of Thelma and the kids since Tony was born . . . . Now, why I rang . . . . Could you arrange for one of your minions to keep an eye on the flat for me? . . . . Oh, no, tell Thelma there's no need for that; let it gather the dust . . . . No, just look in now and then and pay the "Last Demand" bills. I don't want to come back and find the telly and the gas stove re-possessed. If you need any funds ask Pri; I've given him power of attorney while I'm away . . . . The whole summer, I should think, at least until the autumn term starts. After that, it will depend on how well I've revised my trigonometry and my structure of the atom and my olfactory system . . . . Have you? I've got to try and remember how they work as well . . . . Get the sack, I should think. Watch out – I'll have to come and work for you after all . . . . Yes, it might be a chance to find out at last what exactly it is you do . . . . O.K. . . . Yes . . . . Thanks, Parry . . . . Bless you . . . . Love to Thelma.'

Well, that was that. All he had to do now was cancel the newspapers and buy a pair of sunglasses. He was practically on his way.

It suddenly hit him with tremendous forcefulness that for the first time in his life there was no external discipline, no structure, no timetable. Whatever structuring there was going to be was going to come from him. At least, that's what Smoothie Glenmorangie had said.

The whole scheme took on a more challenging aspect than he had hitherto suspected. It also occurred to him for the first time that that could explain why so many members of his family seemed to think it a good idea. He couldn't remember a decision of his in recent years which had met with such general approval.

They hadn't put it like that, of course.

Dad was pleased to see him teaching again.

'Imparting knowledge and wisdom, son. Opening people's minds – there is no finer activity on God's earth.'

Mum, down to earth as usual, homed in on the almost embarrassing financial advantages.

'It'll be good to get a bit behind you. Never does any harm to have a bit behind you.'

Pri, with that slightly motherly air that many eldest brothers adopted towards their juniors, was pleased to see him occupied, and away for a while from the scenes of his recent troubles.

Parry flashed his dazzling smile and said, 'You wouldn't have liked working for me anyway.' What he probably meant was, 'I shouldn't have liked employing you under these circumstances.'

Aunt Jane had made her views clear over the knitting needles and tea-cups.

Even Joy had no criticism to offer. He felt he owed it to her to tell her where he was going.

'You'll probably find it more congenial than the last few years.' Her lips tightened and the corners turned down. 'Ironic, isn't it, that it's only now that you're being so well paid.' The lines either side of her mouth were becoming deeper and more permanent. He noticed it more now that they were separated.

But suppose everyone were wrong. Suppose – well, to put it crudely, suppose it was a colossal con. It was conceivable. Certainly, the interview bristled with suspicious features. And smart-ass Glenmorangie was about as genuine as a nine-pound note. It had also crossed his mind, the more he looked back and considered, that the meeting and conversation he had had in the pub – that chap who 'just happened' to have been looking down the 'Personal' column – the whole thing could have been set up.

Then what if it was? Why? What was so special about Hector Bliss, B.A. (nearly failed)? Aunt Jane's faith in him was gratifying, but he was not the only man qualified to be private tutor to Master Alan Sherrif.

And the boy did exist. So did his school. He had

checked. Pri and Parry had both confirmed his information on the boy's father too.

'Paul Getty, Don Juan, and Mr. Bountiful all rolled into one' had been Parry's summary. Apparently, Sir Alec's devastating effect upon the opposite sex and his sporting interests were also well known. A truly dazzling combination, then, of cash, dash, and charity.

A pretty ponderous cheque ('to cover immediate expenses') had thudded on to his doormat with faultless timing.

So why was he hesitating?

Well, he wasn't now; he'd committed himself. A couple of weeks with Joseph and Sylvie in Languedoc, to renew his French and get his knees brown; then pack his mortar-board and away to the heavy oak front door (or the tradesmen's entrance) of 'Ste. Sophie-les-Mimosas'.

And even now, if someone had asked him why he was doing it, he couldn't have said.

Money?

A change?

A challenge?

Because he liked kids?

To save being a burden to his family?

An escape?

Or was it because of a pair of expensive gold cufflinks set in immaculate white cuffs? He couldn't for the life of him place them, but he knew he had seen them before, and he knew it went back a long time. And he knew it was something to do with Sarah.

Chapter Two

BLISS WALKED THROUGH the booking office out into the sun-drenched yard. Why was it that so many French railway stations looked under-constructed? Everything seemed flat and open and windswept. The few station buildings cowered together apologetically on the edge of a small desert of wide platform and open track rather like the minimal superstructure on the flight deck of an aircraft carrier.

He gazed familiarly about him. Civic pride, in the shape of fondly-tended flower plots, jostled for attention with civic neglect, in the shape of the same noisome 'WC Hommes' in the corner. The *Café de la Gare* looked open as usual, and, as usual, the *Hotel de la Gare* looked shut. Two small urchins, who should have been in school, kicked up dust as they practised dirt-track skidding with their bicycles. Sun beat off bare walls and paint peeled off shutters.

A new hospital was being built, with special accommodation for psychiatric patients, it seemed, judging by the forest of iron bars set into some ground-floor windows. A pall of white dust hung around the base as if someone had just been quarry-blasting. Storey after storey of faceless concrete, with rows of black rectangular eyes, were rearing up towards the cloudless sky, dwarfing the convent church behind. Which set of inmates, shut away in their own brand of seclusion, would envy the other?

Bliss sat down inside the *Café de la Gare* and treated

himself to a long, delicious *cassis à l'eau* – a tall, gracious glass, plenty of ice, a generous jug of cold water, and a long shiny spoon to stir the equally generous measure of *cassis*. That hadn't changed either, praise be. Too often, in station cafes in far more sophisticated towns, he had been subjected to a dull, squat tumbler containing a faint solution that tasted like tepid, quarter-strength Ribena.

He then treated himself to a taxi. It was a good ten miles or so, but he had all that 'immediate expenses' money burning a hole in his pocket. Joseph and Raymond, he knew, would be busy in the vineyard, and he did not wish to pull them out just for one person. Sylvie had never learned to drive. And Monique, who had jumped behind a steering wheel at the very earliest moment that the law allowed, had left home to become the wife of a hotelier in Normandy. Couldn't blame her, really. It wasn't much life for a growing girl stuck out there among fading, shuttered villages and endless acres of vines.

Bliss looked out of the taxi window. The town was spreading along the main road – bright new bungalows, a telephone exchange, two caravan parks, a restaurant, and a huge, new complex put up by the local wine co-operative, with the letters displaying its name half as tall as the roof itself. It all bespoke self-confidence and optimism.

A change from the early days of their family holidays just after the War, when they rattled and bumped over rural roads in a succession of clapped-out Fords and Austins and Standards. Places looked a good deal greyer and less cared-for then, if not actually in disrepair, even ruin. Dad would take them on obscure routes 'to save petrol', and would usually get lost. Mum would snort and say, 'You know your way round Ancient Greece better than you do France.'

But there was some method in Dad's madness. It may not have saved much petrol, but it often saved on other costs. Foreign travel allowances in those days were pitiful, and, by staying away from large towns and main roads, Dad kept eating costs as low as possible – a large consideration with three ravenous boys in the back seat.

They camped of course – fields and orchards mostly. It was in the days before the camping craze had become rigidly organised and classified. Toilet facilities under hedges were often an improvement on what rural cafes had to offer, and lack of running water was never regarded as an inconvenience by at least three members of the party.

Farmers were generous. Probably felt sorry for them. And it was still close enough to the War for most Frenchmen to be well disposed towards any Englishman (or American). Being in a sense both, Dad used to say that he was made to feel he had personally liberated France single-handed.

When Joseph Gommard offered them his barn, almost apologetically, they jumped at it. After what they had been doing, it represented four-star luxury.

God knows, Joseph didn't have much then himself – a mortgage, a prehistoric lorry, a vineyard to get back into business after two years of German occupation, and a new wife and even newer baby to keep.

One thing had led to another, and they found themselves going back time and again.

The taxi turned off the main road where the signpost said 'St. Martin de Villefort' and 'St. Martin la Forêt'. How often had they bumped along here, tired and grubby after a long day in an overheated car, but singing their heads off as they looked forward to Sylvie's cooking and Joseph's wine.

There was a new signboard beside the gate – 'St. Martin les Puits' – picked out in bright greens and reds. Above the name was a most flattering impression of the house, slightly out of perspective. Only four feet away from the pictorial grandeur lolled the old *'Chien Mèchant'* sign, grey and pitted with age, the letters burned with an old poker. Parry had done that for them in about 1952, and had put the accent on *'méchant'* the wrong way round.

Bliss smiled. Most of Joseph's *'chiens'* were about as *'méchants'* as teddy bears if you went anywhere near them with a biscuit in your hand. Fortunately for the security of the place, very few gipsies, tramps, or unwanted tradesmen had ever found that out. The postman never came beyond the box on the front gate, and the baker chose to do business from the comparative security of his driving seat.

Perhaps their caution had something to do with the fact that Joseph's preferred breed was Alsatian, and wild-eyed, rangy Alsatian at that.

The latest in the line came bounding out of the front door as the taxi pulled up. The driver swiftly wound up the window and lit a shaky cigarette, thus making it clear that on this trip the niceties of etiquette, like getting out to open the passenger door, were not going to be observed.

'Bijou, tais-toi!'

Sylvie's voice preceded her. By the time she appeared, the slavering beast was sitting decorously by the doorstep, enabling Bliss to get out and pay the watchful driver, whose cigarette was clamped tightly under his moustache. By the time Sylvie had released Bliss from her welcoming embrace, Bijou was rolling on her back with all four legs in the air. The driver, glowering and shame-faced, ground his gears, narrowly missed the gatepost, and sent a shower of dust from his spinning rear wheels over the '*Chien Mèchant*' sign.

* * * * * *

'Hello, Mummy. You're early.'

'Yes, I had this shopping to do, and I've no supervisions today. And do you know what? The college have actually found some money for re-decoration. They start on my rooms at the end of term.'

'Crumbs! I shouldn't think they've been done since Darwin and Huxley.'

Connie resisted the scholar's compulsion to point out that the reference was scarcely apt, since Darwin and Huxley were biologists, not mathematicians. Ruth was only twelve, and had done well to quote Huxley, never mind Leibniz or Lagrange. Perhaps she expected too much of her daughter.

She dumped her purchases on the hall table and watched Ruth skip towards the kitchen to put on the kettle.

I don't care what the experts tell us about equality and over-regimentation, thought Connie; school uniforms are good for children. Ruth looked lovely in hers, and adored wearing it. David would have been proud of her. It was such a joy to see her take so much pleasure in everything to do with her new school – though, come to think of it, 'new' was hardly appropriate. God – was it nearly a year? Well, nearly a complete school year anyway. University term finished in a couple of weeks, and Ruth's school broke up about six weeks after that.

Connie looked in the hall mirror and suddenly saw extra lines and the odd grey hair. Term ended in two weeks; the sick ghost was looming again.

Noises came from the lounge – the nasal banalities of a cheap American computer-drawn cartoon. It brought Connie back to practicalities.

From the mirror faded the image of the busy lecturer, the widow, the haunted victim; in their place reappeared the zealous parent.

'You haven't changed your clothes yet.'

Tea-cups clattered virtuously.

'I haven't been in a minute.'

'Long enough to put the telly on.'

Always a parent's long suit – tiresome, irrelevant logic.

The click of the top cupboard being opened. Silence while Ruth reached for the tea-caddy and thought of an evasive reply.

'There's a letter for you – on the coffee table.'

Connie smiled. A neat, if only a temporary, solution. She had a last glance at the mirror, decided that the grey hairs were perhaps not so conspicuous after all, and went into the lounge.

The familiar blue envelope, with the irritatingly detailed nomenclature:- 'Dr. C.E. Marshall (Ph.D. Cantab., B.A. Exon.)'. She snatched it up and tore it open with a finger, ignoring the paper-knife that Ruth had laid beside it from the bureau.

A last desperate hope fluttered feebly as she unfolded the expensive paper. It died as she saw the address.

'Dear Dr. Marshall . . . . '

Voices intruded upon her concentration.

' . . . . evil genius of the Universe . . . . '

49

Connie grimaced in irritation and switched off the television.

'Dear Dr. Marshall,

May I take the liberty of reminding you . . . . '

The same sickening politeness.

' . . . . as soon as it is reasonably possible after the closure of your university term . . . . '

The same sinister confidence in total compliance.

' . . . . shall we say, early to mid-June?'

The same empty courtesies.

' . . . . car to meet you at the station, or the airport, whichever mode of transport you should prefer . . . . your usual rooms . . . . every facility . . . . '

The same spurious generosity.

' . . . . cheque to cover immediate expenses, travel arrangements, and your daughter's fees for next term.'

They had never been so barefaced as that before. There was even a reference to the fact that 'consideration' had been 'taken' of the 'current rate of inflation'.

Connie sat down, almost gagging with rage.

Ruth came bustling in with sugar bowl and biscuit tin.

'Oh, Mummy, you've switched it off, and there was something on after – '

She saw her mother's strained face and the letter crumpled in her hand.

'Is it – ?'

Connie nodded.

Ruth put down the sugar and biscuits.

'Will you ring Aunt Meg or shall I?'

'No. I'll do it.'

Ruth smoothed out the front of her school dress.

'I don't mind, Mummy, really I don't. And I like Aunt Meg's cats.'

Connie wanted to fling both her arms round her daughter.

Half a mile away a kettle whistled.

*   *   *   *   *   *

The doorway darkened.

Bliss looked up. After nearly forty years he still felt a sense of awe when Joseph entered a room.

It was not merely the height, or the weight, or the breadth of shoulders, although they were impressive enough. Nor was it the steadiness of the eye, or the unhurried nature of all his gestures and movements.

The handshake was engulfing, the welcoming hug was of bear-like proportions. The eyes twinkled, and the mahogany face shone with pleasure at seeing him.

Yet there was something about Joseph – a massive stillness, perhaps, a watchfulness, a colossal sense of potential force – that made Bliss feel that, however relaxed he became, and he did, he must always take care to be on his best behaviour. He must work hard to gain and keep Joseph's respect. After ten or twelve years of schoolmastering, Bliss still felt at times like a schoolboy out to impress a much-loved teacher. Indeed there had been the odd occasion when he suspected that Sylvie herself was slightly afraid of her own husband.

However, he sat comfortably enough, in one of the ancient armchairs beside the fireplace, while Sylvie fussed round with aperitifs and the local paper, laid carefully at Joseph's elbow. Her pale skin contrasted strongly with Joseph's deep tan; Sylvie did not like the sun, and went out of doors only when she had to, and then rarely hatless.

As they sat back and sipped and exchanged family

51

news and gossip, Bliss let his eyes wander round the familiar room. The same dark-framed photographs of grandparents in high, stiff collars and high, stiff poses; the bruised television set on its rickety stand, wires trailing everywhere; the same dark wood furniture, the table fairly dappled with ring-marks from negligent wine-bottles. Clumps of dog's hair clung to cushions. Incongruously tidy, a large, neat pile of back numbers of the local paper was set behind Joseph's chair. The piano still lay open, though nobody had played it since Monique gave up lessons in 1964.

Bliss smiled, and heaved a great sigh of contentment.

Outside, there were signs of change. Joseph showed him round while Sylvie put the final touches to dinner.

A couple of workmen were humping the last of a large consignment of green plastic crates. Bliss passed comment on the extent to which plastic was invading the wine business as well as every other.

Joseph lifted his huge shoulders fractionally.

'Progress,' he said, with no inflection in his voice to indicate his view of it. 'You should see the wine shelves in the supermarkets.'

He lit a cigarette.

'Come and see this.'

He led the way to a new building in soulless concrete and breeze blocks.

'Refrigeration,' he said. 'For cooler fermentation, greater control. And we have maturing vats now lined with glass.'

'Glass?' said Bliss incredulously.

'Glass. Stainless steel and lined with glass. My father would turn in his grave. But I'm forced to admit – it's passable wine. I don't drink it much, but it sells well, even to you English.' The bantering smile hovered round his mouth. 'You can try some later.'

'Why start making it? You once had all your work cut out simply growing the grapes. You sold your crop *en bloc* to the *négociant* or the co-operative.'

'I was practically on my own then. Times change. I was getting fed up with the deals I was getting from the *négociants* and the co-operative. Raymond was back home from college, full of modern ideas about chemicals and glass and enamel and new types of grape and so on. We had made some money from our holiday flats in the barn.'

Bliss remembered seeing the newly-converted barn for the first time. Their barn. Still, he had realised that Joseph could not afford to be sentimental. A franc was a franc.

Or, as Joseph put it, 'There was no future in remaining as a quaint peasant for tourists to take snaps of from their motor car. I decided to get them out of their motor car and get some francs out of their pocket.'

There was a touch of Ebenezer Scrooge in Joseph's make-up, the result no doubt of grinding poverty when young, and years of scrimping and saving in the early years of his marriage. He had lent money to Monique and his son-in-law to help them get their Normandy hotel on its feet, but he now drew a percentage of the profits.

'So I give Raymond his head.' he said. 'You should see the things he does.'

'Don't you mind?'

'No,' he said flatly. 'I built up this place from nearly nothing after the War. I took my own decisions. What I have created I pass on to Raymond. I cannot expect him to do the same things as I did; he does not start with the same conditions. He will go on from where I leave off, so he must do it his way. And he will make money.'

Another cigarette was lit.

'I have given him the means of profit, so I expect to share that profit. And he still needs my labour and my experience. We are now a working partnership.'

It sounded somewhat grasping, but Joseph was only complimenting him by being perfectly honest. He chuckled.

'You should see the things he does,' he repeated. 'We make white wine now.'

'White!'

'Yes. Not all, of course, but an increasing percentage. *And* we bottle it ourselves. *And* we sell it abroad. We've even had English buyers down here. Bijou took a lump out of one of them; he dropped her biscuit down a drain.'

He glanced at the declining sun much as a city-dweller looks at his watch.

'Come on. Sylvie will have dinner ready.'

As they ambled back, Joseph said, 'I'll show you some of our new labels. Pretty impressive.' He put on a pompous accent. ' "*St. Martin-les-Puits*" – "*mis en bouteilles à la propriété*".'

He chuckled again.

'Of course the joke is we don't use the wells now. Raymond has installed a whole new pumping and piping system.'

*　　*　　*　　*　　*　　*

'Mummy?'

Ruth took the dried plates and put them away.

'Yes?'

'When are you going to tell me about the letters?'

Connie wrung out the dishcloth.

'I don't know.'

'You said you would one day.'

'When you're a bit older.'

'You said that last time. I am a bit older than last time.'

Connie wiped her hands.

'I know, chick, but I don't want to involve you.'

'I know they make you unhappy and they take you away every time, and I have to go and stay with Aunt Meg. I am involved.'

Connie whirled on her.

'You haven't said anything to Aunt Meg, have you?'

'No, no. Only what you tell me to say – about lecture tours and special foreign courses, and so on.'

Meg was wonderful, and Connie loved her, but she couldn't keep her mouth shut. Ruth was different. Connie found herself increasingly reliant on her – almost as an equal – ever since David had been killed.

Ruth, however, was only twelve, and it was not right to burden a child with such terrible details. It was burden enough for her to know that a problem existed.

Connie put a hand on her daughter's cheek.

'Believe me, my pet, I will tell you, but not just yet. I was hoping that the problem would not arise again.'

'But it has.'

'I know, and I must go again. Please don't worry. I promise there is no danger and nothing that is not right. And I shall be back in four or five weeks.'

'Promise?'

'Promise. I've never had to stay longer before.'

Ruth looked at her.

'Will you answer me one question then?'

'I'll try.'

'Is it to do with me?'

Connie hesitated. Ruth pressed home her advantage.

'Is it to do with me being adopted?'

Connie took off her apron.

'You said "one question". All right – I'll answer you. Yes, in a roundabout sort of way, it is.'

'Is it to do with Daddy?'

'Good Lord, no.'

The reaction was so spontaneous that Ruth knew she had heard the truth.

'All right, I'll stop. But I promise you, I shall ask questions again next time.'

'If there is a next time. Don't be so pessimistic.'

'There'll be a next time, and a time after that – unless we do something.'

*   *   *   *   *   *

'It is a pity Raymond is not here. He will be sorry he missed you.'

Sylvie cleared his soup plate and went to fetch the *cassoulet*.

'Where exactly is Raymond?' asked Bliss.

'Perpignan, Narbonne, Montpellier, Nîmes – he's doing a round trip – shippers, *négociants*, and so on. Casting his net wider. Trying to get better deals. He'll go to England if necessary if he thinks a deal is there. Thanks to the English he learned staying with you.'

The dark wine flowed.

'Mind you, he won't be selling this. This won't get any further than the plastic bottles in the Carcassonne supermarkets that I was talking about.'

'Why do you carry on making it if the white is so profitable?'

'Habit,' said Joseph. 'I've grown up with it. I know

where I am with it. Too much chemistry in the new stuff – they're refined it into total paralysis. Just like the bread.'

'The bread?'

'Yes. The bread isn't what it used to be. You've been coming here for over thirty years; surely you've noticed.'

Bliss hadn't – well, hardly; but he did not wish to seem inadequate in Joseph's eyes. Nor did he wish to lie to him. So he said, 'I thought perhaps it might be simply fond reminiscence. You know how our memories invest the past with qualities it may not have possessed.'

Joseph growled, and would have said more, but Sylvie brought in the *cassoulet*.

During that, and during the rabbit which followed, they caught up on further family history from each other.

Neither Joseph nor Sylvie mentioned Sarah's name. They didn't refer to Joy either, though Bliss knew that Sylvie would get it all out of him in the next few days when he helped out in the kitchen, or drove her into town in one of the three vehicles parked in the yard.

They reminisced about previous holidays, as the regiment of wine bottles did its loyal duty. Sylvie, Bliss noted, still took water with hers.

Over cheese and dessert, Bliss told them about his new job.

'I agree with your Aunt Jane,' said Sylvie decisively. 'It will be good for you. You will like it.'

'And if you don't,' said Joseph, leaning over with a bottle in his huge brown hand, 'you can come back here and help us with the harvest. Make some more of this.'

Bliss said nothing about cufflinks or shirtcuffs. Instead he asked a question.

'What is all the bunting for, by the way?'

Joseph frowned.

'What did you say?'

Bliss was afraid he had used the wrong word; his French wasn't that good. For a split second he half expected Joseph to punch him on the nose for having offended Sylvie.

'Flags,' he said hurriedly. 'You know – strings of flags, rosettes, baskets of flowers on lamp-posts. They're all over town.'

'Oh, that.'

Joseph grunted and pushed away his plate.

'Don't you remember what year it is?'

Light dawned.

'Yes, of course – the fortieth anniversary.'

'We've had D-Day and nothing but D-Day all over France for weeks. Surely you've had it in England too.'

Bliss nodded.

Joseph lit a cigarette.

'Some of the *préfets* and *sous-préfets* have gone mad. Local councils have surpassed themselves with flamboyant schemes – competitions, displays, shows, films. Our lot are going to have piped music from every lamppost on every street leading to the square, right through the summer. They think it will bring in the visitors. Can you imagine? It'll drive the shopkeepers crazy.'

'There will be plenty of reunions too, I expect,' said Bliss. 'A lot of our people are coming for D-Day itself, on the sixth – from Canada and America too.'

'They'll be having them without me,' said Joseph.

'You fought,' said Bliss.

'Yes,' growled Joseph. 'For about five minutes. Six months' training in Algeria, two weeks in trains to get to the front, and three days' marching backwards while our corrupt generals negotiated armistice. Then I spent two years in prison camp and two years in hiding here after I escaped. What have I got to celebrate?'

Bliss lowered his eyes.

Sylvie's chair scraped over the tiles as she stood up quickly.

'I'll get the coffee,' she said.

*   *   *   *   *   *

Connie looked at Ruth over the top of the evening paper. Funny how children could sit on their legs without any discomfort. Ruth had only recently stopped kneeling on dining-room chairs.

It had been a quiet evening, but not a strained one. They had accepted each other's word, and that was that.

Ruth turned a page in her book, totally absorbed. Connie lowered her eyes to her newspaper.

A chill went through her as she saw the heavier print – 'Lift Bomb Disaster'. It was not a long article and it was near the bottom of the page, but those three words might have been written in fire.

Revulsion and hideous fascination fought each other, and revulsion lost. So many of the same phrases leapt out at her – 'five victims' . . . . 'must have died instantly' . . . . 'identification from jewellery and half-burned documents and dental records' . . . . 'Liberation Front rang up and claimed responsibility' – that it might have been eighteen months ago.

Connie gazed in horror at the casualty list, half expecting to see David's name there.

It wasn't, of course. But another one was – Foster, Sherman Foster.

Connie laid down the paper. Where had she come across that name before?

*   *   *   *   *   *

Joseph leaned over and poured another cognac.

'Thank you.'

Bliss sat back, rested and replete. The clatter of plates reached them faintly from the kitchen, but he knew that in this household it was far more polite at this stage to leave Sylvie alone than it would be to help her and leave Joseph alone.

He took a deep breath and savoured the rich atmos-phere – a mixture of spices, wine, cigarette smoke, dust, doggy carpet, and cognac.

'I'm sorry if I gave offence about D-Day.'

'D-Day?'

'You know – talking about reunions and everything.'

Joseph waved his worries aside.

'Oh, that. It was nothing. I was forgetting your English passion for celebrating everything – even tragedies.'

'D-Day wasn't a tragedy.'

'It depends where you were,' said Joseph.

Bliss could have bitten off his own tongue, but Joseph came to his rescue.

'I wasn't meaning D-Day,' he said. 'I mean your English love of commemoration. Look how you celebrate Dunkirk – a colossal military disaster, redeemed only by fishing defeated soldiers out of the sea they'd been driven into.'

'It helped in the long run,' said Bliss lamely. 'We couldn't have won the War without those men.'

'All right. What about Hastings then? Your biggest ever military and political defeat. Yet in 1966 you went crazy on the nine-hundredth anniversary. Did Hastings "help in the long run"?'

Bliss grimaced ruefully.

Joseph sat back and took a long pull on his cigarette.

'You won't find Frenchmen celebrating the Battle of Waterloo.'

'D-Day did lead to the Liberation,' said Bliss, counter-attacking.

'No,' said Joseph. 'It led to reprisals first, as you well know. The longer we waited for you and the Americans to arrive, the higher the price we paid.'

Bliss remembered this time to keep his mouth shut.

'Even the Liberation,' said Joseph, 'was not all celebration. It brought out the worst in Frenchmen as well as the best. Revenge on alleged collaborators, recriminations, tale-bearing, betrayal, rough justice, old private score-settling dressed up as public punishment. We saw it all here.

'You didn't have that in England – no occupation, no living with the enemy day by day, no division of loyalty between family and country, no hatred, no willingness to kill.'

Joseph had so rarely spoken about the War that Bliss searched for a way to keep him going without incurring his wrath by arguing with him. So he said, 'I didn't know there were that many Germans round here.'

'The place wasn't swarming with them, if that's what you mean,' said Joseph. 'They didn't come out often into the countryside – there was nothing here. They were more interested in the railways and the Canal.'

'It must have made it a little easier, then, for the Resistance to operate,' said Bliss, fishing.

There was a pause, as Joseph puffed and looked at him through the smoke, as if sizing him up.

'In answer to your question,' he said, 'yes – I was.'

For the next two or three cognacs, Joseph held him enthralled with tales of bravery, and suspense, and patience, and betrayal, and flight; daring and cowardice; success and bitter failure.

'I had a slight advantage,' he said, 'because I was not supposed to be here. I was officially rotting in a prison camp in Bavaria. We used the woods round here a lot.'

Bliss remembered many happy hours up there with Pri and Parry and the young Raymond.

'But we paid the price of over-confidence,' continued Joseph, 'and in the end we were betrayed.

'We were trapped here. We all escaped, except one, who thought he would be clever, and hide down one of the wells.'

Joseph puffed.

'Instead of pulling him up and taking him away, the officer in charge gave orders to throw grenades down.'

The cigarette smoke billowed again.

'We caught the soldier later – the one who dropped the grenades.'

'What did you do?'

'Does it matter? It is what one has to be prepared to do that matters. Could you kill, like that?'

'I have commanded men and given orders to fire,' said Bliss.

Joseph shook his head.

'Not the same.' He mimicked the Guards officer, even for a moment speaking English.

' "Range – twooo hundrahd – et yaw enemy in front – fahr!" '

He made an explosive noise of disgust with his lips.

'It was the fate of the many to be in my position,' said Bliss. 'It was the fate of the few to be in yours.'

'True,' said Joseph.

'We were the lucky ones,' said Bliss. 'You, however,

are the deeper ones; you faced a sterner test, and yours is the greater strength for having passed it.'

Joseph looked keenly at him.

'You understand more than I thought,' he said.

'You did not give me the chance to listen and judge before,' said Bliss.

'Perhaps there are other tests that make a man able to understand,' said Joseph, which was as near as he came to referring to Sarah.

'What happened to the officer?' said Bliss, bringing the conversation to earth again.

Joseph refilled the glasses.

'We laid our plans,' he said. 'It was – '

Sylvie came in, and Joseph at once changed the subject.

* * * * * *

How long ago was it? Four years? Five years?

A great big beefy American, with freckles on his arms. Obsessed with his daughter; always showing photographs of her.

Pretty child, Connie remembered. Lustrous eyes, dark hair. She couldn't recall the name. It might have been foreign.

What she could recall was a remark that Sherman Foster made when he showed his photographs for the first time. He was one of those strangers you meet on travels who insist on providing you with enough material for a detailed biography of them in the first five minutes.

' . . . . no, she's the only one. She's adopted . . . . Well, we couldn't have kids. We had these tests, see? Bette was in a helluva depression, and we went on this holiday . . . . I'm not boring you, am I?'

When she got a chance, Connie remarked that she too

was the parent of an adopted child, and it was a funny coincidence because –

'Is that a fact?'

And off he went again, about his Italian holiday, then about his work. Hydraulics engineer. There followed a pulverising gazeteer of his technical training and early experience. Called in specially, he was. Sure – he'd put in the entire system. You name it; he'd installed it.

'Jesus! The money that guy is prepared to spend. It would have been cheaper to build the whole goddam mansion some place else. Forest and scrub all round it. But I tell ya this: I'm that sure of it – the whole Coat d'Azooer can go up in flames and that shack of his will be safe.'

Connie met him once more, about the same time the following year. He seemed more preoccupied, less good-humoured. When Connie asked him about his wife and daughter, he just said 'Fine, fine', and that was that.

Later, when Connie tried to break the ice by asking to see any new photograph of his daughter, he pulled one out of his wallet and looked at it for a long time before handing it to her. When she gave it back, he stuffed it away and changed the subject.

He was not there long – just enough time to service the water system he had installed twelve months before. The system he was so proud of.

He made only one reference to it.

'Some day I'm going to tell that bastard where to shove his whole goddam system.'

Now he was dead.

Connie laid her glasses on the bedside cabinet.

David had been going to 'have it out with him' too. She had beseeched him not to.

'It's not so very long, after all. Four or five weeks in the summer.'

'Yes – and odd weeks at any other time, whenever he snaps his fingers.'

'He is generous with his money.'

'He can afford to be. And we can manage without his money.'

'Think of Ruth, David.'

'I am thinking of her, and I'm thinking of you. I see the look on your face every time you come back. I see the look on Ruth's face when she sees you. It can't go on, Connie.'

'But Ruth!'

'What can he do, for God's sake? She knows she's adopted; we have no problems there. How can he stir up trouble?'

'By threatening to uncover legal irregularities about her adoption.'

'Bluff. There aren't any.'

'By revealing details of her true parentage then.'

'Bluff again. And even if he does, what harm can he do? She's secure with us. She's one of the most mentally stable children I know.'

'What about her physical security?'

David gazed in disbelief.

'You mean – violence? Oh, come on, Con. This is England, not some crime-ridden ghetto in Naples. And he's a respected pillar of British society.'

Connie could not go on arguing, without burdening David with what she knew. All she could do was beg him to leave things alone.

Suppose he hadn't? Suppose he had ignored her warnings? Suppose he really had gone to 'have it out with him'? It wouldn't have been difficult; he was always away on foreign conferences and meetings. She would never have known.

He had died in that lift disaster in Paris, and Sherman Foster had died in a lift disaster in Marseilles.

Connie's hand shook as she lit a cigarette.

What had started as a ghastly coincidence was turning into a monstrous possibility.

*   *   *   *   *   *

Bliss gazed at the last of a deep red sunset.

'I had forgotten how peaceful it was here,' he said.

'When you have more peace inside you, you don't notice it around you,' said Sylvie.

Trust Sylvie – clattering to and fro with plates all evening, but she hadn't missed a thing. She would get it all out of him before long.

Joseph laid a great paw on his shoulder and pointed towards the darkened rows of vines.

'When you've done a few hours out there, you will remember once again how hot it was too.'

Bliss smiled.

'True. Funny though, but the thing I most remember from a lad is not the sun but the rain. Out there with a sack over my head, and smelling to high Heaven.'

The incongruous detail once again, the stray recollection – like shiny cufflinks and white cuffs.

*   *   *   *   *   *

'There'll be a next time,' Ruth had said. 'And a time after that – unless we so something.'

Connie had been prepared to think in terms of evasion, argument, bargaining, even protest.

Now – that item in the evening paper had shifted the

whole problem into a different dimension. Part of her stood back amazed at the coolness with which the rest of her was contemplating this different dimension.

She had fully expected a wakeful night; now she felt sure that she would have no trouble in getting off to sleep.

It was no longer a question of mere suffering and endurance, but of sheer survival. She was no longer a frightened animal entering a trap, but a newly-released one entering an arena. Their wits would meet as equals; their wills at last would cross as equals too.

First, of course, confirm or disprove that monstrous possibility, that swelled with potential horror and obscenity with every minute.

And, if she proved it . . . .

She had one other invaluable weapon too, she realised, as she pulled up the blanket: Alec Sherrif had absolutely no idea what was coming to him.

In the small bedroom next door, it was Ruth who lay awake . . . . surely there was *something* she could do to help?

Chapter Three

THERE WAS A discreet knock on the panelled door.

Bliss called out 'Come in!' but noticed that the handle had already begun to turn. The door swung open.

'Ah! Good evening, Mr. Bliss. I trust you had a pleasant journey.'

A manicured hand was extended. Gold gleamed in the silk cuff.

'Max Bowman. The London office, remember?'

The humourless, hundred-teeth smile flashed momentarily.

Bliss shook hands.

'I remember. Yes, very comfortable, thank you. I'm afraid second-class French trains often put English railways to shame, never mind first-class. The comfort and the service were excellent.'

'Good, good. You came on the TGV?'

Now, you know damned well that I haven't come from Paris; my letter last week told you that.

'No. I came across country from Narbonne.'

'A pity you missed the TGV. It is a great experience.'

Why the compulsion to put me down all the time, I wonder?

'Some other time, perhaps,' he said evenly. 'I have been staying with friends in Languedoc.'

And you know that too.

'Ah, yes, of course. Now I recall. A little peasant vineyard. Near Carcassonne, I believe?'

A little wearily, Bliss told him, so precisely as to leave no scope for further empty questions on local geography.

The tactic was deftly switched. The capped teeth gleamed.

'I trust Sir Alec's cellar here will be an improvement on their rustic hospitality.'

You patronising bastard. I'd just like to see you say that to Joseph's face.

'If there is anything you require?'

Bliss flashed a gleaming smile back.

'You appear to have thought of everything.'

A head was inclined in gratification, but the smugness showed.

'A matter on which we pride ourselves. Dinner will be at seven-thirty, when I shall introduce you to the household and our one other guest. Sir Alec is looking forward to meeting you.'

Bliss bowed in return.

'I shall be there.'

A smooth, pale hand adjusted the silk handkerchief about a millimetre in the breast pocket.

'Nothing formal. In this current unseasonal heatwave, Sir Alec wishes his guests to feel comfortable.'

Which is more than you do.

'I have rarely known it so warm here at this time of the year,' said Bliss.

That'll save you the trouble of telling me that May and June are usually the ideal months.

'Until seven-thirty then.'

'Seven-thirty.'

A slight, almost military bow, and all that was left after the door had closed was a faint whiff of Cologne.

Bliss sought the fresher evening air on his bedroom

balcony, where the view was, naturally, stupendous. The lights of Cannes were going to be even more stupendous when it got dark.

Barely a flicker of breeze ruffled the deep blue curtains behind him. A riot of dazzling shades and tints was spread below him in the packed flower beds. Even allowing for the greater horticultural potential of a Mediterranean garden, Sir Alec seemed to have a most un-English taste for strong colour. Decor, paintwork, soft furnishings – everything Bliss had so far seen had revelled in strong primary and secondary hues. Nothing tasteless of course – perish the thought. All was carefully blended and contrasted so as to produce effects which were constantly striking but never jarring. The furniture and fittings, equally expensive and equally impressive, had that tinge of flamboyance that spoke of an aesthetic taste to which England had contributed only a part.

There were clearly many sides to his new employer. What was it Parry had said? 'Paul Getty, Don Juan, and Mr. Bountiful all rolled into one.'

Well, you could add a touch of the Count of Monte Cristo – the opulence, the faultless correctness of taste and behaviour, the exotic, almost incense-laden atmosphere.

It extended to the car that had picked him up at the station. A Rolls, of course. But a deep scarlet one? The only person of position whom Bliss had ever seen to favour such a style and colour had been the Sultan of Zanzibar. The chauffeur's uniform would have made a West-End hotel commissionaire look like something out of an Oxfam shop.

The chauffeur himself, though, had been a little more earthy. Tucked and buttoned into that ridiculous jacket, with his beetling brows and three broken noses, he would have been more at home behind the wheel of a ten-ton truck. Indeed there were times on the bends of the road up from Cannes station when he handled the purring Rolls as if it *were* a ten-ton truck; the drive had not been without incident. It seemed odd that a man with Sir Alec's resources could not have employed someone more – well, more discreet.

So the chauffeur didn't make sense. There was something about Sir Alec himself that didn't make sense. And there was a great deal about Mr. Max, Smoothie, cuff-link, Glenmorangie, one-up Bowman that didn't make sense.

The name, for a start. It was so obviously ungenuine that Bliss felt almost annoyed at the man's effrontery. It was as if he were saying, 'I know my name isn't Bowman, and so do you, but I dare you to try and prove otherwise.' He was so damned cocky that he had not even bothered to change the un-Englishness of the Christian name. He might as well have called himself Wolfgang Hopkins. Had he simply stuck a pin in the telephone directory? It looked like it.

His manner was unpleasant, of course, but that was probably because he was simply an unpleasant human being. However, there was something devious too, as if all the time he knew something that Bliss didn't. As if he was, moreover, enjoying that superiority of knowledge.

Then there was the accent. Only slight, but it was there. Could it be German? Bliss found himself wishing he had listened to more of the language on his postings to B.A.O.R. Or was it that the very name 'Max' was steering him towards thinking of German? Perhaps 'Max' also was false, and the obvious incongruity of the two names side by side – 'Max Bowman' – by stimulating his annoyance, was in fact designed to throw him off the scent.

On balance Bliss didn't think so. The man was too obviously arrogant, and vain. His tendency would be to underestimate other people's capabilities, not overestimate them. Something worth remembering.

Worth remembering because Bliss felt he might have to reckon with this man. He didn't know when, or how. But it was to do with Sarah. To do with Sarah's past. This was the second time now it had happened. The bells of memory were not ringing yet; only the cords on the ends of them were twitching. But they would ring – one day. And Bliss sensed that he would need to be prepared in some way.

He braced his hands against the wrought-iron railings of his balcony, then stood up, stretched, and eased the fatigue of travel from his shoulders.

First things first. Unpacking, a shower, then change into something 'informal', before going down to meet the redoubtable Sir Alec Sherrif, K.B.E. – tycoon, philanthropist, and heartbreaker – and see what he had to say for himself.

*   *   *   *   *   *

'Yes, young lady, what can I do for you?'

'Do you print letter-paper as well as books?'

'We do.'

'Can you do it raised? You know, embossed?'

'Yes.'

'Good.'

Ruth dropped her head and fished in her shoulder bag.

The printer smiled gently and sucked the end of one arm of his glasses.

Ruth took out a largish text-book and extracted from between its pages a carefully-laid-out sheet of paper. She passed it across.

'I'm sorry it's only a photo-copy, but could you do some sheets like that? Blank, of course. With the address and all laid out like that?'

The printer put on his glasses and had a good look.

'Yes, I should think so.'

'Embossed?'

'Yes.'

'In black?'

'Yes.'

'Like that?'

'Yes.'

'On good paper?'

'Depends on what you want to pay.'

Ruth hesitated.

'I – I think I can afford it. You see, I don't want very many.'

The printer took off his glasses again.

'I'm afraid the price isn't always to do with the number of sheets; it's more to do with the type-face and the time taken to set it up, and the quality of the paper.'

Ruth became businesslike again.

'Ah, yes, I was wondering. Could you use a type of paper that they use in France?'

The printer looked quizzically at her, but refrained from asking a question. Instead he wagged his head to one side and made a face.

'I'm not much of an expert on foreign stationery, but I think we could get close enough to what you want to fool most people.' He smiled. 'After all, that is what you are planning to do, I should imagine.'

Ruth blushed, but held her ground. When she saw the printer still smiling, she conjured up a smile herself.

'In a way, yes. But it's quite harmless. Sort of birthday surprise, as you might say.'

It would be a surprise all right, if it all came off. And Mummy's birthday was soon. So the truth was still, roughly, intact.

Ruth smiled again.

'And you're quite right; I'm not planning to fool a printer.'

Only a headmistress.

'In that case, young lady, my fellow-practitioners can rest easy.'

The printer picked up a scrap of paper and a stray, capless biro.

'Let's see now. Embossing, good paper, minimum number . . . . '

He pointed at Ruth's sample sheet.

'This size?'

'The size of the original, not the one it's copied on to.'

'I see.'

He scribbled a calculation, then quoted a figure.

'Oh.'

Ruth's face fell.

'And you'll want some good envelopes too, won't you, for this – er – surprise?'

Ruth brightened again.

'Oh, no,' she said. 'Only plain-type blue. They always come in – ' She checked herself. 'I can get some French envelopes sent to me by my pen friend. I'd thought of that. I didn't think the paper would be so expensive though.'

The budget was not a big one, and the most costly item was yet to come. Would it be worth trying another printer? If indeed there was one. Unlikely, in Aunt Meg's district, and she didn't want to visit one nearer home, for obvious reasons.

The printer cleared his throat.

'I'll tell you what I'll do.'

He scribbled on another piece of paper and held it out to her.

'How about that?'

Ruth looked and widened her eyes.

'Oh, would you! Oh, that's so kind. Thank you ever so much.'

'On one condition.'

Oh, dear!

'What?'

'You tell me where you live and I can ring up your parents to check.'

'My mother.'

'All right, your mother.'

Ruth thought fast.

'Well, the surprise is actually for her. Could you ring up *after* her birthday?'

'All right. When is it?'

'June 26th.'

What a relief to be able to say the total truth.

The printer picked up his pen.

'What's the number?'

He mustn't start checking yet, behind my back. And if he finds the number ringing and no answer, he might get suspicious. If I give him Aunt Meg's number, it will involve so many explanations in so many different directions . . . .

'Um, could I tell you when I come to pay for them? Then you could still decide whether to give them to me or not.'

The printer looked at her.

'I could wait while you check the number really is in the book,' said Ruth, 'so you know I'm telling the truth.'

She met his gaze unflinchingly.

'I can give you a deposit if you wish.'

The printer laughed.

'No – that won't be necessary.'

If half his casual customers were like this one, he would never get through his evening meal telling his wife about them.

'I'll have them ready next Wednesday. Will that be all right?'

Ruth thought.

'Yes, that'll be fine, thank you.'

She hitched up her shoulder-bag.

'Goodbye.'

'Goodbye.'

Ruth blew out her cheeks as she walked down the street.

So far, he had trusted her. He couldn't ring up until she gave him the number. When she did, he would ring two or three times before he suspected anything. If he then bothered to take any action, there seemed to be no way he could trace her to Aunt Meg; and even if he could, she would be out of his reach by that time.

She made a mental note to go and explain and apologise to him when she got back, and heaved a big sigh of relief.

So far, so good.

*   *   *   *   *   *

There was still over half an hour to go before dinner. Time for a closer look at the gardens.

Bliss enjoyed gardens. His mother had green fingers, and some of his earliest recollections were of trotting behind her holding trowels and packets of seeds. Dad characteristically knew the Latin name for every weed, bloom, and shrub as far as the distant horizon; the scholarship had gone in one ear and out the other, but the interest and enthusiasm had stuck. Of the three boys, Priam had turned out to be the gardener. Parry was always out playing games somewhere, and Bliss himself had never seemed to find the time. Army postings were rarely extended enough or in a congenial enough place to allow for long-term horticultural plans – another source of friction with Joy. When he went into teaching, he could rarely summon up the nervous energy after a day in the classroom. Joy liked going out too. So that was that.

Perhaps now that he was in changed circumstances and more able to please himself, he might get around to it some day.

He sauntered across emerald carpets of princely vastness. My God – the watering arrangements here must be prodigious. If the French run their system on a meter basis, Sir Alec's bills must be astronomical. The general effect of this lush panorama of green seemed a combination of a Cambridge college garden and a Georgian cotton millionaire's golf course.

As for the colours . . . . shrubs, flowers, bushes, creepers, and trees, in clumps, clusters, lines, bays, avenues, and hedges, produced fresh sensations for eye and nose at every turn – all in the most harmonious order, naturally. Under the glass of a conservatory of Crystal Palace proportions, yet more exotic plants vaunted their rare, unpaintable beauty.

Bliss reached the limit of wonderment long before he

had circled the house. He found himself longing to catch a glimpse of a simple scattering of dead leaves, or a mole-hill, a wormcast – anything.

The only jarring note was struck by what looked like wire mesh fences all round the property, and he was not even sure of that because they were so far away. He squinted in the bright light – they seemed very substantial for a private house.

He had put one foot down a path to go and have a closer look when he heard someone laugh. A woman. Then rubber-soled shoes running up stone steps. Getting closer.

Bliss stopped and turned back. She reached the top, burst through a gap in the bushes, and almost fell into his arms.

'Oops! Sorry.'

A sea of suntan, sweat droplets, and sensuality swam before Bliss' eyes. His nostrils recoiled from the combined impact of perfume, grass cuttings, and moist flesh.

He did his best to disengage himself, and wrenched his eyes up to the level of hers.

'That's all right. You can do that any time you like.'

Bright blue eyes sparkled and blond hair waved. She laughed again.

'I'm Dolly Vartan. Who are you?'

'Bliss. Hector Bliss. I've – er – just arrived.'

'Ah!'

She was still puffing slightly, which caused the most disturbing undulations under her white tennis kit.

She patted the undulations.

'Sorry,' she said. 'We've been playing tennis.'

'We?'

'Yes.'

She waved a tennis racket unnecessarily. Every movement this creature made seemed to set off the most suggestive ripples somewhere else.

'By yourself?' said Bliss.

She glowed with enough life for this stupid remark to seem possible.

She simpered.

'Silly!'

She looked over her shoulder.

'No, I had a partner a minute ago. I s'pose he was parking the – ah, here he is.'

Up the steps, three at a time, came another vision – dazzling white shorts and sweatband, no stomach, and four perfect profiles.

'This is Cass,' said Dolly. 'And we've been playing tennis. Haven't we, Cass?'

The vision was frowning slightly as it caught sight of Bliss, but it answered civilly.

'Ya! And we have had good time.'

I'll bet.

'You are tennis player?' asked Cass, the frown poised to come down again in the presence of a possible rival.

Oh no, not another accent. Now where the Hell do you come from?

'No, I'm afraid not. At any rate, not any more, and almost certainly not to your standard.'

'You see, Mr. Bliss has only just arrived,' said Dolly, by way of logical explanation. Even that produced shimmers, this time of eyelashes.

Bliss held out his hand.

'Pleased to meet you, Mr. – er – '

'Call him Cass,' said Dolly. 'It's Casimir really, and his other name is even more impossible. Nobody can say it properly, so we've given up trying.'

'Cass.'

'Bliss.'

The vision gripped Bliss' hand in a chocolate vice, then released it like a pump handle.

Dolly held her racket in front of her like a convent girl going home with her satchel.

'That's that, then.'

She sighed with the satisfaction of a job well done. Yet more heart-stopping pulsations made their way towards fascinating extremities.

'Are you a guest?'

'Sort of. I'm the new tutor for Sir Alec's son.'

Dolly's eyes widened.

'Oh!'

Then she giggled.

'What's so funny?' said Bliss, keeping his eyes up with tremendous difficulty.

She had put her hand up to her mouth. Now she took it away and flashed a conspiratorial glance at the vision, who, now that he knew no competition across the net was in the offing, had also allowed himself the luxury of a grin.

'Promise you won't be cross.'

'Promise.'

How could he deny her anything?

'Well, we've all been talking about you and wondering what you'll be like, and we worked out a nickname for you.'

'I see.'

She leaned forward expectantly.

'Don't you want to know what it is?'

Fresh acres of moist cleavage glistened.

Bliss smiled.

'I think that might be a good idea – yes.'

'We called you the "Brain Train". '

She put her hands on her hips and looked pleased with herself. Thank God she had almost got her breath back by now.

Bliss forced a grin. If only her repartee could have matched her physique.

'Well, what do you want me to do – give you fifty lines?'

Dolly grinned back.

'No. It's just that – well – you don't look like what we had in mind.'

'Sorry to disappoint you.'

The eyes glowed.

'Oh, no disappointment, I assure you.'

I wonder how good Cass' English is?

'Um – if it isn't too rude a question, what do you do here?'

Dolly looked genuinely surprised.

'Me?'

She placed a brown hand demurely across the moist cleavage.

'Oh, I'm just staying here. I'm a friend of Sir Alec's.'

'Are you now?'

What does Adonis here, with his imperfect English, make of the situation? Or Lady Sherrif, if it comes to that.

'I'm sure Sir Alec, with his legendary hospitality, is giving you a good time.'

Dolly simpered once more, and pretended to slap him on the wrist.

'Silly!'

I wonder if Cass is up to translating that one?

'What's the time?' said Dolly, becoming practical.

Before Bliss could answer she had picked up his slapped wrist and peered at his watch.

'Lord! Is it that late? Come on, Cass, we must get our skates on.'

'Skates?'

He peered in puzzlement at his tennis racket. Dolly grabbed Cass by the wrist now and yanked him off towards the house. She flung a last glowing glance over a gleaming brown shoulder.

'See you at dinner, Mr. Brain Train.'

Seen from the rear, in full retreat, Dolly had just as many disturbance areas as she did from the front.

Bliss grinned to himself as he remembered the last line of a vulgar limerick from college days . . . . *'with a bum like a jelly on springs.'*

*   *   *   *   *   *

Molluscs . . . . arthropods . . . . vertebrates . . . .

Ruth yawned. That was enough Biology for the evening. She would have another look before breakfast.

She took her right leg out from underneath her and put the left one there instead. She glanced up at the clock on her beside cabinet. There was time for that French exercise before Aunt Meg called up to her for supper.

She opened the text-book and flicked over the pages till she found Exercise 14 – 'La famille Berthier go on holiday'. She yawned again. More feeble drawings of pudding-faced parents and goppy kids. And the number of times 'la famille Berthier', or odd members of it, went to the airport or through the customs you'd think they were smuggling drugs or something.

Ruth shut the book again, rolled over to a kneeling

position, and went on all fours to a bottom drawer. She pulled it open, and paused to listen for tell-tale noises from downstairs. Some panel game or other was in full swing on the telly, and Cousin Colin had taken his acne off to a disco, so the coast was clear.

She lifted the clothes and slid a folder out from underneath. She took out some sheets of paper and used the folder on her knees as a desk top.

The first sheet was headed 'Budget'. Underneath, in her clear, careful hand, was written 'Postal charges' and 'Stationery'. After some thought she added 'Travel Estimates'. She put the printer's figure against 'Stationery', then took out a largish envelope containing a letter and several other plain airmail envelopes.

Henriette's English was not much better than Ruth's French.

' . . . . here is the envelopes you are demanding. As you see they are for aeroplane . . . . I think it is a adventure very exciting that you are figuring . . . . tell me when you are ready and I will hurry myself to help as fast as possible . . . . '

Perhaps after supper she could get down to the business of composing the letter.

She entered a sum against 'Postal charges' and put 'Henriette' in brackets after it; then she added 'International Money Order'. Henriette would have to be recompensed for all this.

The gentleman in the Post Office had been very helpful. She had blinked innocent eyes, and he had fallen over himself to tell her all the details she requested. Even gave her two or three 'Withdrawal' forms to practise on.

With any luck she wouldn't need to go more than about five or six times. At fifty pounds a go, she should have enough. She decided to use the same post office. Some eagle-eyed clerk might spot from the date-stamps what she was up to if she went to six different ones on consecutive days, whereas this man was so nice. And after her story he was so fatherly and helpful she thought she had better stick with him. Better the devil you know, as Daddy used to say.

So she wrote '£300.00' in pencil on the right-hand side, then considered what she had been told by the travel agent. She could not remember all the details about charter flights and 'Pex' flights, and Gatwick and Heathrow, and night schedules and mid-week rates, and British Airways and Air France, and so on, but she had grasped the general idea that cheaper travel meant pinning yourself down to a definite hour and day weeks in advance. Cheaper still standby tickets were available, but she didn't like the idea of waiting for hours in an airport, perhaps at night; even if she did, she would never convince anyone that Mummy would have made such an arrangement for her.

No – it had to be a scheduled flight; it was safe and proper, and it allowed flexibility. But it meant more money. Ruth sighed and entered a figure.

There was still the rest of the journey – to and from the airport, especially at the other end. Money could be changed on the spot, but she had to have enough sterling with her to do it.

She felt in the file again and pulled out a passport. For the tenth time she checked the expiry date. She looked at the photograph and grimaced. Why were passport photos always so awful? Back it went into the file.

What a lucky thing it was they had had that school trip last year – unusual for primary schools. But it had meant Ruth having her own separate passport. Had she not gone, Mummy would still be using a joint one and would have taken it off to France with her.

So she could take no credit for that piece of good fortune. However, she had been sharp enough to make contact with Henriette. After the trip the school had suggested pen friends, and by that time some sort of vague hope was already stirring in the back of her mind. If a correspondent was available in Nice, just up the coast from Cannes, it might be an idea to establish contact; not much point in having one in Nantes or Limoges. Henriette was a bit older, but Ruth was so insistent about Nice that the school gave in – 'after all, she is above average for her age, and her mother is a university lecturer.'

More to Ruth's purpose, an older girl would be likely to understand more English.

'Ruth! Supper.'

Ruth listened. The telly had stopped. She hadn't noticed.

'All right!'

She stuffed everything back into the file.

'Coming, Auntie.'

Clothes were rearranged and the drawer carefully shut.

Ruth paused by the door and checked.

One stray sheet still lay on the rug.

After a glance downstairs, Ruth pounced on it. It was covered with crossed-out versions of a signature – 'C.E. Marshall (Mrs.)' Ruth opened the drawer again and thrust the sheet into the file.

A bit more practice was still needed, especially on the capital letters.

*   *   *   *   *   *

It was a curate's egg of an evening.

The good parts chiefly involved the weather, and what was on the table; Bliss didn't think much of the people round it, or of the atmosphere.

After freezing in a typical English spring and then sweating among Joseph's vines for a fortnight, Bliss found the warm, scented leisure of 'Ste. Sophie-les-Mimosas' anything but oppressive. And Dolly had already provided memorable, if momentary, light relief.

Every wine was, of course, perfect. It had begun with the *apéritif.*

'One of our lesser-known sparkling wines, Mr. Bliss, but, in my opinion, very much underrated. *Blanquette-de-Limoux* – I don't suppose you will have encountered much of it in England.'

There you go again – bumpkin Bliss belongs to that nation of plonk-swillers who barge round Boulogne supermarkets on day trips with their baskets bulging with two-litre bottles of *Vin de Table Français.*

'As a matter of fact, I know it quite well. And I agree, it is underrated. It is the *méthode champenoise* of preparation which adds to its virtue, of course.'

He took a sip, and flashed one of Max's own surgical smiles back at him.

'Chilled to perfection too. And so refreshing to see it served in the correct glasses.'

Put that in your pipe and smoke it.

A delicious German wine followed; Max, having burned his fingers once, refrained from telling Bliss where the Rheingau was.

Which was lucky, because the claret was frankly above Bliss' head. Neither his experience nor his pocket had put him in a position to judge the nectar that seduced his nose and palate with such a bewildering range of subtleties. It confirmed what the label at least had told him – that he was in the presence of real class – but that was about all.

And so it went on, right through to the cognac and liqueurs.

The food was the same, from the sea-food salad to the *soufflés*. Plates and glasses were presented and removed through sheer sleight of hand by a small cohort of ghostly servants.

My God, thought Bliss – do people actually get used to living like this?

Lady Sherrif certainly had. She treated wine and food alike as if it were chewing-gum. She rarely said 'Please' or 'Thank you', and she never so much as looked at any of the serving staff. Bliss could see, though, that it was not the assurance that comes from breeding; it was bored indifference.

He knew she was American; her accent proclaimed that. Max had confirmed it, in the course of providing a potted biography when he made the introductions.

'Lady Sherrif is from Ohio, in the U.S.A. Like yourself, Mr. Bliss, she is a university graduate – though, unlike yourself, from an American university.'

Max contrived, by the word 'though', to make it sound third-rate. Lady Sherrif's eyes flashed dangerously, but Max had not finished.

'You may have seen Lady Sherrif's photograph in the newspapers some years ago; she was formerly married to Senator Congreve Sheridan at the time he was campaigning for the presidential nomination.'

In Max's view, therefore, she was not only indifferently educated; she had dumped her previous husband after his political failure.

So Max did this sort of thing to everybody. Bliss felt almost sorry for her – for a moment.

It soon became clear, however, that Lady Julia Sherrif ('call me "Julie"'), formerly Sheridan, was well able to take care of herself. She dismissed Max in pithy, if somewhat earthy, style, and grabbed a second glass of *Blanquette* from a passing tray.

'So you're going to be the resident egghead?'

Does everyone round here treat you like a doormat? Better start as you mean to carry on.

'You have a degree yourself.'

Julie waved the empty glass. A battery of diamonds flashed on several fingers.

'Oh, that. It means I can swear in three languages. What the Hell?'

The grooming was correct, and expensive. The mind was intelligent. The eye showed interest, though Bliss suspected that the interest sprang only from the attraction that novelty offered to boredom. The lines round the mouth were hard, and the jaw was like granite. Glasses of *Blanquette* went down like Russian toasts to *glasnost.*

Bliss could hear one of his mother's most condemnatory judgments: 'Educated brass.'

Julie had done most of the talking till they sat down at the table, then Bliss had managed to get in some polite comment about 'looking forward to meeting your son'.

The blue eyes went several shades colder.

'He's not my son. He's my husband's heir.'

She made an exaggerated gesture towards Sir Alec at the opposite end of the table.

Oops! Slipped up there.

There was no need to dredge up a face-saving remark;

Julie had turned away to the vision on her right. Cass obligingly said 'Yes' and 'No' at the right intervals, and submitted to having his face patted.

So Lady Julie had more than the grape to console her in this featureless desert of riches; and thumping it from the base line was not the only type of service required from profile Casimir.

Bliss glanced to the head of the table, where Sir Alec was deep in technicalities with Max and some visiting VIP from international industry. He glanced back at Cass, who was now having the back of his left wrist stroked.

Nobody took the slightest notice.

Bliss looked across at Dolly, and gestured with his eyebrows. She glanced at the patted wrist, and Bliss thought he detected a moment of genuine pain on her face.

She looked back at him, made a face, and shrugged.

On Bliss' right sat a stolid, dark-jowled Frenchman, sweating in a heavy, dark suit. Bliss had long since forgotten his name. He had very little English, and even less conversation. Bliss had tried French, but the man seemed unable to talk about anything except his work as hydraulics engineer, and how proud his firm was that they had won the servicing contract for Sir Alec's estate. It would mean promotion for him if Sir Alec put in a favourable report. And so on and so on.

Julie had tried, briefly, to do her duty as hostess, but when the man produced photographs of his children from a fat leather wallet, she recoiled and took refuge with Casimir's wrist.

Bliss could think of no French conversation relevant to computerised sprinkler systems and gravity-feed swimming pools, and the poor man spent the rest of the meal in Trappist isolation.

Across the table from Bliss, and between Dolly and Casimir, sat a lady who had been introduced as 'Mademoiselle Aline'. Bliss was not quite sure of her status; as far as he could make out she was a sort of mixture of poor relation and housekeeper.

Max and Sir Alec treated her with the matter-of-factness that came from very long acquaintance, but they both inserted the 'Mademoiselle' before the 'Aline', he noticed. So did Dolly, in an awful French accent. The servants deferred to her; it was to her, not to Sir Alec or to Julie, that they looked for glances of instruction during the evening. Julie, characteristically, practically ignored her.

Mademoiselle Aline was interesting, because she wouldn't fit easily into a category. She was no beauty, but no frump either. Her face certainly showed more character than either Dolly's or Julie's. She was not dressed from a *couturier*'s; nor did she look like Mrs. Danvers. Her conversation did not sparkle, but she was obviously no mouse.

It was she who showed the most genuine interest in the work Bliss had come to do, though her questions had a note of steely interrogation about them.

She fixed him with a stern eye.

'Do you think all your tuition will turn him into an English gentleman?'

'Mademoiselle, I understand he is already English, and, coming from such a household as this, he will already be acquainted with the qualities required of a gentleman.'

A slight frown of puzzlement appeared on Mademoiselle's brow.

'However,' continued Bliss, 'in answer to the spirit of your question, I can only say that I see my work not as training and constricting, but as opening and liberating. Truth and knowledge open the mind to greater enjoyment and understanding. A teacher's aim is that a child should have life and have it more abundantly.'

My word – quite a speech! Where had it all come from? The wine? Or Dad?

Bliss saw from Mademoiselle's face that the answer was not one she had been expecting. She wiped the sides of her mouth with her serviette, shot a last watchful glance in his direction, and turned away to give some instructions.

That left only one other person to talk to – the lady on his left. It should have been easy, but it wasn't.

Dammit, she was English, and had more brains than all the rest of them put together – Cambridge Ph.D. She ought to have a lot to talk about.

Every entry that Bliss tried led to a dead end.

Was she on holiday here? No.

Was she a guest of Sir Alec's? Not exactly.

Was she an employee? Not really. Sort of consultant, you might say.

Oh? What sort of consultant?

Her degree was in mathematics.

Bliss tried a feeble joke.

Was she selling calculators to Sir Alec's office staff?

No, she wasn't. (A frigid stare.) Her work was of a confidential nature.

Ouch!

Bliss looked desperately round the table . . . . the VIP and Max were drawing diagrams on serviettes for Sir Alec. Dolly was tucking into a second helping; her appetite was all right then. It needed to be, with a figure like that. Mademoiselle Aline had her head down. The Frenchman was mopping blue jowls with a checked handkerchief; Cass had just got his wrist back; and Julie was guzzling *Château Pétrus* as if it were lemonade.

So Bliss came back for more.

Was Dr. Marshall here alone or with her family? (He had now recalled the name.) Alone. She was a widow.

Bliss said he was very sorry. Had she any children?

Lips tightened. Yes, one.

Boy or girl? A girl.

How old? Twelve.

A pity she had to miss these lovely surroundings, ventured Bliss, waving vaguely towards the open window, with its inevitably marvellous view.

'I should not want my daughter here!'

Bliss gave up.

As he took off his 'informal' jacket in his room, he wondered what he had let himself in for.

Smoothie Max didn't like him, though he probably didn't like anybody very much. Mademoiselle Aline disapproved, though he did feel that he had impressed her more than she had expected to be impressed. He had got off on the wrong foot with Julie – which, on balance, was probably just as well; she wouldn't feel like making a pass when the vision was away on the tennis court. The vision would be no problem as long as Bliss stayed away from tennis rackets and didn't wear a white sweatband. Dolly? Dear Dolly! You couldn't take Dolly seriously any more than you could have taken Marilyn Monroe seriously.

And the fearsome Dr. Constance Marshall – he now remembered the Christian name. God knows what would have happened had he used it at dinner. What she had against him he couldn't imagine. She made him feel

like an old man who had wheezed an improper suggestion to her on top of a bus.

That left Sir Alec Sherrif, K.B.E. He had smiled pleas-
antly while Max made the introductions; he had bowed
slightly to acknowledge Bliss' compliments about the
house and gardens. He had listened intently while
Max went through trivial administrative arrangements
concerning accommodation and preparation for Alan's
arrival and coming tuition. Bliss was conscious of a pair
of dark, glowing eyes, almost orb-like. The skin was dark
too, for an Englishman; it threw the thick grey hair into
greater contrast. Trimly built. Slightly smaller than Bliss
had imagined.

Alert. Very alert.

But charming. No question of that. Bliss could understand the women falling for him, and not only because of
his money.

He had gallantly stood back for Bliss to precede him
through the door into the dining room, and waved him
graciously to his chair.

Bliss hung his tie round the coat hanger and put it into
the wardrobe.

Odd, though – during the entire evening Sir Alec
Sherrif had not uttered a single word to him.

Chapter Four

'I DON'T GET it, Aunt Jane.'

Aunt Jane stacked her picture postcards into a neat pile and took out some stamps from her tiny handbag.

Bliss sighed.

'It's not the men; it's the women.'

Aunt Jane wiped the first stamp across her tongue.

'You never were very good at females, Hector.'

'You mean choosing them, or handling them?'

'Both.'

If almost any other human being had said that to him, he would have felt like punching them on the nose. Instead he sipped his martini.

'Well, that's as may be. But look at 'em, Aunt Jane. The men I can understand. Smoothie Max – two-faced, probably three-faced, for all I know. But at least he's consistent – a permanent bastard. The chauffeur does nothing but skid his Rolls round corners, and he has such a thick regional accent I can't understand a word he says. Alsace, I think he comes from. Dreamboat Casimir has only two things on his mind, and they're both on his hands, as you might say.'

Aunt Jane thumped delicately with her fist on the drying stamps.

'What about your employer?'

'Bit of a mystery, I agree. But he's the boss; you don't expect to have many dealings with him. Smart-ass Bowman is the one I do business with. No – Sir Alec comes and goes. When he's there, he holds doors open and smiles charmingly, and that's about it.'

Another sip.

'No. I repeat – it's the women. There's diamond-drip Julie, who is all over me to begin with, and then freezes stone-cold when I mention her son. "Oh, no – not my son," she says. "Sir Alec's heir." She's hardly spoken since.'

'Perhaps he isn't.'

'Isn't what?'

'Her son. Didn't you say Sir Alec was a ladies' man?'

Dolly rose before his eyes – Dolly, all a-quiver.

'Maybe. But he wouldn't have his bastards about the house. Sir Alec is a pillar of the Establishment – honorary K.B.E. and all.'

'Perhaps he was married before.'

'Could be.'

'Couldn't you ask the housekeeper?'

Bliss pointed with the glass in his hand.

'Now there's another one. Looks down her nose and jangles her jailer's keys until I start talking stuff about the noble aims of education. Then she goes all mysterious. She's hardly spoken since either.'

'What about this – what's her name – Dolly?'

Bliss chuckled reminiscently.

'Dolly! If ever a young woman was the victim of her own hormones it's that one. But she's up to something too, and, if it's what I think it is, she's playing a dangerous game. Sir Alec does not look to me like the sort of man who would tolerate infidelity in the woman he's being unfaithful with.'

'Going from bed to hearse then, is she?'

'Oh, very good, Aunt Jane. No – it's not as bad as that. I don't think she's in severe physical danger. But there are too many charming smiles around for anyone to feel safe. Remember that limerick about the young lady from Niger?'

Aunt Jane chimed in.

' – "Who smiled as she rode on a tiger"?'

' "They came back from the ride – " '

' " – With the lady inside – " '

' " – And the smile on the face of the tiger." All I'm saying is, Dolly may live to regret it, and it's a pity, because she's so harmless.'

'Harmless! Hanky-panky twice over?'

'If you could see Dolly's combination of energy, gormlessness, sex drive, and kindness of heart, you'd understand what I mean. That girl must live in perpetually seduced circumstances. I tell you, she's harmless.'

'Is your Dr. Marshall harmless too?'

Bliss winced.

'I never got past the barbed wire entanglements. Not to begin with. But I kept trying, largely because I didn't want to speak French all the time to people who didn't want to listen. I got nowhere at all until I showed her a photo of Sarah – '

' – and told her she was dead. Going for the sympathetic angle, eh?'

Only Aunt Jane would attempt to put it in perspective by making light of it.

'That's the funny thing. She never turned a hair.'

'Didn't she react at all?'

'She just said "what a shock it must have been", and that was about it. Anyway, we went on about this and that – I'd talked her into having a lift with me into Cannes. Arranged a captive audience, as you might say. She was tolerating it in a bored sort of way. And I let slip that Sarah was adopted.

'The change was remarkable. She suddenly became human. So, obviously, did I, in her opinion. I was no longer something from under a paving-stone.'

'There you are then.'

'What do you mean – there I am then?'

'She likes you.'

'Rubbish.'

'Sorry for you, then.'

'Not even that. Just intrigued, I'd say. Still watchful, and pretty frigid. But definitely intrigued. I may not be acceptable humanity, but I am humanity. At least I'm now out of the Neanderthal classification.'

Aunt Jane finished her *thé citron*.

'I think it's time I had a word with this Dr. Marshall. What's the Christian name?'

'Constance.'

'Hmm. Connie, I expect.'

'I wouldn't know; I've never dared.'

'And she has a daughter?'

'Yes. I did get that out of her.'

Aunt Jane picked up the bill, peered at it, and passed it across.

'Your turn. We used my expense account last time.'

Bliss grinned.

'I'll stick it on the bottom and call it blackboards and pencil sharpeners.'

Aunt Jane stood up and handed the pile of cards to him.

'You can post those, and then escort me to the marina. I'll arrange for you and Connie to come on board tomorrow for coffee. We're not sailing until Tuesday.'

'Where to this time?'

'Only Nice.'

Aunt Jane smiled demurely.

'And perhaps a spin in the Mercedes to Monte and Ventimiglia.'

*   *   *   *   *   *

'Dear Miss Crosby,'

Ruth pulled her knees up higher and made sure there was a space beside her under the bedclothes into which she could thrust things quickly if she heard Aunt Meg coming. She poised her pencil again over the paper.

Be careful. Don't be greedy, and don't overdo it. And remember – adult language.

'I'm sorry this request comes at such short notice – '

Mustn't give them too much time to consider things or ask questions.

' – if you could let – ' No. Ruth erased it with the rubber on the end of her pencil. ' – if you could consent to Ruth having a week – ' Ruth crossed out 'week' and put 'fortnight', then changed it back to 'week'. She would probably know within two or three days if she could help to get Mummy out of her trouble.

' – a week with me here in Cannes. My boss – ' No. Rubber. ' – my employer.' Better. 'My employer says – ' No. ' – informs me that my work is now ahead of schedule – ' That's good – 'ahead of schedule '

Ruth sat back, cocked her head, and admired her own handiwork so far. She bent down, stuck out her tongue, and resumed.

' – is now ahead of schedule, and has offered his hospitality to Ruth for a week, here, at his expense.'

Ruth paused. Now for the sympathy bit.

'It is so kind of him that it would seem – ' Ruth

searched for a word. Suddenly there came back a phrase which she had heard Daddy use.

' – would seem cherlish to refuse.' Must look it up in the dictionary.

No. Do it now; you'll forget. . . . Ah.

' – churlish to refuse.' Ruth grinned. Next, we put Miss Crosby on the spot.

' – and I'm sure you will agree that it is a terrific chance – ' No. ' – a splendid opportunity for Ruth to improve her French.' So if you don't agree, Miss Crosby, you're a killjoy and a rotten educationist.

Ruth turned over the page. Now we must make it sound terribly reasonable.

'I understand Ruth's summer exams will be over by the time you receive this, and that a lot of things – ' No. ' – activities now take place out of the classroom on trips and camps.' True. They do. So if I wasn't in Cannes, Miss Crosby, I'd be shivering in some drippy tent on the edge of the New Forest.

And now – Ruth grinned smugly – the 'good parent' part.

'I can assure you that I shall have Ruth back well in time for Sports Day and the Swimming Gala.'

Turn that down, and you're an old meanie.

Time for the travel arrangements.

'I have told Ruth to draw the necessary money from her Post Office Savings account – '

Better have a separate letter about that all prepared in case they ask to see it. Come to think of it, might be a good thing to show to the man in the Post Office as well. Where was I?

' – her Post Office Savings account. I should then – ' Posh people said 'should', not 'would' ' – should then be most grateful if you would let Ruth purchase an airline ticket from London to Nice – ' She paused and added the word 'single'.

Of course, single! That'll save money. Why didn't I think of that before?

' – I shall buy Ruth's return ticket here.'

How far dare she push Miss Crosby? Was it asking for trouble to go any further?

If I were Mummy, would I leave it at that? No, I wouldn't; I'd want them to escort my daughter to the airport lounge. It had to sound genuine, even if it did sound a nuisance.

' – As a last favour, I should be – ' I've said 'grateful' once. What else could – got it! ' – I should be most indebted – ' She remembered the 'b'. ' – most indebted if you could arrange for Ruth's transportation to the airport. Ruth will have the money to pay for the bus.'

Dash it! They weren't all that far away from Heathrow. If the worst came to the worst, she could run away and walk there.

Nearly finished. A few more details about 'being met' at Nice – she would write to Henriette, and perhaps Henriette's parents could manage something. That way, Ruth felt she was only misleading Miss Crosby, not actually lying to her.

Finally, some sugary remarks about 'sincere thanks for all the trouble, apologies for all the inconvenience', and how much 'Ruth has enjoyed her first year with you', and how pleased Mummy is with 'her excellent progress' – Ruth made a face.

She sat back.

There. That should do it.

Think about it tomorrow, check it on Friday, and type

it on Saturday. Make some excuse to Aunt Meg about going home and getting some fresh clothes. The typewriter had a new ribbon; she had persuaded Mummy to change it two or three weeks ago – just in case.

She slithered out of bed and opened the drawer. From the bottom she took a package, undid it, and looked at the sheets of freshly-printed stationery.

' "Ste. Sophie-les-Mimosas", Ste. Sophie-en-haut, Alpes Maritimes.' She ran her finger over the embossed letters. Mr. Partridge had done a super job.

She looked again at her rough notes. Practise on some rough paper first. Should take two sheets if nicely spaced out.

Well satisfied with her evening's work, she packed everything away and went back to bed.

'Ruth!'

Ruth jumped.

'Yes?'

'Ruth, I've been calling you Do you want anything else to drink?'

Crumbs! And she hadn't heard.

She scrambled out again, rushed to the door, and called downstairs.

'Sorry, Auntie. I had my stereo earphones on. No – no more, thanks.'

'I'll be up soon, to say goodnight.'

'Thank you, Auntie.'

Phew! That could have been close.

And what a good thing I checked 'cherlish'. That would have been a terrible give-away.

*   *   *   *   *   *

'A small world, Mr. Bliss.'

Bliss felt suddenly so annoyed that he wished he had pushed the glass swing door into his face instead of giving way to allow him through. The man was insufferably cool, and poised, and in command. And now Bliss had been caught stepping back for him.

He searched for a remark that would put him back on a level, to extricate himself from the position Max had put him in by implying that he somehow ought not to be there.

'We all have to post letters – even you, it seems.'

Max refused to take offence. A white cuff waved airily.

'There are some errands of a certain confidentiality that one would be ill-advised to entrust to a subordinate.'

Again that well-modulated English that was just a fraction over the top.

Max pointed to the postcards in Bliss' hands.

'The post box is outside, you know.'

God, you annoy me! And you do it on purpose.

'I am aware. However, I need some more stamps.'

'There is no need, Mr. Bliss, for you to go to this trouble in future. Any correspondence you have can be left to Sir Alec's office staff. I shall be happy to show you where. The stamps will cost you nothing.'

So that you can have a damn good look at them. That last letter you brought me from Parry looked tampered with. Who does the actual steaming, I wonder? Mademoiselle Aline-jailer-Danvers with her copper kettle?

'I make it a habit, Mr. Bowman, always to post my own letters. Like peeling one's own oranges, you know?'

The expression remained blank.

'Nevertheless, should you wish to reconsider . . . .'

'I shall bear it in mind.'

Enough of this one-way traffic. Time to turn it.

'I should not have thought you were one for the sun.'

Bliss gestured towards the open sky and smiled.

In other words, what's a dough-faced, cuff-trimmed smoothie like you doing out in this heat? See how you like it.

The thrust was easily dealt with, followed immediately by counter-thrust.

'Your official duties have not yet begun, Mr. Bliss. Mine – alas – are with me all the time. I am due to meet another associate of Sir Alec's. You will probably be introduced this evening. Boring business, I'm afraid, but Sir Alec is a stern workmaster.'

Caught you there – for the first time. You should have said 'taskmaster'.

Bliss smiled devilishly.

'When my duties do begin in earnest, I only hope I can match your conscientiousness, Mr. Bowman.'

The faintest of reaction appeared in the cold eyes.

'We shall see, Mr. Bliss. We shall see. And now, if you will excuse me . . . .'

As Bliss watched him leave, a scarlet Rolls Royce pulled up with a sigh and a whisper at the kerb. The Ruritanian broken nose got out and held open the door. Bliss could see the sweat on his jowls even at that distance.

The pale blue eyes gave a last fish glance through the window as the red wraith faded away. Bliss found himself looking at the shop fronts on the other side of the street. He jumped; one of the figures there seemed familiar, but withdrew at once into a shaded doorway.

Bliss continued into the Post Office, bought his stamps, came out, posted his cards, and looked across the street again.

He was still there.

Bliss ambled along, pretending to look at the shop windows full of espadrilles and sun-tan cream. The other man followed.

Bliss turned right at the *Syndicat d'Initiative* office and went in the direction of the car park.

There could be no doubt about it. What was more surprising, and more annoying, was that the man made little attempt to conceal himself.

Bliss found his rage at Max Bowman growing with every glance over the shoulder. This swine was not only snooping at his mail; he was monitoring all his movements – and he didn't care who knew. The arrogance was breathtaking. How could he be so sure that Bliss wouldn't turn round and tell him where to shove the whole thing?

Because that was what Bliss felt tempted to do at that particular moment.

He was not only annoyed; he was saddened too. Bowman, he knew, was two-faced. Julie – diamonds-forever Julie – he didn't care if she was two-faced. Mademoiselle Aline wouldn't even show him one face. But, when he had privately marked down a person as pretty straightforward, he felt sad when they turned out to not to be. He didn't much like sweatband Casimir, but had not imagined him to be anything more than a dour, humourless bed-hopper imprisoned by his own good looks. Now, it seemed, he was a hired snooper of Max Bowman's as well. Pity.

*   *   *   *   *   *

'Dear Henriette,

'Here is the letter – *voici la lettre* – I was telling you about. I write in English to make sure I say everything

104

clearly. Now this is what I want you to do.

'Put the letter – both pages – into the first airmail envelope with my address on it. My address here at Aunt Meg's. Put the envelope addressed to Miss Crosby, folded but unsealed, into the same envelope. And also put Mummy's letter to me in the same envelope. Seal it and post it to me as soon as possible.

'That is, if you haven't got a typewriter.

'If you have got a typewriter, do you think you could copy the two letters on it? Use the blank sheets of paper that I have enclosed – four for practice and four for the real thing. Only type on one side. If you do type it, please, please type it exactly – *exactement, très exactement.*

'Then post it all back to me as I said, and put in my typed letters as well.

'I think it might look very good done on a French type-writer, but if you can't do it, we'll just have to hope for the best. I think it will be the French envelope and the French stamps that will do the trick – make the joke.

'Then can you write a separate letter to me saying that you and your parents will meet me off the plane at Nice Airport, and asking me to tell you what time I shall arrive.

'Say something about how much you are looking forward to my visit.

'Oh – and it would be a good idea to write it all in French. Send it to me here.

'Thank you. I am enjoying the adventure, and I hope you are too.

'Please, please do it *exactly*, and please hurry. As soon as possible. *Vite que possible.*

'Thanks ever so much. Hope to see you soon.

Love,

Ruth.'

Ruth checked and re-checked.

'P.S. Please put in some spare French stamps in case I need them.'

Now, have I thought of everything?

There is no real need to send out the second envelope, the one addressed to Miss Crosby, because it's only coming straight back again. But at least I can tell the truth when I say I've just received it. The more truth I can tell the better it will be.

Ruth looked at the two handwritten addresses on the two envelopes. It was a good idea to use block capitals; apparently people often did on letters to foreign countries. It was easier to forge, and Miss Crosby would have no idea what most of Mummy's capital letters looked like.

That left only the signature to work on. It had taken time. It wasn't hard to get the shape of the letters, but it was hard to iron out the wobbles where she had copied slowly and carefully.

Luckily Mummy did not make round letters like a lot of women. Her writing was small and inclined to be a bit spiky. She had read somewhere once that people who were on the quiet side and who liked working on their own often had small spiky writing. Whatever the reason, it was a piece of luck, because spikes were easier than loops and curves.

Anyway, there it was – 'C.E. Marshall (Mrs.)'

She stroked one of Aunt Meg's cats; it purred smugly, half buried in the bedclothes.

Ruth heaved a deep breath. It was the best she could manage. If it didn't work, she would have to think of something else.

*　　*　　*　　*　　*　　*

Bliss went through his letters when he got back. One from Mum and Dad, full of domestic gossip and homely advice. A brief note from Pri enclosing some old Common Entrance examination papers – it seemed as good a place as any to start with young Alan. A bank statement re-directed from his flat by Thelma.

Sherlock Bowman could turn those inside out till he was blue in the face.

Bliss turned and looked at the furniture in the bedroom, almost expecting to see socks and ties dangling from half-open drawers, in the manner of all Hollywoood film sets depicting broken-into homes.

Max wouldn't find much there either; there was nothing in his clothes except sew-in labels from St. Michael's.

Bliss scratched the back of his neck.

Over and above the annoyance was the mystery.

Why?

What was so special about Hector Bliss, Major, retired, that you had to chat him up with malt whisky, and con him into accepting an overpaid job – a job for which hundreds of other men must have been equally qualified – just so that you could be rude to his face and snoop into his mail and his underclothes behind his back?

The only clue so far had been a pair of gold cufflinks. That had stirred distant chords about Sarah. Very distant. Before the hospital and that hideous machinery. Before the crash – long before. Before the courts, before the outraged teachers, before the offended guests and neighbours. In fact before the pain and bafflement had begun.

Bliss struggled, but he could grasp nothing beyond the cufflinks. Nothing visual, that is. Aurally, there was something – a well-modulated voice that lulled him into security.

'All the formalities have been taken care of. She starts a new life with you.'

Vague impressions of black faces, automatic rifles, burning wooden bungalows, a tumbled cross, a blackboard and easel lying askew . . . .

Now there had come a second jab to the seat of the memory, something Smoothie Sherlock had said outside the Post Office – 'should you wish to reconsider'.

That took him back only eighteen months or so, when Joy and he were at least still talking to each other.

He had been away on a school adventure expedition in the Pyrenees, and virtually incommunicado for two or three weeks. Not that Joy bothered to write much anyway.

A week or two after he returned home a letter came through the box with a Buenos Aires postmark. He couldn't make head or tail of it, and asked Joy.

'Oh, some letter came while you were away, offering you a splendid job abroad.'

'What did you do with it?'

'Threw it away.'

'Why, for God's sake?'

'You wouldn't have taken it.'

'How can you be so sure?'

'No pension.'

'What is that supposed to mean?'

Joy sighed wearily.

'It means, my dear, that you would have looked all round and prodded and probed it until it had lost any bit of attraction and adventure it may have possessed. Then you would have turned your nose up at it.'

There had followed the usual tiresome scene, so repetitious that each knew what the other was going say seven sentences in advance.

Even more infuriating, at the end of it all, Joy said, 'As it happens, I agree with you this time. I would have turned it down too.'

There! After all that.

'Why?'

'He brought Sarah into it somehow.'

'Sarah?'

'Yes. I can't remember how, but it was unpleasant. I didn't like it. So I told him what to do with his job. It wasn't permanent anyway and you might have been out on your ear.'

But only just now you said – oh, what the Hell!

'Who was this man?'

'I forget now.' She thought. 'Foreigner,' she said, as if that settled it.

'Was it this name?'

Bliss held out the new letter.

Joy peered at the signature – 'M. Torres.'

'Could be.'

Bliss read part of the last paragraph aloud with heavy irony.

' "Should you wish to reconsider . . . ." '

'I should ignore it,' said Joy.

For once Bliss agreed with her.

'Should you wish to reconsider.'

Not exactly a unique piece of phraseology. All the same, it was odd that he should remember it.

He remembered too that Mr. Much-Travelled Bowman had had books in Spanish on his office shelves, and he had also referred to Sir Alec's offices in Buenos

Aires, amongst other places. The name 'Bowman' wasn't genuine, so perhaps 'Torres' wasn't either. The initial 'M' was the same. Did crooks like to stick to their own Christian name even while ringing the changes on aliases? Ha! A haven of stability in an ever-changing world?

Bliss shook his head. This was getting nowhere. He was tying a few strands of memory and hypothesis together, but he was only making knots.

Facts, Watson, are what we need.

Bliss went out into the garden; air was what he needed even more.

Company was what he got.

Dolly was crying her eyes out.

Bliss crouched beside her on the grass and looked around them. The park-like lawn was empty.

'Dolly, what on earth's the matter?'

He put an arm round her heaving shoulders, and struggled to keep his eyes away from the volcanic effects the sobs were having on her upper torso.

'That bastard!' she hissed, between eruptions. 'All because I wouldn't chuck away me pills!'

The Wandsworth vowels were showing, under stress, almost as much as the cleavage.

Bliss shook her.

'Dolly, I can't help you unless you talk straight.'

Dolly nodded, and sniffed bravely. Bliss fished a handkerchief out of his pocket.

'Ta!'

Bliss gazed nobly at the sky as Dolly took deep breaths and blew.

'Now, what is it?'

Bliss released her shoulder and sat down properly on the manicured grass.

Dolly began kneading the handkerchief.

'I know I'm not much of a girl really.'

That was the understatement of the year. However, Bliss listened solemnly.

Dolly wiped her eyes.

'I mean – you know – I haven't got any O-Levels or things like that. All I've got is a body.'

You can say that again.

Dolly blinked.

'Men don't come after O-Levels; it puts 'em off.'

Bliss thought of the fearsome Dr. Marshall and her string of degrees. Thanks to Aunt Jane, though, he had got around to speaking to her, if only to utter a hesitant invitation.

Dolly sniffed again.

'But they do come after people like me.'

'So it would seem, Dolly.'

'I don't mind, in a way. I mean, it's flattering really. But then you find out that they're all the same. They think that because you're full up here – ' a pat on the subsiding superstructure ' – you're empty up here.' A touch on the temple.

'I may not have the brains for O-Levels, but that don't mean I've got none at all. Men always think simple, have you noticed?'

For someone with a lowly-estimated IQ, Dolly was managing the soliloquy on philosophy pretty well.

'You were saying about – ' began Bliss, but hesitated. He didn't want to upset Dolly again by saying the wrong name.

'Sir Alec, yes.'

Sir Alec, eh? The 'Don Juan' part, obviously.

'How did you meet him?'

'Oh – we went on one of them club coach trips to Spain – Allicanty. Whole lot of us. We thought it was wild – no clothes on the beach all day, and in and out of bed with each other all night. I suppose it was like – well – raising two fingers to everything back home. Though I didn't want Dad to know – not really.

'Anyway, I got fed up with being half-plastered all the time, and I bumped into Sir Alec. 'Least, I met Max, and he introduced me to Sir Alec.'

Yet another way in which Mr. Fixit was of inestimable service to his employer – talent-spotter. Was there no end to the man's uses?

'What were they doing there?'

Dolly waved vaguely.

'Oh – Sir Alec owns about a million hotels up and down the coast.'

'Why do you still call him that?'

'What?'

' "Sir Alec." You surely can't say "Sir Alec" when you. . . .'

Dolly grinned for the first time, and pretended to slap his wrist.

'Silly!'

Then she became serious again.

'No, I made that mistake once. I called him "Alec" or "love" or something at the lunch table. You should have seen how quickly Max got on to me afterwards. I had the bruises on my arm for a fortnight.'

'Didn't he – Max – ever make a pass at you?'

Dolly shook her head vigorously.

'No. More than his job's worth. He's scared of Sir Alec, you know. Deep down. No – he wouldn't touch me, not like that. Besides, it's not his style. I reckon he gets his

112

kicks being nasty.'

In addition to being a philosopher, Dolly was a perceptive student of human nature.

'If you didn't like it,' said Bliss, 'why didn't you go back home?'

Dolly widened her eyes.

'Have you seen Earlsfield?'

'Earlsfield?'

'It's where I come from, halfway between Wimbledon and Clapham.'

Ah, so it was Earlsfield, not Wandsworth. Close though.

Dolly waved a hand at the blazing flower beds and the groves and the alcoves, and the garden furniture set out with discreet artistry. Artificial streams tinkled joyously over imported pebbles.

'Now look at all this.'

She blew her nose again.

'Besides, Max said I couldn't go.'

'Couldn't go?'

'Sort of. Said, if I did, he'd tell my Dad all about Spain and Sir Alec and everything.'

'That's blackmail.'

'Yes, it is, isn't it?' Dolly agreed readily. 'But I worked it out; if I played my cards right, Sir Alec would get fed up and pack me off soon enough anyway.'

Dolly was a tactician too.

'You mean,' said Bliss, 'a few "headaches" in the evening?'

'Something like that. There are ways and means.'

There were ways and means all right, and Joy had known all of them.

'Mind you, he was generous,' admitted Dolly. 'I had

more spending money in a month than I had in a year at the supermarket. So I thought I could save a bit. Take 'em all presents when I went home and still have plenty left over for a deposit on a flat or something. You know – a place of me own.'

'What went wrong then?'

Dolly became wary.

'How do I know I can trust you?'

'I trusted you with my handkerchief.'

Dolly gave him a gentle push.

'You know what I mean.'

Bliss took her hand.

'Dolly, you will trust me because you're bursting to tell somebody something and I'm the only one around who's English, and hasn't made a pass at you.'

'What about Dr. Marshall?'

'You won't tell her because I'll make a level bet she disapproves of you.'

Dolly grimaced.

'You're right; she does.'

'She disapproves of me too.'

Dolly stared.

'Honest?'

'Honest.'

'But you're nice.'

'Flattery, Dolly, will get you anywhere with me. As a matter of fact, I think you're very nice too.'

'Get on with you!'

Another, almost shy grin.

'So,' said Bliss, 'we have that much in common; we think we're both nice. Not a bad start. And I'll tell you something else.'

'What's that?'

'I don't like Max either.'

'What's he done to you?'

'A long story. Right now, you're doing the story-telling. I have now proved to you beyond any shadow of a doubt that we are practically twin souls. And if that isn't enough, I have an elderly widowed aunt who is staying on a yacht near Cannes – right now – who will assure you that I was an officer and am still a gentleman.'

'Honest?'

'Dolly, I could never have invented my Aunt Jane in a thousand years. I'll tell you how to find her, and you can go and see her any time you like. I've already told her about you.'

Dolly looked him straight in the eye for a moment, then decided to take the plunge.

'Well, it's Cass.'

'Cass?'

'Yes. You see, things were going fine until Cass came along.'

'How did you meet?'

'He's Polish, you know.'

'Casimir.'

'Yes. It's Casimir Broc – something or other. I still can't spell it. Can't even say it properly. Sir Alec picked him up somehow and offered to get him out of Poland.'

'Sir Alec goes behind the Iron Curtain?'

'Where?' said Dolly blankly.

'Sir Alec deals with Communist countries?'

Light dawned.

'Oh. You mean, like Russia. Yes. He'll do business with the Devil. You should see the string of Yids and wogs who come to the house. Straight out of James Bond, some of 'em. Anyway, I was saying – Cass. He'd been in some political trouble with the police – something to do with trade unions, I think. At least the police were after him; I don't think Cass understands it himself, poor love. Still – '

Bliss held up a hand.

'I can guess; don't tell me. Friend Max fixes up a fake passport and identity papers, smuggles him out, and Sir Alec has another willing worker whom he can blackmail if he shows any sign of independence.'

'Something like that.'

'Then he comes here and Lady Sherrif thinks he's dishy and she says, if hubby can have his girls I can have my boys. Sir Alec doesn't care, so everything's fine. Am I right?'

'Julie's a cow,' said Dolly with great vehemence.

'I've no doubt.'

'Even Sir Alec doesn't like her – not now. He only keeps her for appearances – sort of wears her like human jewellery.'

And Dolly reckoned she wasn't very bright! Bliss' regard for her intelligence was going up by the minute.

Dolly sniffed.

'And Cass isn't a boy; he knows what he wants, and it isn't Julie.'

'Julie doesn't seem to think so.'

'Julie changes her men like pants. Besides, what choice did Cass have? Any trouble, and he's back to Warsaw or wherever.'

'You like Cass, don't you?'

A soft look came into Dolly's eyes.

'He's a love. And he likes me for what I am. He's a bit thick, like me; we understand each other.'

She gazed fondly at nothing for a moment.

'He's teaching me tennis. It's fun.'

'Service with a smile?' prompted Bliss.

Dolly nudged him good-humouredly.

'He's lovely.'

Bliss remembered the furtive figure following him earlier that day. It was a shame to shatter Dolly's dream, but the sooner he did it the better. Dolly, with her kind heart and her brimming body, had gone and fallen in love – a dangerous thing to do in this glittering world of wealth and selfish calculation.

'Dolly, there's something you ought to know, before you go any further.'

'What?'

Bliss hesitated.

'Look. I don't like saying this, but believe me I'm doing it for your good.'

Dolly frowned.

'Come on – out with it.'

'Cass works for Max.'

'You're joking.'

'It's true. I noticed him following me only this morning, as soon as Max left me. He must have been doing it for days.'

Dolly laughed. Bliss felt slightly nettled.

'What's so funny?'

'Of course Cass has been following you. He's been trying to talk to you, only he can't quite make up his mind, poor love.' Dolly grimaced. 'My fault really. I told him you couldn't be trusted.'

'Thanks.'

'Well, how was I to know? You turn up out of the blue, all ready to teach the young master. You weren't some poor devil on the run with a fake passport, were you? You can tell Sir Alec to go to Hell any time you like.'

'So can you.'

'Maybe, if I don't mind me Dad finding out. But Cass can't. Not until he can get to somewhere like England and get some proper papers and ask for – what is it?'

'Political asylum.'

'That's it. He thought you might help, being English and all, and knowing a thing or two. But we can't let Max find out. Or Sir Alec. It's no fun – all this waiting and wondering.'

'Does Julie know about you and Cass?'

'Don't think so. She wouldn't care.'

'I bet Sir Alec would.'

Dolly frowned.

'Yes, that's the trouble. When we realised it might take some time, I had to change round a bit with Sir Alec.'

'You mean, go back to being nice?'

'Yes. I couldn't have him getting fed up and kicking me out and leaving Cass here by himself. He might do something desperate, poor love.'

Bliss noted the motherly element creeping into Dolly's affections. Talk about lie back and think of England – or rather Poland.

'Did you manage it?'

Dolly looked glum.

'Yes, that's just the trouble. I made too good a job of it.'

Bliss' mind boggled.

Dolly glowered.

'D'you know what? He wanted me to have a baby. His baby!'

'Cass?'

Dolly tossed her head in annoyance.

'No! Sir Alec. Said he'd provide for me and all. Julie

won't have any kids, he said, and he felt his – what was it? – his "best years slipping away".'

Dolly shook her head in wonderment.

'Said I'd never want for the rest of my life. Bloody cheek!'

'What did you tell him to do with his suggestion?'

'Told him to stuff it.'

Bliss kept his face straight with an effort.

'What happens now?'

Dolly's eyes flashed fire.

'I'll tell you what happens now. Sir Alec drops me like a hot brick. I'm in my room cooling off and in comes Max and says that a "foreign business associate" of Sir Alec's is coming to stay and I'm supposed to "entertain" him. You know what I mean?'

Bliss nodded sadly.

'And Max says I'd better not leave, because something nasty might happen – telling my Dad and all that.'

'Nothing else?'

'He didn't hurt me this time, no. Says he didn't want our visitor to be handling broken goods. Bastard!'

'Does he know about Cass?'

Dolly shook her head.

'No. 'Least, I don't think so. He went on making vague threats, about my family. And me. But he can't do anything. I don't care if Dad does know now.'

She began crying again, in rage and humiliation.

'I'm know I'm not much of a girl, but Christ! D'you know who this bloke is?'

'This "business associate"?'

'Yes. Some fuzzy-wuzzy from Egypt or Sedan – I don't know – somewhere in the Far East.'

Bliss resisted the schoolmaster's urge to correct her

geography and anthropology; she was in full flow.

'And this Sherrif sod wants to farm me out. I don't mind being someone's woman, kept private sort of – ' Dolly breathed fire ' – but I'm buggered if I'm going public.'

Chapter Five

BLISS PASSED THE binoculars, and pointed with his free hand.

'See? I think that's the *Canberra*.'

He watched her twiddle the focus rings and push a strand of hair from her eyes.

If she were not so tight-lipped all the time, she wouldn't be bad-looking. He realised too, now, that the set of the jaw and the downward edges of the mouth came not from disapproval but from tenseness.

Half an hour on deck amid the coffee cups had demonstrated that. Aunt Jane had stage-managed everything with her usual aplomb.

'Now, you two will stop behaving like shy children at your first party. You, Connie, I can see, are a very nice person, and most attractive. Hector, why didn't you tell me she was attractive?'

'I –'

'Hector, sometimes I despair of you.'

She turned back to Connie.

'It's all that bachelor living in officers' messes and school common rooms. Stunts the personality. But I can assure you he is quite harmless and very used to behaving himself. Hector – pull up the chairs and get a cushion from over there.'

The coffee was brought by a servant in a freshly-laundered white monkey-jacket and tight black trousers.

'Isn't he gorgeous?' whispered Aunt Jane like a

conspirator when he was out of earshot. 'Moves like Valentino.'

Connie was forced to grin.

'Now,' said Aunt Jane. 'You will pass each other sugar and biscuits and you will call each other "Hector" and "Connie" and let's have no more of this formality nonsense. Hector – pour!'

After a start like that, neither of them had much of a chance. By the time Aunt Jane saw them off and back to the marina, the Christian names at least tripped fairly easily off the tongue.

Bliss still felt that there was a sort of 'coiled-spring' air about her, rather similar to the slightly absent air one notices when talking to someone who is going to have a tooth taken out in half an hour.

He also caught her looking searchingly at him once or twice, as if trying to make up her mind about something.

However, when he suggested a drive to Cannes and a walk along the front, she accepted readily enough.

She followed the liner for a while, then swung the binoculars upwards to catch an aeroplane whose engine she had heard.

'Why do those odd-looking things keep flying to and fro? They've been at it some time.'

'They scoop up great dollops of water, fly inland, and drop it on any forest or grass fires. There's nothing serious at the moment – just the odd patch.'

'I've heard of them, but I've never seen them.'

'You've been here before then?' said Bliss.

'Yes,' she said shortly. 'Quite a few times.'

'Business?' he prompted.

'Yes.'

Again that sidelong, searching look. Bliss unscrewed the tension.

'I expect they want the place nice and tidy for the Film Festival. Can't have our starlets' complexions ruined by smuts in drifting smoke, can we?'

Connie managed a grateful grin. She gestured to the sunburned seal colony of gorgeous shimmering bodies on the beach.

'They certainly look all right at the moment.'

Bliss laughed.

'It's a job to know where to put your eyes, isn't it?'

'I wouldn't know; I'm not a man.'

'But you're human at least; that's the first time I've seen you smile – really smile.'

'Thank you.'

'Look,' said Bliss on impulse, 'would you like to go somewhere quieter? Let's get away from this bare breast barbecue and go and have lunch. There's a nice place back in Ste. Sophie; I can recommend it. The locals use it.'

'Don't tell me,' said Connie. '*Le Restaurant des Mimosas.*'

They both laughed together.

'It's like a bear garden in there,' said Connie. 'I've been past it sometimes.'

'Nice friendly creatures – bears. Have you ever tried it?'

'Well, no.'

'Then it's time you did. It'll make a change from the caviar and the *premier cru.* Come on.'

It was cool inside. It was also noisy and crowded. All the side tables were taken, and they had to squeeze on the end of a long row of tables joined together. It stretched from the back wall right down the middle of the restaurant almost to the open doorway. Every seat except the bottom two was occupied, so it seemed, by a large Frenchman in a check shirt, blue trousers, and cap.

Connie looked furtively up the length of this huge banqueting board. Tiny sprays of flowers stood in empty mustard jars; bowls of vegetables steamed; droplets of condensation shone on tall bottles fresh from the fridge. A multi-limbed octopus of brawny brown arms reached constantly for bread, salt, wine and mineral water. Crumbs were spilt; wine was poured into soup; lumps of bread were wiped round plates to get the last of the gravy.

In the corner, to the left of the door, was the bar, policed by its regulars on their high stools. All Connie could see of them was hunched shoulders, blue overalls stretched over ample buttocks, and cigarette smoke.

'See?' said Bliss. 'It's not so bad, is it?'

Connie smiled.

'It's certainly very French.'

Bliss nodded.

'You won't get tourists in here. So for an hour you can forget Sir Alec and Max and everything, and just enjoy plonk and wodge for next to nothing.'

A bright, busy young woman in a black dress and flip-flop sandals bustled round them with a new sheet of paper to cover the red-check tablecloth. She took their order, dumped a bottle of red wine and one of mineral water in front of them, and dashed off to the kitchen.

Bliss looked at Connie's face. She was trying bravely to enjoy herself, but not succeeding very well. If he pressed her at this stage, she might go back completely into her shell. Perhaps if *he* did some talking, it might prompt a reaction. Make it look as if *she* could help *him*.

'Look, I'm the new boy here, and you've been here

before. There are one or two things about the general set-up that I don't quite follow. I wonder if you could help.'

The eyes were watchful.

'How do you mean?'

'Well, for example, the boy himself.'

'Alan?'

'Yes.'

Connie looked surprised.

'Haven't you met him?'

'No.'

'You took him on blind?'

'I've always taken classes on blind. What's the difference?'

Connie shrugged.

'Not much, I suppose.'

'I don't suppose you can choose the students you lecture to.'

'All right. Point taken. But I don't think I can help you much.'

'You can. For instance, I put my foot in it with Julie the first evening by assuming that Alan was her son.'

'Oh, dear.'

'Ah, you understand then.'

'Yes. Julie and Sir Alec have only been married for about seven or eight years, I think. And . . . .'

Connie hesitated. Bliss finished it for her.

'. . . the first flush of passion has now faded?'

'I should imagine so.'

'And they each take consolation elsewhere?'

Connie's jaw tightened.

'If you call a little madam like Dolly "consolation", yes.'

'Little' was hardly the word Bliss would have used

for Dolly, but he let it go. Nor did he wish to antagonise Connie at this early stage by an argument over Dolly's moral stature.

'Do you think Julie wanted children once?' he asked innocently, keeping Dolly's recent revelations to himself.

'I suppose it's possible. Or perhaps he did and she didn't – hence the rift. Or perhaps she couldn't. That happens sometimes.'

The jaw tightened again, and Bliss sensed he was on delicate ground. So he shifted.

'Who is the boy's mother then?'

'Sir Alec's first wife, obviously.'

'What happened to her?'

'She was killed, I believe, in an accident. It was before I started coming, you understand. So far as I can make out, the official version – '

'You mean, Max's version?'

It was a shot in the dark, but, as it happened, not a bad shot.

She looked at him oddly.

'Yes, now that you mention it. Why?'

'Never mind. Go on.'

'Well, the story is that they were visiting some South American country where Sir Alec has mining interests. Brazil, I believe. His wife was actually declaring something open, I think. There was an explosion and – '

Connie broke off suddenly. A look of disbelief settled on her face. Bliss was quite alarmed.

They were interrupted by a large basket of bread appearing between them, and an even larger tureen of soup. Plates and cutlery clattered in from nowhere, and there was a hasty 'Bon appetit' before the girl scuffled off again.

By that time Connie had pulled herself together.

'Anyway, there was an enquiry, but they found nothing untoward. They couldn't even recover the bodies; half the mountain had fallen in. Sir Alec shut the whole place, gave a million to the relatives' distress fund, named a new hospital after his wife, and that was that.'

She had recovered from whatever initial shock it was. She was under control, but she was obviously thinking of something else all the time.

'What about the boy?'

She came to with an effort.

'Alan? He was only a baby then. Mademoiselle Aline looked after him while he was small.'

'Ah, that explains something else,' said Bliss.

'What?'

'I don't think Mademoiselle Aline approved of me much, until I started talking about Alan. I think she imagined I was some sort of Mr. Squeers who was going to brainwash the boy into becoming the perfect knuck-le-head public-school Englishman. You know – cold baths, shooting-sticks and point-to-point, and solid wood from the neck up.'

Connie smiled.

'Is the public school system really as bad as that?'

'No. But a lot of people still think it is.'

'Ruth's school isn't.'

That was the first chink of light she had let out. Don't pounce, or you'll lose her again.

'There are a lot of very good ones,' he agreed. 'And you can't lump the day schools with the boarding schools.'

'Yes. Ruth's is a day school.'

The chink was getting wider. Let it open of its own accord.

'Anyway, Mademoiselle Aline was the only one round that table who showed the slightest interest in Alan. I mean real interest, not polite inquiry.'

'She is very fond of the boy.'

'Have you ever met him?'

'Only once. My – er – visits don't coincide with his holidays as a rule. Nice little fellow.'

Bliss broke some bread. Connie finished her soup. Patience, patience – the chink might be widening again.

'The story is,' said Connie, 'that Mademoiselle Aline didn't want him to go to school in England. Not so young anyway. Mind you, I think, thanks to her, he's almost bi-lingual. She's very good with children. I've seen her with some of the staff boys and girls.'

'She looks pretty forbidding to me.'

Connie smiled.

'So did I, you said.'

That's more like it.

Bliss smiled back.

'Remember what Aunt Jane said? I'm not very good at judging that sort of thing. More soup?'

He proffered the huge soup ladle.

'No thanks.'

The plates were whisked away, to be replaced almost instantly by the *plat du jour* – a colossal pork chop and a mountain of Brussels sprouts.

Bliss refilled the glasses.

'You'd have thought Sir Alec might show some interest. After all, it's his son. And he hired me. But do you know – he hasn't said a word to me since I got here. Just smiles charmingly and stands back at doorways.'

Connie paused with her fork midway.

'D'you mean to say you don't know?'

'Don't know what?'

'About Sir Alec.'

'What about him?'

'He's dumb.'

Bliss stared.

'You're kidding!'

'No. It's true.'

'But there's nothing wrong with his hearing.'

'He hasn't been dumb from birth. And I think it's some psychological thing, not a physical defect. It goes back, apparently, to that accident I was describing, when his wife was killed. The shock must have been colossal.'

She broke off again .... accident .... shock .... colossal .... how pathetically inadequate. A whole library of dictionaries could not produce the words to describe the sheer awfulness. She caught sight of Bliss' keen look, and recovered quickly.

'They say his hair went grey, and he lost the power of speech.'

'I've never seen him use sign language.'

'He's vain,' said Connie, with surprising definiteness. 'He hates showing the slightest sign of physical weakness. Hence the trim figure, the healthy glow, the passion for sport. Besides, Max does all the negotiations. Max is his voice. Max is always there.'

'Max,' said Bliss. 'It always comes back to Max. He was the one who told you about the accident.'

'Yes. Sir Alec couldn't, could he?'

'True. But it *is* always Max, isn't it? Max makes the appointments; Max greets the VIP's; Max runs the shop; Max hires the staff. He hired me. I bet he hired you.'

'Yes.'

No details. Careful with that chink of light.

'I bet he runs the house too.'

Connie shook her head.

'Mademoiselle Aline has more influence than you imagine. And if you are thinking that Sir Alec is a mere cipher, let me assure you that nothing could be further from the truth.'

That was said with great intensity. We were close to a nerve here.

Bliss recalled Dolly's shrewd comment on Max – 'He's scared of Sir Alec, you know. Deep down.'

Bliss tried to move away from a sensitive area.

'All right, so Max is the number two.' He tried to make light of it, watching carefully however for any flicker of reaction. 'That man and his white cuffs. Did you ever see such a smoothie? Such glossy English? And yet he's foreign; I'll bet my boots on it.'

'He's foreign all right.'

The answer came sharply enough. Bliss drank his wine, waiting tensely for the follow-up. He could feel Connie watching him, examining him, struggling to come to a decision about him.

The chink of light was as wide as it had been all morning. If he didn't do something to get his foot in the door, he was afraid it would swing shut. It might shut on his foot anyway, but it was surely worth a try. Couldn't he let her see that he was at least willing to help?

He put down his glass and looked around. There was no need for discretion; everyone else was totally absorbed in eating, drinking, and laying down the law. Nobody was paying the slightest attention to them.

'Look, Connie, tell me to mind my own business if you like, but my guess is you're worried about something and you badly need someone to talk to about it. Wouldn't I do?'

He made a face.

'Bring your problems to good old Mr. Chips and get a sympathetic ear.'

Connie gazed down at her plate.

'It's nothing – really it isn't.'

Bliss tried once more.

'One of the tricks I learned as a schoolmaster was a certain facility in detecting deceit. I don't mind your not telling me what your problem is; that offends only my pride. But please don't tell me there isn't a problem; that offends my intelligence.'

Connie looked up.

'Sorry.'

'So we'll leave it at that, shall we? You have a problem, but you don't trust me enough to tell me. Is that right?'

Connie winced.

'Come on,' said Bliss. 'Honesty, at least, if you can't manage openness.'

'Yes, that's about it,' she finally admitted.

'Good. I'll settle for that – for the time being. Now let's try some of the cheese these gentlemen are wolfing. We might as well have our money's worth.'

$$* \quad * \quad \times \quad * \quad * \quad *$$

The travel agent lady was a bit stern but clear and straightforward.

'I'm afraid I couldn't sell you an airline ticket just like that,' she said.

'Not even if I show you my passport?'

'It's not a question of a passport, dear; it's a question of parental control.'

'Well, if I show you a letter from my mother?'

'I'm afraid it's not as simple as that.'

'You mean there are laws?'

'Not exactly laws. But we in the travel business must act in a responsible manner; we can't sell airline tickets to any ch – any young person who comes in and asks for one. Surely you see that. It could be dangerous for them on such long journeys, especially out of the country.'

Ruth thought.

'What if an adult buys it for me?'

'That's different. But you must also be put on the plane by an adult and you must have arrangements to be met at the other end.'

Ruth nodded.

'Right. Thank you very much. Goodbye.

That wasn't too bad, then. She would just have to get Miss Crosby to send someone down to buy the ticket, that's all.

She stopped outside Boot's. Might as well get the sun oil. It was supposed to be very hot on the Riviera. Might look a bit silly, though, asking for 'Ambre Solaire' in England in early June. Better stick to 'Nivea'.

Then to Marks to look at sleeveless blouses, and round to the Post Office for the last fifty pounds.

Please God! Make Henriette's letter come soon.

*   *   *   *   *   *

'Hallo, Pri? . . . . Yes, fine thanks . . . . Yes, she's fine too. On great form . . . . 'Matter of fact, I'm speaking to you from her yacht . . . . Yes, she's arranged it. She's got the whole family eating out of her hand. The crew are devoted to her as well. She's having a whale of a time – off to the Film Festival soon . . . . Look, I've got to be quick, cos this is costing a fortune. Get a pencil and paper . . . . I can't; I don't want them to know at the house what I'm up to . . . . because I might be folowed, and anyway cafés have ears. Just get the pencil and paper like a good chap, will you? . . . . Right. Now, as you may have guessed, there could be a spot of bother here . . . . No, she's all right; she's safe on her yacht, and she has her own private navy round her. No, I've met someone who I think may be in trouble, and I'd like to help.

'But I need information. So I want you to wake up your firm's private eye, tell him to put away his infra-red telescopic lenses and get out his magnifying glass . . . . Yes, yes, I'll pay. Take it out of my pension. I've got money to burn here. I want the lowdown on – ready? – Dr. Constance Marshall. Married. Widowed . . . . What? . . . . Oh, late thirties, I suppose. She's a Cambridge Ph.D. in Mathematics and she lectures in a college somewhere in or around London. She did tell me which one, but I've forgotten . . . . Well, I'm sorry. Your man has lists and things, hasn't he? If I knew everything I wouldn't be paying him to find out. It's personal rather than professional detail I want, though anything he can find will be welcome – you know, education, background, husband, family – that sort of thing . . . . No, there's another. Much more interesting, this one. Calls himself Max Bowman . . . . Max Bowman – B-O-W – Bowman, but it's probably an alias. He might have another alias – Torres – T-O-R-R –E-S – . . . Yes. He's almost certainly a crook . . . . blackmail, fake documents, possible violence, maybe sharp business practice – try mining or the hotel trade . . . . Hotel trade . . . . Poses as a lawyer . . . . Well, I'm sorry, Pri; he does. It's not my fault if all legal practitioners are not Sir Galahad like you . . . . Late fifties, maybe sixty or more. Very well preserved. Almost certainly speaks Spanish, and probably other languages as well. Near-perfect

English, but I can't place the accent. Works ostensibly for Sir-You-Know-Who, KBE . . . . What? . . . . Don't have much to do with him; he's a man of few words, as you might say . . . . sorry, private joke. I'll explain some other time. Now get your nosey-parker into his hansom cab and tell him it's a three-pipe problem and we want some results pretty fast . . . . Oh, come on, Pri. He'll jump at it; anything like this must be a welcome break from poison pen letters and suspected infidelity. I'll give you another ring in twenty-four hours . . . . It's not; it gives him a full working day. What more does he want? . . . . Yes, yes, all right. Just see to it, please, Pri. It could be important.

'Oh, one other thing – get on to Foyles and order two copies each of the first two books in the series "The Cambridge Introduction to the History of Mankind". The first is called *Men Become Civilised*. Got that? . . . . The second is called *The Romans and their Empire*. . . . Yes, "Empire". They're both by Trevor Cairns – C-A-I-R-N-S . . . . Cambridge University Press, of course. Get them out to me as soon as possible; put them in the diplomatic bag or something . . . . Yes. It'll be a novel experience to teach two of the great Mediterranean civilisations in the Mediterranean . . . . Yes . . . . I will . . . . Thanks again, Pri . . . . Love to Joan. Tell Mum and Dad I'm fine . . . . 'Bye.'

*　　*　　*　　*　　*　　*

The vehicle swung round the corner and jumped the lights.

Bliss saw it, but the woman half-way across the road did not. She was trusting the lights. Foolish, thought Bliss; you would have thought the French knew better.

He leapt from the pavement, caught the woman by the elbow, and practically frog-marched her to the other side.

She turned, furious, and opened her mouth to say something, when the familiar two-tone siren burst forth. The huge red machine rushed by, sprinkled with firemen in varying stages of undress.

Immediately the woman understood. She recognised him too, and for a moment suspicion and gratitude fought a battle on her face.

'Thank you, monsieur,' she managed at last.

'I'm sorry, Mademoiselle Aline,' said Bliss, 'but there was no time to explain. Are you all right?'

'Yes, thank you.'

Another fire-appliance vehicle rushed noisily by. Owners and customers came to the doorways of shops.

'I see no smoke,' said Bliss, pointing to the Tanneron Massif above them.

'The fires are not here,' said Aline. 'They are in the forests behind Fréjus and St. Raphael. It was on the local news this morning.'

'Early for fires,' observed Bliss.

'Yes. But the police say it could be deliberate – the work of terrorists.'

'Terrorists?'

'Basques, Corsicans, Arabs – who knows? Perhaps they time it for the Festival.'

'The utter selfishness behind the cloak of noble patriotism,' said Bliss.

Aline looked keenly at him.

'You speak good French, for – '

' – for an Englishman?' said Bliss.

I've caught her on the hop, figuratively as well as literally. If I don't jump in now, I'll never get another chance like this.

'I'm also quite acceptable – for an Englishman,' he said.

Before she could reply, he went on. 'I really do want what is best for Alan, you know. I am not what you think I am.'

He fell into step beside her. She made no attempt to escape him.

'Are you married, Mr. Bliss?'

'Divorced. May I carry your bag for you?'

To his surprise, she agreed.

'Have you any children?'

'I had one – a daughter. She was killed about a year ago.'

'I am sorry. I did not know. It must be a great loss for you.'

Bliss did not pursue that line.

'You must be very fond of Alan then?' he ventured.

'I cared for him until Sir Alec – until he went to school.'

You were going to say 'until Sir Alec took him away'.

'How old was he then?'

'Five.'

'Too young, do you think?'

The eyes grew watchful.

'I did not say that.'

So you are wary of Sir Alec too. You have that much in common with Max, but that's all, I'd say. Let's try you.'

'I'm surprised you did not know more about me. Max interviewed me pretty thoroughly.'

'Sir Alec and his – secretary do not confide their business secrets to me,' she said.

Ah, I thought so. So nobody likes Max. I don't blame them.

They had reached the pedestrian crossing.

'May I, Mademoiselle?' said Bliss, taking her elbow. 'This time, with your permission?'

At last he got a soft look out of her. Not exactly a

smile, but the features definitely eased. She had been beautiful once, judging by the bone structure. Then there had come some tragedy or shock. Connie's strain looked intense, immediate. The strain on Mademoiselle Aline's face looked as though it had its origins in the deep past.

Think fast, Hector.

'I was wondering, Mademoiselle, if you have finished your trip, whether I could give you a lift back to the house?'

'I have a car here, waiting for me.'

You don't mean 'no'; you mean 'give me an excuse not to use it'.

'I was rather hoping you could help me about Alan. I have to plan outdoor activities as well as indoor ones. You know Alan so well – all the things he is fond of. I should like to build on his preferences if possible.'

She was melting by the minute.

'I should be so grateful, Mademoiselle, for your assistance. Nobody else knows the boy as you do.' Bliss tried an extra tactic. 'Tell me where the car is and I'll dismiss the driver.'

Mademoiselle Aline thought deliberately before she spoke.

'That will not be necessary, Mr. Bliss. I shall ring him up on the car phone when we get back and tell him I came home by taxi from the other end of the town. I shall be pleased to accept your invitation.'

My word, Bliss, me boy! You're becoming quite a charmer. If only Aunt Jane could see you now.

Interesting, though, that she didn't want the driver to know she was travelling with me. Who is she afraid of – Max? Or Sir Alec? Or both?

*   *   *   *   *   *

137

'How did you get on?'

'Not bad at all. She told me quite a lot about Alan.'

'Alan?'

'The boy I'm going to be teaching.'

Aunt Jane looked up from her knitting.

'Hector, who are we talking about?'

'Mademoiselle Aline, the housekeeper. I think I've unfrozen her. She's obviously very fond of the boy, and I used that to get her to talk. I think I've convinced her I'm not one of Sir Alec's minions.'

Aunt Jane waved a needle in annoyance.

'It's Connie I want to know about. Have you convinced *her*?'

Bliss looked glum.

'No – at any rate, not yet.'

'I'm not surprised, if you're all over the housekeeper.'

'That's not fair, Aunt Jane.'

'She is a woman, isn't she?'

'Who? Aline?'

'Ah, so it's "Aline" now, is it?'

'Don't make snide remarks. As a matter of fact, we took some care to make our conversation discreet.'

'Furtive meetings in dark corners too?'

'Aunt Jane, stop it!'

The eyes twinkled over the spectacles.

'All right. Now, what did Connie say?'

'Not much. But she did admit she has a problem. She kept wondering whether to tell me or not – you could see. But in the end she decided against it.'

'Not good enough, Hector.'

'No, I know. So I'll have to try again.'

'It had better be something different this time.'

'Why?'

'You've tried the charm. and that's obviously working. She came on board for coffee. She had lunch with you. She hasn't refused to see you again. And I expect you've shamed her too.'

'Yes, I think I have.'

Aunt Jane punched the air with her fist.

'Good. She's cracking. Come at her now from another angle and she'll fall to bits.'

'Any ideas?'

'She wants proof, Hector.'

'Proof?'

'Proof you're on her side.'

'How do I do that?'

'Think of something. You're the tactician. I'm only the strategist.'

*　　*　　×　　*　　*　　*

'May I spik with you?'

Bliss jumped.

Cass had materialised form some shrubbery so suddenly that Bliss almost fell off the chair he was lounging in. As it was, he dropped his book.

Somewhat flustered, he motioned the young man to another chair. He looked about them. Apart from a distant, and most assiduous under-gardener, they had the lawns to themselves.

'Mister Bliss, I must tell you things about myself.'

Bliss stifled a sigh. Oh, well – if you must. Why was it that the people he wanted to talk wouldn't, or at any rate not much, while others whose confessions he could have done without seemed only too willing to confide half their life story? It was not so far from this very spot that Dolly – admittedly under great provocation – had

139

used his presence as an opportunity to get a lot off her ample chest.

However, he listened while Cass, having removed his sweat band and carefully stowed it in his pocket, embarked on a lengthy, involved, and over-detailed story of the circumstances which had brought him to his present parlous position as resident gigolo to the wife of a multi-millionaire.

Cass' English could not really stand up to a sustained narrative, and Bliss' memory could not cope with the recital of names from Polish politics, industry, and geography. What he really wanted to do was concentrate on finding a way of getting into Connie's confidence. He didn't dislike Cass; the dourness had faded with lengthier acquaintance, and he had had glowing testimonials from Dolly. But frankly he could have done without him at this particular moment.

As a means of shortening the monologue, which was becoming increasingly mid-European and impenetrable, he cut in with some questions, and elicited a few clear facts. Cass and Dolly were 'in the love', they wanted to run away, and Cass wished to know how to get into England and find legitimate work.

Bliss told him about the Foreign Office and about basic immigration regulations. He warned him of the likelihood of interrogation, and suggested total honesty if the young man were to avoid possible deportation back to Poland. He taught him how to pronounce the words 'political asylum', and gave him the name of an ex-brother officer in Counter-Intelligence at the War Office. As an afterthought, he wrote out Pri's name, address, and telephone number, explained how he could be contacted through Aunt Jane, and drew a diagram of the marina at La Napoule to show where the yacht's berth was. He made a mental note to apologise to his brother later.

Cass was profuse in his thanks.

'You are so kind, Mr. Bliss.'

'Not at all.'

'So kind. Dolly is right. She said to me you are the nice man.'

Not at first she didn't. However . . . .

Cass wrung his hand.

'You give me courage, Mister Bliss. Some day soon, I know, I shall talk with Dolly's father in the Field of Earl. I shall tell him we are the lovers, and ask to give to me her hand in wedding.'

*   *   *   *   *   *

'Hallo, Pri? . . . . Yes, I've just been talking to her . . . . Fine . . . . What have your Baker Street irregulars got for me? . . . . Yes, I know about the degrees . . . . Oh, *that* college? . . . . Yes, got that. Research too, eh? Bright girl, our Connie . . . . Mind your own business. What else? . . . . Yes, I know that too. What happened to him? . . . . Where? . . . . Did you say "in a lift"? . . . . A bomb, in a lift? . . . . No, nothing. It's odd, though. I've read about a similar incident somewhere, and quite recently . . . . Anyway, what's the daughter's name? . . . . Ah! . . . . Yes, I know the age. She told me . . . . What? . . . . Good Lord! . . . . No. She never told me that . . . . Is that all? . . . . Hmm. What about Smoothie Max? . . . . Max Bowman . . . . All right, I only asked . . . . Yes, I'll wait. Give you another ring tomorrow . . . . Thanks, Pri . . . . 'Bye.'

*   *   *   *   *   *

'What did you find out?' said Aunt Jane.

141

Bliss told her.

'Well,' she said, 'that's something you have in common. Might be a help.'

'Yes,' agreed Bliss. 'It might explain why she was hired to come here.'

'I didn't mean that.'

'No, I know.'

Aunt Jane frowned.

'I don't follow.'

'Well, I'm not sure I can make sense of it yet,' said Bliss. 'But it's odd, isn't it? We are both English, both to do with the academic profession, we both have adopted children – or had – we both are hired to work here for the summer season, and we are both overpaid for duties that nobody could call burdensome.'

'Is she overpaid too?'

'She hinted as much. Oh – and one other thing. She doesn't like Max either. I wonder . . . . '

'What?'

'I wonder if she's met Max before?'

'You mean some love affair?'

'Oh, good Lord, no! I mean, to do with Ruth, the daughter.'

'Why on earth should you think that?'

'Because, Aunt Jane, I'm almost certain that Max is connected with Sarah and it goes back a long way.'

Aunt Jane stared.

'Sarah?'

'Yes.'

She threw a sharp look over her glasses.

'So that's why you came here.'

Bliss shrugged.

'Could be.'

'Do you want to tell me?'

'Not yet. It's too vague. But it's given me an idea.'

'For a new tactic.'

'Yes.'

Bliss finished his drink, stood up, and kissed his aunt.

'Tell your dreamboat waiter with the tight trousers to put a drop more *cassis* in it next time. Only five out of ten for that one.'

He picked up his jacket.

'Are you off to the Festival again?'

'Tomorrow evening – big reception. My employers are invited, so of course . . . .'

Aunt Jane smiled smugly.

'Have a nice time at the ball,' said Bliss.

'I shall avoid your horrid Sir Alec if he's there,' she said.

'Why, have you met him?'

'Vile little man. Smells awful – and no scent that I know. When he bowed and kissed my hand – ugh!'

'It is alleged that numerous ladies find him extremely attractive.'

Aunt Jane snorted.

'Any female turned on by a smell like that is no lady.'

Chapter Six

RUTH TOOK THE stairs two at a time. She rushed across the landing into her bedroom, and took the envelope across to the window to have a better look.

At first sight it looked good – stamps, 'Par Avion' label, style of paper. The postmark stood out clearly – 'Cannes, Alpes Maritimes'. Bless her! Henriette had taken the trouble to go from Nice to Cannes in order to post it.

Ruth glanced at her watch. Cousin Colin was at cricket practice, Aunt Meg didn't get back from her part-time job until five, and Uncle John wouldn't be home for ages. She had twenty-five minutes, maybe half an hour. It had to be done now. There might not be a chance this evening. Aunt Meg must have seen the envelope before she left, and would want to know what was in it.

Down the stairs again, into the kitchen, kettle on. Quickly into the lounge and turn on the telly – ITV. Not so loudly that the door catch can't be heard. Back to the bedroom, get the bag, bring it down, and put it on the settee, so that it looks as if I've gone straight in there to read it.

Kitchen again, turn up the gas. Cups and saucers out, ready for Aunt Meg when she comes in. Biscuits out – leave the lid off as usual so that she can tick me off as usual. Come on, kettle, come on!

At last!

Ruth held the envelope to the steam. It was easier than she had thought, but she had to take care that the flap did not curl back on itself and stick in the wrong place.

Better do the next bit upstairs, just in case anyone came back early.

She took out each item carefully, laid it on the bed, sat back, and surveyed them together. First, Mummy's letter to herself; then *the* letter – the one from Mummy to Miss Crosby; thirdly, Henriette's own letter arranging to meet her; finally, the envelope addressed to Miss Crosby. Ruth tipped up the empty main envelope; four stamps fell out. Henriette had remembered.

Ruth unfolded the first letter. Bless her – Henriette had re-typed it. Ruth laid the original beside it. The type-face certainly looked different. It was not very likely that Miss Crosby was an expert on the differences between English and French typewriters, but one could never be too sure. Ruth scanned it anxiously for errors; if Henriette had had the slightest lapse of concentration, it would look odd to Miss Crosby that a lady of Dr. Marshall's education had misspelt a simple word.

No – it was all right.

Ruth went through it again, checking the main points – the news of Sir Alec's offer; the time; the duration. The travelling arrangements – airports, tickets, a rendezvous at Nice, including a reference to Henriette's letter. Details concerning the Post Office withdrawals.

Ruth had thought of Aunt Meg too; 'Mummy' had said in paragraph five that she was 'writing today to Auntie' and the letter would 'probably' arrive at the same time.

At the end were more trivial and intimate details of clothing, toilet, and hygiene; about security of valuables, passport; about talking to strangers, and so on – the 'worried parent' section. Ruth was especially pleased with this part. The first part – the 'excited parent' section – had been easier.

Ruth turned to the 'Miss Crosby' letter. She ran her fingers once more over the embossed address in the top corner – 'Ste. Sophie-les-Mimosas'. Her heart gave a jump as she realised that she might well be there in a few days, actually seeing the house with her own eyes, the house she had pictured so often in her mind during the last few years.

'Dear Miss Crosby . . . .'

Ruth checked and re-checked. On the second run through she tossed her head in distress; there were two mistakes. Feverishly she read the letter for the third time. No, that was all. Henriette had tried, she really had. But those two errors stood out like sore thumbs. After all the planning and thinking, to have it ruined by two misplaced letters on a typewriter. Ruth could have cried in vexation.

She looked at her own original. Had the error been hers? No. It was Henriette's mistake. But she couldn't blame Henriette, she knew that.

Of course she could go back and use her own original, but that meant having to use her original for the other letter as well, and it seemed such a pity to waste Henriette's successful efforts there.

She read Henriette's version of the Crosby letter once more. Perhaps she could get away with it. After all, it was a typing error, not a handwriting error, and Mummy was not supposed to be a typist.

Too late now. Might as well give it a go and see what happened.

Ruth went to the bottom drawer and took out the pen she had used to forge Mummy's signature on the two original letters. Time to sign the new ones.

She practised a couple more times, to make sure, on a piece of rough paper, then laid the two new letters on the dressing table.

As she poised the pen over the space under the 'Yours sincerely', she stiffened.

Of course! Stupid! Why hadn't she thought of it before? Mummy would pick up the pen to sign and probably read through the letter first. If she found a mistake, she wouldn't put it back in the typewriter, would she? She'd simply cross it out with the pen.

Ruth bent her nose close to the paper, and stopped again. No! It wouldn't be a tiny crossing-out, a 'Ruth-type' crossing-out; it would be a 'Dr. Marshall-type' crossing-out. Mummy never altered an error carefully; she slashed her pen right through it. Probably the result of having to mark so many stupid mistakes in higher mathematics.

Ruth hesitated. To make such a bold stroke across neat work prepared in such detail. She set her jaw. It had to be done.

Then the two signatures. The 'Mummy' one was easier – nearly all spikes.

She held the two sheets at arm's length. They looked all right.

Now – the 'Miss Crosby' envelope. When she looked at it again, she blessed Henriette once more. Her friend had not folded the envelope across the middle, but only fractionally at the two ends, so as to get it flat into the overall envelope. Ruth hadn't thought of that, but realised now what a good idea it was. All she had to do was crinkle the ends of the 'Crosby' envelope, the creases would be masked, and it would all look like the general wear and tear of a routine journey – and no tell-tale crease in the middle. It avoided any clumsy folding of the letter to fit it.

Into the envelope with it. Lick it and stick it down.

Next she read Henriette's letter and made as much sense as she could from it. She recognised enough French words to understand that her friend had arranged the rendezvous at Nice Airport exactly as she had asked.

Now it was time for re-assembling.

Henriette's letter, Mummy's, and the 'Miss Crosby' envelope – all went back into the outside envelope which she had steamed open. She took some Stephen's 'Golden Gum' from her drawer, and, with a paintbrush, carefully laid some on the underside of the envelope flap, taking great care not to spread it beyond the limits of the original glue.

She stuck it down, and held it while the gum dried. She looked for any blobs of surplus glue that might have been squeezed out. She went to the bathroom, washed the gum out of the paintbrush, and put it away, along with the 'Golden Gum'. The spare stamps she stowed carefully with her remaining clean sheets of 'Ste. Sophie' notepaper in the bottom of the drawer. Underneath and out of sight went her original two letters which Henriette had so faithfully copied, and the piece of rough paper on which she had practised the signature.

She looked at her watch. Time was getting on.

She took the re-sealed letter downstairs and put it on the sofa. She refilled the kettle and put it on a low gas, ready for tea.

Well, that was that. The preparations were made; the machinery set. All she had to do now was put it into motion the minute Aunt Meg walked through the front door.

She heaved a big sigh and sat completely still for a moment.

Then she stood up, turned up the television to normal volume, sat down again, and picked up the *TV Times*.

When she heard her aunt's key in the lock, she picked up the letter and went into the hall.

'Look, Auntie. A letter from Mummy. I was just going to open it. And I've remembered to put the kettle on.'

*   *   *   *   *   *

Connie came out of the computer room, pulled the door to, and locked it. As she was putting away the key, Bliss pretended to pounce.

'Carry your bags, Miss?'

Connie smiled in spite of herself.

'Only one bag.' She held it up.

'In that case,' said Bliss, 'it'll have to be dinner out. Let's play hookey.'

Connie hesitated.

'I promise I won't poke my nose in any more,' said Bliss, 'and I won't ask what goes on in there.'

He pointed at the locked door. Connie still hesitated. Bliss gestured at the dazzling sky.

'Now come on. You've done your homework for the day. I've bought my exercise books and written out my marksheets and timetables. So let's enjoy the place, for God's sake. Not even Max can make the sun go in.'

'All right. Just let me go to my room. I shan't be a minute.'

When they met again in the drive, Bliss waved towards the cars.

'Which do you fancy – the Renault or the Volvo? Or perhaps the Citroen?'

Connie chose the Citroen.

Bliss laughed wryly to himself as he started the engine.

'I must hand it to Sir Alec. He does things in the grand manner. An array of cars always at one's disposal – keys and all. Doesn't he ever worry about theft?'

'Have you counted the security guards around here?' said Connie. 'Or the dogs? Have you ever walked round the wire perimeter? It can be electrified, you know. You wouldn't get out of here with a wheelbarrow, never mind a car.'

'Why the passion for security? What does he have to hide?'

'Your guess is as good as mine.'

It jolly well isn't, but all right, we did promise, didn't we? Let's just talk about the cars.

'I can understand that here,' said Bliss. 'But I've seen his Rolls parked outside the Carlton, with the front window open and the keys in the lock.'

'Sir Alec is well known, and so are his vehicles,' said Connie. 'You might as well try and steal the "Rocket" from the railway museum.'

She still looked tight-cheeked. Let's get on to something really harmless.

They passed the 'Ste. Sophie-en-haut' sign at the roadside.

'Who was Ste. Sophie?' he asked.

'Patron saint of the village.'

Bliss changed gear for a tight bend.

'Oh, come on, Connie, you're not in the witness box now; you can do better than that.'

Connie smiled.

'We're coming to her church now. See? There.'

Bliss pulled up.

'I'd like to have a closer look. Do you mind?'

'No.'

They got out and walked across the road. The doors were unlocked, so they walked in. It was a little on the bare side, though Ste. Sophie's small side chapel was well cared for. Dozens of candles flickered before an altar above which hung a painting of dubious artistic value in a frame of ornate, grubby gilt.

'You were saying,' said Bliss, as he peered up.

'As far as I can make out,' said Connie, 'she was a village girl. She had a lover who was a soldier. He went away to fight in a crusade.'

'What, Jerusalem?'

'No, much closer than that. In Languedoc.'

'Ah – the Albigensians. The Cathars.'

'Yes. I'm not sure of the century.'

'Thirteenth.'

'Ah, you know?'

'A bit. Go on.'

Bliss sat in a pew. Connie came and sat beside him.

'Well, I expect you know, then, that the Pope declared a crusade against the Cathar heresy, set up the Inquisition to root it out, and sent in armies to crush any resistance. They were amazed by the power of the faith that they found. There were scores of cases of ordinary people who were prepared to accept death by burning rather than recant their Cathar faith.'

'What is the connection with our Sophie?'

'According to the story, she ran away from home here to join her lover in the punitive army, but by the time she found him, he had become sickened by what he was having to do. In fact, he was so touched by the faith of the Cathars that he became one himself – at the risk of his life.

'He deserted from the army and joined the Cathars in their last stronghold at Montségur, in the Pyrenees. Sophie, faithful Sophie, went with him. During the siege Sophie in her turn became converted. The armies of the crusaders at last forced them to surrender, and offered them all their lives if they would recant. Over two hundred refused, knowing full well that the punishment was burning. Sophie and her lover were among them.

'They were burnt together – all two hundred – near the foot of the rock they had defended. It must have been terrible.'

'It must indeed,' said Bliss grimly. He had seen burning bodies in Africa, and smelt them – at the mission station.

'Anyway, the village sort of adopted Sophie as their local heroine.'

Bliss looked surprised.

'How could they do that if she was a condemned heretic, excommunicated?'

'Don't ask me,' said Connie. 'I'm only the story-teller, not a theologian. Perhaps the Church turned a blind eye in the interests of peace and quiet. Perhaps she was never really canonised. Perhaps it was another Sophie altogether, and they got mixed up. I don't know. All I do know is – it's a strong local tradition, and many of the local people believe that Sophie protects them from fire.'

'Forest fires?'

'Yes. You know how easily they can start. Take a look round you. You'll always find it full of candles when the temperature goes up.'

'Like now.'

'Like now. Light a flame in here for Ste. Sophie, and the flames outside will never touch your house.'

Bliss stood up, walked to Sophie's altar, put a coin in

the box, and lit a candle. As he stuck it in a holder, he felt Connie come up beside him.

She too put in a coin, took a candle, and held it to the flame. She paused fractionally before fixing it in the holder, as if something had just occurred to her. Bliss could have sworn that a gleam came into her eye that had nothing to do with the reflection of the candles. Her hand trembled slightly. She knelt and said a short prayer.

By the time she stood up she was in control again.

'I'm hungry,' she said. 'Are you?'

She preceded him to the door and across the road.

As Bliss sat beside her in the car, he said, 'Look – just one question, and then I promise – I really promise – no more prying.'

'I don't guarantee to answer.'

Bliss held up a placatory hand.

'Just listen, that's all. If I set up a little experiment to try and convince you I'm on your side, will you go along with it? I promise there will be no trouble, or awkward-ness, or embarrassment for you. Will you do that much?'

Connie tightened her lips.

'Please,' said Bliss. 'If it doesn't work, I'll leave you alone.'

He put a pompous hand on his chest. 'Word of an officer and a gentleman.'

Connie nodded.

'Good,' said Bliss. He turned the ignition key. 'Now let's go and see what the *Restaurant des Mimosas* has to tempt our jaded palates.'

*   *   *   *   *   *

'Where's the letter to Miss Crosby?' said Aunt Meg.

'Here.'

Aunt Meg turned it over in her hands, looked at the name and address on the front, and the sealed flap at the back.

Ruth had a sudden ghastly fear that she hadn't stuck it properly.

'Keep that safe, then.'

'I will, Auntie, I will.'

Aunt Meg read Mummy's letter once more, and looked at Henriette's. She glanced at the single envelope.

'I expect she and Henriette wrote their letters together to make sure their arrangements coincided for you.'

Ruth swallowed.

'Yes, I expect they did.'

'I suppose my letter will come in a day or two.'

'Yes.'

'I wonder why she didn't put it in with yours?'

'Perhaps there were one or two things she wanted to keep private from me. You know – grown-up things.'

'Mmm.'

Aunt Meg nodded vaguely.

'All the same,' she said, 'it might be an idea to ring her up.'

Oh, no!

'Oh, I shouldn't think so. It's ever so expensive. All the details are in the letter.'

'Mmm.'

'Besides, you might have to speak French to someone to go and get her and you might have to wait ages. And you don't speak French.'

'No, but you do.'

Ruth felt her palms going damp.

'Oh, only a bit, Auntie.'

All those quizzes and word games with Daddy – in

154

French – as early as she could remember. 'Take it in through the pores of the skin,' he used to say – whatever that had meant.

'Go on – *you* ring her up. I don't mind paying.'

Oh, dear!

Ruth stood up.

'Have we got the number?'

A feeble last effort.

'Of course we've got the number. It's in the book on the hall table. You dial and get through, have a word with Mummy, then call me and I'll come and speak.'

Ruth went out into the hall with lead in her shoes. She didn't bother with the book; she knew the number perfectly well.

Taking a deep breath, she picked up the receiver.

' *'Allo? . . . . ça c'est la maison "Ste. Sophie-les-Mimosas"? Je voudrais parler avec ma mère, Mme. Marshall . . . . oui, s'l vous plaît . . . . oui, j'attends . . . . merci . . . .* Hallo, Mummy? I got your letter . . . . yes . . . . yes . . . . it sounds super . . . . I can't wait . . . . oh, I'll give it to Miss Crosby all right, first thing in the morning . . . . I'm sure there won't be any trouble; I know quite a few girls whose parents are going to take them off for holidays. They just write letters in advance like yours. There's never any snag as far as I know. You're allowed a fortnight, I believe . . . . Oh, and thanks for Henriette's letter . . . . What? . . . . Yes, she's nice, isn't she? . . . . Yes, I've got all the details. I've read it three times already .. . . Yes, it's all clear . . . . Don't worry; I know what to do . . . . Yes . . . . Yes . . . . I'll tell her . . . . She wants a word with you, by the way . . . . Auntie!'

She heard Aunt Meg coming.

' . . . . What? . . . . Oh, I see . . . . Yes, sorry . . . . Hallo?'

Ruth looked puzzled at the receiver.

'What is it?' said Aunt Meg.

'I don't know,' said Ruth. She turned back to the receiver. 'Hallo, Mummy?'

Ruth looked at her aunt, the frown still very evident.

'We've been cut off. Listen.'

She held the receiver to her aunt's ear. Aunt Meg nodded.

'That's the dialling tone.'

Ruth replaced the receiver.

'Mummy said we were not to spend your hard-earned money on expensive foreign calls unless it was an emergency. That's why she put it all in the letter. I got a bit ticked off.'

Aunt Meg hesitated.

Ruth added a desperate last touch.

'Mummy said they're not too keen on foreign calls coming unless it's really important.'

'Oh.'

Ruth pressed her palms against her thighs. This was it!

'It is all in the letter, I suppose,' said Aunt Meg.

'And in Miss Crosby's letter, I expect.'

'Yes.'

Aunt Meg lingered for more agonising seconds.

'Oh, all right. I'll get some dinner. Your uncle will be in soon.'

She moved off to the kitchen.

'We'll have to see about your clothes.'

'Yes, Auntie.'

'Now, switch off the television and come and give me a hand. It's telly, telly, all the time. You even had it on before you opened your mother's letter.'

Ruth drew a colossal, silent sigh.

Telly had its uses though. It was from one of the hundreds of American comedy shows that she had learned the trick of holding down the knobs under the receiver while you dialled the number.

'Oh, Ruth! You've left the top off the biscuits again. How many times have I told you.'

Ruth smiled to herself.

'Sorry, Auntie.'

*   *   *   *   *   *

'Here, she's nice, isn't she, your Auntie.'

'Aunt Jane?'

'Yes. She made a great fuss of Cass.'

Bliss grinned.

'She makes a great fuss of anybody she likes, especially good-looking young men.'

'D'you think she liked me?'

'I'm sure she did, Dolly.'

Dolly sighed with contentment.

'It was lovely talking to her. She somehow helps to clear your mind when you've got lots of things on it.'

'I've noticed that too.'

'And she told me all about your brother who's going to help Cass.' Dolly frowned in the effort of recall. 'What's his name – Pram?'

'Priam. It's a name from Ancient Troy. My father is an expert on it. I have another brother called Paris.'

Dolly's eyes glazed slightly.

'Oh.'

Oh, dear – the number of times he had had to explain this.

'In the legends, the King of Troy was called Priam, and two of his sons were called Hector and Paris. My father has spent his life studying Troy and the Trojans, and named his three sons accordingly – Priam, Hector, and Paris. Paris was the one who ran away with the Greek princess Helen.'

Dolly's face lit up.

'Helen of Troy? Oh yes, I've heard of her. The wooden horse and all that.'

'Yes,' said Bliss, surprised.

'Oh, yes,' said Dolly authoritatively, 'I know all about that. We did it in history – 'bout the only thing I remember.' She paused and frowned. 'Wait a minute though. Your lot lost, didn't they?'

'Pardon?'

'Your lot – the Trojans. They lost.'

'Yes, as a matter of fact, they did.'

'Ah!'

Dolly might have pondered that debating point for longer if Bliss had not brought her back to the agenda.

'I only gave Cass my brother's address. I cannot guarantee that he can help.'

'No, but it's a start, isn't it? And there's that other one you gave him in the War Office.'

'I've tried to help.'

'But it was your Auntie Jane.' Dolly shook her head in amazement. 'She's a one. D'you know what? She's made me realise how I can get my own back.'

'How?'

'Well, she didn't exactly *say* it, but she made me feel good enough to think of it myself. "Stand up to him," she said. "You have dignity too." Ha! Me! Dignity!'

Dolly made a face.

'Yes. "You're as good as he is," she said. "Give him a dose of his own medicine." She doesn't like him, does she?'

'Not much,' agreed Bliss.

'Anyway, that gave me an idea. D'you know what I'm going to do? *I'm* going to fix *him*.'

Bliss waited patiently for the great revelation. Dolly looked each way towards distant, unhearing gardeners.

'I'm going to tell the *News of the World* all about him – Sir Alec Robin 'Ood Sherrif is nothing but a randy black-mailer. How about that?'

'I wish you luck,' said Bliss, wondering vaguely what the repercussions of this Fleet Street sensation would be on his own professional position as private tutor in this vice baron's household.

Dolly leaned forward intently.

'Cass and me, we're going. Straight home to Dad. And we're taking the Renault too. Don't worry; we'll leave it at the airport. I'm not taking anything that doesn't belong or what I haven't earned. I'm not leaving anything behind either.'

'Like your honour, perhaps?' said Bliss innocently.

Dolly flashed back.

'I'm only a call-girl here; I can be married back home.'

Bliss laughed.

'Well answered, Dolly. I asked for that.'

'Oh, by the way. I nearly forgot. Cass asked me to give you this. He's down buying tickets. It's a message from your Auntie Jane.'

She groped inside the top of her cotton dress.

'Here.'

It was folded very small.

'Thank you,' said Bliss solemnly.

'She said "be careful with it".'

Bliss felt the paper; it was still warm.

'Oh, I'll do that, Dolly.'

'Good.'

Dolly smoothed down the front of her dress.

'Tell me,' said Bliss, 'do you often do that?'

'What?'

'Put things in your bra.'

'Oh yes. I remember them, see? I've got an awful memory, and I don't often have pockets. Besides, they're safe there.'

Oh, really?

'There's always room to squeeze something in.'

You could have fooled me.

Dolly leaned forward and kissed him.

'Thanks for everything. Be seeing you.'

'Are you going now?'

'Yes,' she said decisively, as she stood up. 'Sir Alec bloody Sherrif and Maxie the Creep can do their worst. I've put a letter in his desk to say what I think of 'im. Wish I could be there to see 'is face. He'll go puce.' Dolly's smug satisfaction cost her a dropped 'h' or two, but not too many . .

'Vain men don't like being rejected.'

'Yes, I know.'

Dolly grinned hugely.

Bliss ventured a question which had intrigued him ever since he had heard Aunt Jane refer to it.

'Forgive me, Dolly, but could you satisfy my curiosity on one small point?'

'What's that?'

'Did you ever find Sir Alec physically attractive?'

'Oh, yes, at first,' said Dolly very readily. 'It's something about him. Sort of atmosphere.'

'You mean smell?'

'Yes – sort of.' Dolly pondered intently. 'He was . . . .

different. It wears off after a while, but – ' she waved a hand ' – well, there's other things by that time. I mean –- ' she looked puckish ' – later on you're puffing, not sniffing. 'Bye.'

*   *   *   *   *   *

The room was totally silent save for the rustle of paper.

The heart was pounding almost enough to cause choking.

After absolutely hours, glasses were taken off and laid on the desk.

'Your mother appears to have thought of everything, Ruth.'

'Yes, Miss Crosby.'

*   *   *   *   *   *

Bliss looked at Aunt Jane's note again.

'Little Bow Peep has lost her bow,
And doesn't know where to find it.
It will come home if she says "Boo",
Says the watchman who designed it.'

Bliss smiled fondly.

'Phone calls from a yacht, private investigators, secret documents by Slavonic couriers, coded messages – Aunt Jane was having a marvellous time.

Bliss doubted, however, whether the subtlety of encipherment would have given sleepless nights to a professional cryptographer.

'Max Bowman', then, was in fact 'Max Booman', or rather 'Bumann', and he was presumably of Swiss extraction. That might explain his international interests, his business skill, and his facility with languages. Nearly everyone in Switzerland seemed to speak at least two;

many spoke three; a few spoke all four official tongues. If you added English and probably Spanish, that made six. And if he was Sir Alec's 'voice' behind the Iron Curtain, you might add a seventh. Conceivably an eighth, judging from Dolly's remarks about the 'string of wogs' that frequented the house.

Quite a chat-man. Capable of violence and black-mail. If he was not averse to inflicting pain on women, he would certainly not shrink from inflicting it on men, especially if chauffeur Albert was around to offer moral support.

'I reckon he gets his kicks being nasty.'

Bliss had enough respect now for Dolly's shrewdness to set some store by a remark like that.

A lawyer too; maybe not a regular practitioner, but knowledgeable and qualified enough to be considered worth employing as a domestic legal eagle by a man of Sir Alec's huge world-wide interests. Did he have any hold on Sir Alec? Hardly.

'He's scared of Sir Alec, you know. Deep down.' Dolly again.

Then the veneer of polish on his speech and manner, like cheap nail varnish. And, like cheap nail varnish, it could crack very easily, Bliss felt. The man enjoyed being 'in the know' about something that others didn't, enjoyed putting people in their place. That was obvious even above the veneer; underneath it could be very nasty indeed.

Well, Bliss could now begin to find out for himself exactly how nasty.

He was going to put Max on the spot. Sting him. Speak his mind like Dolly. Try to produce some cracks in that veneer.

Whatever was going to be revealed might help Connie to make up her mind.

Or was it to help *him* to make up *his* mind? To try and get those bells of memory to ring loud and clear about Sarah? Cuff-links and shirt-cuffs, burnt bodies in Africa, and 'should you wish to reconsider'.

Bliss folded Aunt Jane's note. As he held open his wallet, he bent his head to sniff. The paper still smelt of Dolly's perfume. He smiled and put it in his pocket, just as there came a knock at the door.

'Come in.'

'You said it was important, Mr. Bliss. At the risk of apparent discourtesy, I must ask you to be brief.' A slight caress of the silk handkerchief in the breast pocket. 'I am due at a reception with Sir Alec in Cannes.'

'Ah, yes – the Festival. I am sorry we shall not have the pleasure of your company at dinner this evening, or Sir Alec's.'

'Get to the point, Mr. Bliss.'

A warning shot across the bows. Bliss accepted the challenge, and brought his main armaments to bear.

'I've changed my mind.'

'I beg your pardon.'

'I have been re-considering since I arrived here. To put it bluntly, I don't like the set-up, and I intend to return home.'

The cold eyes narrowed.

'This is – somewhat surprising. May one ask why?'

' "One may ask",' said Bliss, deliberately mimicking, 'but "one" may not necessarily receive a satisfactory answer. I've told you; I don't like the set-up.'

There came another warning shot.

'Could it be that it is not so much the "set-up", as

you put it, as the people associated with it that you dislike?'

Bliss prepared his second salvo.

'Not people, Mr. Bowman – person; there is only one person here I distrust. And from what I have heard from Miss Vartan, I am not alone in that opinion.'

No harm in involving Dolly; she was gone by now. And by keeping Sir Alec out of the conversation, Bliss could make his implication about Max unmistakable.

To his surprise, Max showed no sign of annoyance. Instead, something like a gleam of excitement came into his eye. As if the hunter had scented the quarry.

'Let me be clear about this, Mr. Bliss; you are telling me that you wish to cancel your contract here and return home because of your dissatisfaction with the domestic arrangements here and because of some personal animosity towards myself.'

Bliss nodded, retrieved one of Max's lighter missiles, and tossed it back.

'At the risk of apparent discourtesy – yes.'

The man almost swelled with suppressed excitement. Faint tinges of colour appeared on his pallid cheeks.

'I'm afraid that will not be possible, Mr. Bliss.'

Bliss motioned him to the easy chair, while he himself sat on a small wicker chair near the bathroom door, as far away as he could.

'Would you be kind enough to tell me why?'

Max declined the invitation. It was obvious that it would detract from his rising emotion to sit down.

'I should have thought that was simple enough to understand.'

Bliss flashed one of Max's own spectral smiles.

'You must bear with me – a mere stupid Englishman.

Why can I not tell you what to do with your offer of employment?'

Bliss was enjoying himself too, though he was curious to know the motivation behind Max's unexpected reaction. He would have preferred simple bluster or temper.

Max lit a cigarette, not nervously, like a busy man preoccupied with work, but languorously, like someone about to savour something intensely pleasurable. He inhaled and expelled smoke.

'Because you know what happened last time.'

Max's eyes were fixed on Bliss' face, waiting.

One of the bells of memory began to ring.

'You mean that offer from Buenos Aires? From – who was it – Señor Torres?'

Max smiled.

'I am surprised, Mr. Bliss, since you remember my name on that occasion, that you do not recall the terms of my offer.'

'I never saw them. I was away at the time. My wife threw the letter away before I returned home to read it.'

'Then how did you know my name?'

'I saw your second note, begging me to. . . . "reconsider", I believe, was the way you put it.'

'A great pity you did not.'

'Why?'

The flushes on Max's cheeks grew deeper.

'Because your daughter might still be alive.'

Bliss was completely thrown, the more so as he could not at once see the connection.

'What does Sarah have to do with it?'

The initiative had shifted, and Bliss knew it. So did Max. He inhaled luxuriously once more.

'Can you not work it out for yourself?'

165

'Sarah was killed in a road accident,' said Bliss, blustering slightly, because he dared not face the awful possibility that had come into him mind.

Max looked at the ceiling, as if struggling to recall elusive facts. Just as he did in the London office. Just as the man had done in Africa . . . . 'Let's see, Captain Bliss, if I remember rightly, your wife's name is Joy, and she is the one who is unable to .. . . '

The second bell was ringing.

'As I recall,' said Max, 'Sarah died as a result of a car crash.'

'Nearly two weeks afterwards,' said Bliss, his head full of bells now.

'A young man was killed with her, was he not? He was driving. The car went off the road and down an embankment.'

'He was drunk,' said Bliss, clinging to the official version.

'He was indeed,' agreed Max, 'as the post-mortem examination revealed. But then it does not require many whiskies to take a young man over the limit – especially a young man anxious to impress his girl friend.'

The enormity of it robbed Bliss of speech for a while. The more so as Max was deriving such pleasure from it.

'It had the added virtue,' said Max, 'of providing the perfect mask to the true course of events.'

Max smiled.

'A discreetly-hired lorry, a well-paid professional driver, skilled in these matters. A well-chosen, lonely spot, a late hour, a quiet nudge with the wheels . . . . another sad case of wayward youth paying a heavy price for alcoholic misdemeanours.'

'Albert!'

Bliss could see the ham-like hands so out of place on the leopard-skin wheel of the scarlet Rolls.

'A man of few talents, I agree, Mr. Bliss, but most useful talents. Moreover, his poor command of language renders him admirably taciturn.'

Bliss stared.

'You planned it. Worked it all out – in advance.'

Max spread his hands.

'Alas! An unfortunate necessity. We had to make you realise that we meant what we said.'

'Work for you or you'd commit murder.'

'Rather that the price of non-co-operation could become distressingly high.'

'You were responsible for Sarah's death.'

'No, Mr. Bliss. You were. Had you co-operated. . . . '

'But I didn't even know! I told you; my wife threw the letter away before I saw it.'

Max picked a piece of invisible tobacco from his tongue.

'That, I agree, was an unfortunate mistake – '

'Mistake!'

' – by you. Which should, if nothing else, serve to make you understand the value of co-operation now.'

Bliss' head was spinning. Half of him was on his feet, beating Max's face to a pulp. The other half was telling him that this was totally impossible; he must have misunderstood.

'Look, have I got this right? You provided a daughter for Joy and me to adopt – it was you, wasn't it, in that office in Kampala? You had a moustache then, didn't you?'

Max stroked his upper lip.

'When one wishes to throw someone off the scent, it is often better, I find, to remove features rather than add them. Do you not think so? The emptier the face, the harder it is to place it.'

'But why provide us with a child and then kill her? You must be insane.'

'No, Mr. Bliss. Merely truthful. And we are businessmen. Sixteen years ago we were able to render you a service. Last year we demanded payment for that service in the shape of your labour, for which you would have been amply rewarded. We warned you of the dangers of non-compliance. When it appeared from your lack of response that you did not believe us, we had to convince you that – as I said – we spoke the truth. Your daughter's death is on your head, or rather, on your wife's, since she threw away the letter.'

For a wild moment Bliss conjured up a scene of agonised argument with Joy, in which he would have the perfect reply to her oft-repeated refrain:

'You could have given her another chance. You needn't have told them to turn off the machine so early.'

To which he could have said:

'If it weren't for you chucking away my mail, she wouldn't be *on* the damned machine.'

He fought to quell the imagination and the anguish. He must use his intelligence, find a way to take the smile off the face of this monster. Even accusations of madness hadn't done it.

'Why try and hire me again? Sarah is dead.'

'You are a good teacher, the best available to us. We have looked elsewhere and found none to compare with your all-round record.'

'You mean none whom you can blackmail.'

'It is true that fidelity in our employees is usually better ensured by means of such a combination of intimate knowledge and quiet pressure.'

Bliss tried to force a grin, but it came out more like a leer.

'Sarah is dead. You can't touch me now.'

Max laughed.

'My dear Mr. Bliss, I begin to despair of your powers of perception. There are plenty more members of your family. Where do you suggest we start? With the older generation? Or with your own – those peculiarly-christened brothers of yours? Or shall we continue with the younger generation? For instance, that nephew who is such a promising young player of your game of cricket?'

Bliss was dumbfounded. While his heart reeled from the hideousness of the threats, his brain was spinning in amazement at the extent of the man's knowledge, at his command of detail.

Max took a step towards him. There was such contempt on his face that Bliss could have sworn he intended to inflict a blow.

However, Max controlled himself with a great effort, took a last puff of his cigarette, and put it out in the ashtray on the table. Beside the ashtray was a pile of files and books. Max picked one up and looked at it.

'I see your preparations for Alan's arrival are well under way. When you talked of leaving, perhaps you did not mean what you said after all. However, Mr. Bliss, I hope I have convinced you that we mean what we say. I suggest you continue with the work you contracted to undertake. You will not find us unreasonable or ungenerous employers.'

'Just murderous ones.'

Max smoothed his breast pocket handkerchief again.

'A very subjective opinion, Mr. Bliss. Unfortunately for

you, not provable. And now, if you will excuse me, I must go to Sir Alec; the reception starts very soon. Enjoy your evening meal. May I recommend the *Beaujolais Juliénas* or *Fleurie*? So much more suited to this warm weather than the *Gigondas* or the *Châteauneuf-du-Pape*, don't you think? But do feel free to order what you wish; ask Marcel to bring you the full list.'

The door closed.

Bliss put his head in his hands.

Connie came out of the bathroom behind him and put her arm round his shoulder.

'Hector! I had no idea.'

Bliss sighed, close to tears.

'Neither did I.'

'Come with me,' said Connie. 'I want to show you something.'

Chapter Seven

'WHAT IS ALL this – a geography lesson?'

Connie sat at the keyboard.

'No. This is just by way of introduction, to show you the extent of Sir Alec's interests and organisation.'

'New York – Buenos Aires – London – Johannesburg – Sydney – Hong Kong – I know all that. Max told me. Tell me something else.'

He was still in a state of shock. Connie was prepared to make allowances. At least she could be sure of him now. When she had agreed to hide in the bathroom, it had been with great reluctance; every nerve and antenna had been strained to detect the slightest tremor of elaborate deceit. But she had seen, or rather heard, that the interview had not gone as Bliss had planned it. There was no possible way that he and Max could have prepared such a scene in advance. Besides, she had heard that quiver of excitement in Max's voice before, and knew that it could not be simulated.

Now it was Bliss who was suffering. It was he who needed the immediate help, not herself. She knew too that here was the ally she had never thought to find. No Government agent, no policeman, no special investigator, no representative of any authority whatsoever, was of the slightest use. But a person in the same hopeless trap as herself – that was different. The more hopeless the trap, the more comfort was derived from the mere fact of its being shared.

'How about this then?' said Connie, as she pressed more keys.

A list of names came up on the screen. Bliss recognised some of them.

'What's this – his guest list? I'm impressed, but not surprised.'

'Do you know what they do?'

'Some of them, yes.'

Bliss pointed.

'He's a financier. The one at the top is an oil magnate. The one underneath is in textiles, I think.'

'Would you like to know what else they are "in", as you put it?'

Connie brought up each name one by one; against each name appeared a list of activities.

Bliss snorted.

'I don't believe you.'

'Pick a name,' said Connie, putting up the full list again. 'Go on. Any one you like.'

Bliss did so.

During the next few minutes he sat stunned as the details flickered across the screen – chapter and verse of names, places, shipments, quantities, rewards, deals, cheque numbers, bank accounts.

'Pick another one,' said Connie.

Bliss turned to her.

'It's all right. I'm sorry. I didn't mean to – '

'Pick another one!'

Bliss did so.

The pattern was repeated.

Connie made him sit through seven more case histories.

Bliss was appalled and sickened. There was no murky

172

corner of criminality that had not been penetrated by the organisation represented on the screen in front of him – extortion, assassination, drugs, arms deals, illegal immigration, sale of government secrets, prostitution – it was mind-boggling. Bliss felt his shoulders sagging under the weight of the accumulated, and infinitesimally detailed, evidence.

'For God's sake, Connie, you've made your point.'

'Plenty more where that came from.'

'All right, all right, but please!'

Connie let the screen go blank.

There was silence for a while.

'Now do you see?' said Connie. 'You and I – we're nothing compared with all this. I couldn't begin to tell you about it, now could I?'

'No.'

'If I had, you wouldn't have believed me, would you?'

'No.'

Connie gestured towards the screen.

'That – that is the submerged nine-tenths of the iceberg.'

'Then why bother with small fry like us?' said Bliss.

'We're part of the other tenth. I'll come back to that in a minute. First of all, you see that all this information on crime and illegal profit gives this man the perfect opportunity for yet more crime and even bigger profit.'

'Blackmail.'

'Exactly.'

'He need never fear reprisal or vengeance or doublecross. He can betray too many people to the authorities; he can set too many rivals against each other by carefully rationing the secrets he lets out; and he can levy a charge for not letting out the rest.

'You see, make no mistake, he is clever – clever. He does not wish to eliminate rivals; he sees further than that. He just wishes to know about them. By allowing them to continue in operation he can draw off yet more profit by means of this knowledge that he possesses. By letting them make millions, he can make tens of millions.'

'What about these rivals? Don't they mind?'

'They mind, yes. But they consider the alternative. Better a partner, they decide, who is not an over-greedy blackmailer than a rival who might try to eliminate them altogether.'

'Doesn't any one of them get it into his head to try and take his place?'

'They think again, usually. Thanks to Sir Alec, they can be put in touch with so many other branches of organised crime if they wish. One or two get greedy, step out of their league, and get their fingers burned. It teaches them a lesson. Not one of them has Sir Alec's class, or polish, or connections, or his entry into the Establishment and polite society – certainly not his combination of all that. It would be positively unprofitable to remove him.'

'You mean nobody has tried? Not one?'

'If they have, they're not here to tell the tale.'

'So he runs organised murder too.'

'You know that already – Sarah.'

Bliss winced.

'If I hadn't turned him down – '

Connie stopped him.

'You were not to know. It was not your fault. If you had turned him down knowingly, that would have been a different matter.'

'But if it hadn't been for – '

Connie banged the top of the desk.

'Hector, stop it! You are not responsible for Sarah's death; Alec Sherrif is. Just as he is responsible for my husband's death.'

Bliss stared.

'Your husband's?'

'So I have every reason to believe – now.'

Bliss forgot his own pain.

'Oh, Connie, I'm – I don't know what to say.'

'You can say nothing to comfort me,' said Connie. 'But you might be able to do something to help.'

'What happened?' asked Bliss. 'Can you talk about it?'

'Yes. Oh, yes. I can now.'

Connie told him.

'You see? David was going to "have it out with him". I begged him not to. He thought it was a simple piece of blackmail over Ruth's adoption – you know, threaten to expose legal irregularities. And we'd lose her. When I told him Ruth might be also be in physical danger, he pooh-poohed it. He had no idea what they're capable of. You have – now.'

Bliss shuddered.

'Yes.'

'Max,' said Connie, 'is one of those rare people who say rather less than they mean. David didn't know that; I did. He didn't know about all this.' Connie waved towards the computer screen. 'I did. I couldn't burden him with that knowledge; it was enough that I should have it. I suppose I could have used it to stop him, but I could not be sure it would have worked. It might have made him even more determined to challenge them. Does that put me in a position like yours then? Should I have found a way of stopping him? Am I responsible for my husband's death?'

175

'Of course not.'

'Then neither are you responsible for Sarah's.'

Bliss nodded, and heaved a deep sigh.

'How did it happen?' he asked.

Connie took a handkerchief out of her dress pocket and held it tightly.

'He was blown up in a lift.'

Bliss started.

'Blown up in a lift?'

'Heard it before, somewhere, have you?'

'Yes.'

'I'll tell you where it was too – Marseilles, last month. Want to know who the victim was?'

Bliss said nothing; Connie's voice was like ice.

'A Mr. Sherman Foster, hydraulic engineer from Iowa. Employed by a certain Sir Alec Sherrif to install the fire-prevention and fire-fighting water system here. Married. One daughter called Gina. Adopted. Last time I met him he was going to tell Sir Alec what he could do with his job. Need I go on?'

Bliss shook his head. Then a thought struck him.

'But other people get killed in these affairs.'

'Of course. It's the perfect mask, isn't it? Kill two or three people together, and nobody finds out which one was the intended victim.'

'I thought it was terrorists.'

'That's what you're supposed to think. People are so quick to suspect terrorists and there are so many oddly-named terrorist groups around, that it only needs a couple of 'phone calls to newspapers claiming responsibility to make everyone believe it instantly. "Ah, yes," they say. "Bloody terrorists," they say. "Shooting's too good for them. Same again, Charlie." And that's all anybody wants to know.'

Bliss had never heard Connie swear before. He had never seen that look on her face before either. Even though, as they sat there, he knew Sir Alec held all the cards, he was conscious of relief that he wasn't in Sir Alec's shoes. Give this woman half a chance, one hundredth of a chance . . . .

This explained at last the 'coiled spring' air that she had about her. It was not so much fear or worry or revulsion, although they were all present. It was fury; it was moreover frustrated fury searching for a means of expression. The coiled spring was waiting only for a direction in which to release its pent energy.

Was it up to him to point a way? Now that he shared a similar motivation?

First, he thought, some questions needed answering.

'You have no proof about David, I suppose?'

He gestured towards the screen.

'Not on there,' said Connie. 'Max handles this side of the business – the human weakness and misery side of it. Finding childless couples with useful skills. Locating orphan babies. Arranging the pairing off of the one with the other. Smoothing out the difficulties, cutting the red tape.'

Connie sneered.

'The shirt-cuffs and gold cufflinks bit,' said Bliss.

'Yes. You've had it too, I've no doubt. That's the investment. At some future date, they call in the dividend. Say they need an engineer, or a haulage contractor, or a computer expert – '

' – or a schoolmaster.'

' – or a schoolmaster. Someone who'll come when he's told, do as he's told, and no questions asked. They don't want professional crooks who know too much about the

177

business and know too many people. These poor parents are just the right sort of amateur they need – skilled at their own trade, ignorant of the world of crime –'

' – and vulnerable.'

'You're getting the idea. They may not be required actually to do anything illegal, but they might come face to face with illegality in the course of their work. That's when their silence is necessary. So – Max brings pressure to bear.'

'By threatening murder.'

'Oh, no, not always. There is a whole scale of threats that can be employed. Telling the child it's adopted is one. That is, if the parents haven't already. That can cause no end of trouble.'

Bliss knew only too well. He should have told Sarah sooner, much earlier. But there . . . .

'There's always exposure,' continued Connie. 'You know, discovering legal irregularities in the original adoption procedure. Can't you just hear Max saying it? "I regret to have to inform you that certain unwelcome procedural difficulties have arisen which may make it necessary to . . . . "'

'Yes, I can hear him.'

'And all these couples know in their heart that there might be something in it, because they all came by their child in odd circumstances.'

Bliss looked surprised.

'Really?'

'Oh, yes. I expect you thought you came across Sarah in a uniquely different way.'

'Well, yes. I first saw Sarah outside a burning mission station in Africa.'

'David and I acquired Ruth after a hotel collapsed in

Spain. I could give you other instances. There's another way, too, they can bind you hand and foot.'

Connie took out a packet of cigarettes and lit one. Bliss did not know she smoked. She saw his eyes following her hands.

'Only since David died. It was either that or drink.'

She put the match in an ashtray beside her keyboard.

'Have you noticed how generous they are with money?'

'Yes.'

'All part of the system. Never drive your victims right into the ground. Always give them something to console themselves with. Give them something which will help them to silence their conscience. "Ah, well, I know it's a bit dubious, but the money is terrific." I'd say you were partly attracted here by the money.'

'I must admit it was a factor.'

'But they add a further refinement too. Max keeps the most detailed records, you know.'

'I know,' said Bliss, recalling Max's staggering knowledge of his own family.

'And he regularly updates them. So out of the blue may come a cheque for school fees or medical expenses just when you're wondering how you can afford them. You imagine the temptation of that. So you see, by plying them with so much money, he almost makes his victims into his accomplices. Besides the fear factor there is now the guilt factor. Max had turned blackmailing on its head; *he* gives *them* money'

'You keep saying "Max". Doesn't Sir Alec have anything to do with this?'

'Not directly, no. This is Max's baby.'

Connie clicked her tongue in annoyance.

'Sorry. I didn't mean that.'

'That's all right.'

'You see, it fits with Sir Alec's general policy of giving his subordinates their own little empires. He knows that Max is a good organiser, has a phenomenal memory, and is attentive to detail. He also knows that Max is some kind of psychotic who enjoys cruelty for its own sake. So this is the perfect operation – valuable to Sir Alec, and therapeutic for Max.'

'How do you know all this if it's not in there?' said Bliss, gesturing again towards the screen.

'I've worked it out. I've had five years to do it.'

'You've been coming here for five years?'

'This is my sixth. I've had plenty of time to study Max in action, and I've talked to people who have been through here. You'd be surprised how many turn out to have adopted children, and how many of them were not enjoying themselves here. But they're not in the main computer record. Max keeps all those files in his office.'

'How can you be so sure I'm not in there?' said Bliss, pointing to the screen.

'Because I know what's in there. I put it there. I designed all the programmes for it. Why do you think I'm here?'

Bliss gaped.

'You *designed* them?'

Connie looked disapproving.

'Am I supposed to make some kind of disclaimer? I can't help being brainy, you know.'

Bliss apologised.

'Believe me,' said Connie, 'there have been times in the last five years when I have devoutly wished I wasn't. And I'm a worrier too. Not like my sister Meg. Dear Meg! If the world revolution broke out and the polar ice cap melted, the first thing she would do is put the kettle on and make a cup of tea. She looks after Ruth while I'm away.'

'Does she know anything? Meg, I mean.'

'Good Lord, no. If I would not burden David I certainly wouldn't burden her. Besides . . . . well, Meg is a good sister and I love her, but she does rather enjoy a gossip.'

Bliss tried to marshal all this bewildering array of fresh information.

'Going back to Max for a moment, if you think he killed David – '

'He did.'

'All right, all right, he did. But, that being the case, why didn't he tell you?'

'For the same reason he didn't tell you about Sarah before now; he didn't see the necessity. From what we now know, he killed Sarah in reprisal for your refusal to work. He naturally assumed you would deduce it.'

'Even when I came for the interview for this job? He sat there, knowing that I knew? Or thinking that I knew?'

'You forget,' said Connie, 'you are not dealing with a completely normal person. He enjoys deviousness; he takes delight in the exercise of power; he adores cat and mouse games. Look how much he revelled in telling you just now.'

'True.'

'He hasn't told me yet about David because I have been too obedient. He doesn't need to. But he'll enjoy it if and when he does. I think he had David killed only to get him out of the way, not to frighten me. Ruth is his way of frightening me. And he has always succeeded – up to now.'

'Does Max know what's in there?' asked Bliss.

'Good Heavens, no! Only Sir Alec and I know the entry

181

code. Max doesn't know the code and he doesn't know the contents, except in a general sense.'

'But I thought he was Sir Alec's right-hand man.'

'So he is. He is given great authority and a lot of discretion. That little adoption-blackmail scheme is only one of many. But there is no question where the real power lies. Max and all the others may be let out on a long line, but one twitch on the line and they're down. I've seen it happen.'

'And Sir Alec – this is stupid. Here he is – a master criminal – and we're still calling him "Sir Alec".'

Connie nodded.

'I know. Silly, isn't it? But you've got to call him something. And he really does engage in a lot of legitimate activities too.'

'How does he do it – with no voice?'

'Ask his subordinates. They should know. They never question him. I suppose there are plenty of ways of conveying menace without using the vocal chords. I cannot recall that talkativeness has ever gone hand in hand with deep criminality. Rather the opposite, I should guess. You should ask Max; he's terrified of him.'

Bliss thought of Dolly. Dear Dolly. Who didn`t think she was 'much of a girl'. Dolly had rumbled Max all right: 'He`s scared of Sir Alec, you know Deep down.'

Bliss smiled almost fondly.

'What is it?' said Connie.

Bliss shook his head.

'Nothing. Just a thought. Let`s get back to Max. Doesn't he try to get you to tell him what's in there?'

'No. He knows I would tell Sir Alec. And Max, as I said, is terrified of him. Max is in here too, you know.'

Connie patted the keys.

'Yes, that reminds me,' said Bliss. 'I've found out that his real name is Bumann and he is Swiss by birth.'

Connie's expression radiated scorn.

'Is that all? Watch.'

She tapped the keys.

Bliss received his third shock in half an hour.

'A Nazi!'

'Double-dyed, three-starred. Look – Hitler Youth, anti-Jewish and anti-Communist informer. Joined the Army – not the SS, note. Remember those films which told us that all the real villains were in the SS, that all the regular army officers were jolly good chaps really? Well, here's one that wasn't.'

'What made him leave Switzerland?'

'Crime. Look.'

More figures and letters flickered across.

Bliss whistled.

'He started young.'

'Yes. It's funny to think of a Swiss who is so, shall we say, anti-neutral towards his fellow-man. Or woman. The Swiss spend so much time trying to persuade other people to stop fighting, and having international confer-ences in Geneva, that it comes as a shock to discover that they also have criminals. I should think they were glad to be rid of him.'

'And I don't suppose the Nazis would have asked too many questions about someone who showed such will-ingness to hammer the Jews and the Communists.'

'Correct. So he had a good war – look. Russia, Yugoslavia, North Africa. Made it to colonel. And the decorations .... Then he blotted his copy-book somehow, and was packed off to occupation duty in France.'

'What did he do wrong?'

183

'I don't know.'

'Perhaps he was wounded.'

'Not in the record. But this is. See what he got up to after the war.'

'Argentina!' said Bliss. 'I thought so. The Spanish books in his office. Señor Torres. He took a Spanish name.'

'So did plenty of Nazis,' said Connie. 'And a lot of them, like Max, were drawn to crime. It must be a frame of mind. Max didn't become a criminal psychotic because he was a Nazi; he became a Nazi because he was a criminal psychotic.'

'What about his legal training?'

'Here. And his other qualifications.'

'Yes. And languages?'

'Here.'

'Arabic – I wondered about that. And Russian too.'

'Eighteen months on the Russian Front. I've no doubt he endeared himself to the local population in the process.'

'A remarkable linguist. He speaks marvellous English; I've seldom caught him out.'

'English mother,' said Connie, and added, 'poor woman.'

'Why "poor woman"?'

'I'm not sure,' said Connie. 'There's something pretty hideous in his deep past. It's not spelt out in the record, but his mother appears to have died when he was in his teens, and in mysterious circumstances. He left Switzerland almost immediately afterwards. I have noticed too that he loses no opportunity to sneer at any expression of parental affection, even in general conversation. "Stifling", he calls it. "Stultifying" is another one. Have you noticed, for example, that Mademoiselle Aline is good with children?'

'Yes. I've seen her with the staff kids.'

'Well, Max often sneers at that. He doesn't actually say anything outright, but he leaves you with a nasty taste in the mouth. He cheapens everything. And he certainly doesn't like Aline.'

'It's mutual, I should think.'

'She loathes him.'

'So that would explain why Max enjoys this cat-and-mouse game over the adoptions.'

'Takes to it like a duck to water. He revels in parental anguish. You can watch him almost drawing strength from pain. It makes the flesh creep.'

'And Sir Alec knows this?'

' 'Course he does. He uses it to keep Max amused. And he uses what's in there to keep him under control. One nod from Sir Alec, and Max could be snapped up by any one of half a dozen governments and police forces, to say nothing of Israeli and other Jewish war-crimes investigation agencies.'

'Where did they meet?'

'South America. A natural place to recruit criminal subordinates; it was swarming with ex-Nazis on the run. But Sir Alec didn't just bump into him, you know. There is never anything random about that man. He already had a sizeable organisation by the late fifties. Thanks to his blackmailing skill he had infiltrated one of those Jewish war-crimes bureaux I was talking about. All he had to do was to get his victim to pass over copies of files on Nazi fugitives in Argentina. Then he simply flew to Buenos Aires with a shopping list and drove round digging out whoever he wanted.'

'And they said yes?'

'They said yes please. He offered protection, a new identity, power, wealth, and, as in Max's case, the chance to indulge their cranky little whims. He demanded in return – '

'Total obedience.'

'Yes. But they'd been used to that before. So it was business as usual without the uniform.'

'Shirt cuffs instead of peaked caps.'

'If you like.'

'And Max was his prize pupil.'

'Top of the class, especially since quite a lot have died off.'

'So Max is the only one around the house,' said Bliss, searching for reassurance that the whole estate wasn't seething with ex-Gestapo thugs disguised as waiters and gardeners.

'Yes,' said Connie. 'Apart from Albert.'

'Albert!'

'Yes. But he's a very small cog. They use him for the petty violent jobs.'

'I know,' said Bliss, shuddering at the memory. 'Is he on your machine?'

'Coming up.'

A sickening record of guard duties and torture at transit depots, prison camps, and worse.

Bliss sat back, round-shouldered and limp, struggling to digest it all. Connie had not yet finished with him.

'I could show you a dozen more like Albert, dotted around. And I've shown you the big operators, the ones who make the wheels go round. We – you and me and the other poor parents – we are at the other end. We are merely little drops of oil squirted into the machinery now and then. Time now for the next lesson. Stand by for the men in the middle – not the wheel-winders, or the oil, but the little cogs in between.'

On the screen came a list of staggering variety – policemen, local government officers, civil servants, senators, commissars, harbourmasters, customs inspectors – from dozens of countries right round the globe.

'You see? I told you – he is clever. He doesn't demand too much of them. He rarely gets them to commit blatant crimes; he has his core of professionals for that. All he wants from these people is a blind eye here and a helping hand there. And once he has found the skeleton in the cupboard he can get it.'

'Blackmail?'

'Blackmail.'

There was another silence.

Bliss passed a hand across his brow.

'I can't take all this in. Who is this man? Some kind of antichrist?'

'You're still recovering from the shock,' said Connie. 'Don't worry; it took me quite a while too.'

'What happens when you recover?'

'You try to think of a way to destroy him.'

Bliss gaped.

'Are you mad? To take on that?'

He flung an arm towards the screen.

'We're nothing but a squirt of oil in the machinery; you said so yourself.'

'It's oil that makes machinery go round.'

Bliss gestured impatiently.

'Don't play metaphors, Connie. If we don't do what he wants, he can eliminate us or our families – one by one if necessary – and replace us at the end with someone else. The machinery will always go round.'

'No machinery is infallible, and no one man is superhuman.'

'What are you going to do?' said Bliss dryly. 'Bump him off?'

'Not unless I have to,' said Connie evenly.

Bliss stared.

'By God – you mean it.'

'I've had time to think about it. You haven't – yet.'

'Connie – he has taken your husband's life and he has taken my daughter's. But we have laws about that sort of thing. Private citizens can't go around taking an eye for an eye.'

Connie almost spat.

'What law does he recognise? What law can touch him? Who can prove anything? What shred of evidence have we outside this room? Who is in a position to do anything except us?'

'But private revenge, Connie. Quite apart from the moral rightness, there's the danger.'

Connie stubbed out her cigarette.

'I don't want revenge, Hector. I want destruction, removal, annihilation.'

'Connie, be sensible.'

'I'm being very sensible, Hector. You keep forgetting; I've had time to think. You haven't. Of course I couldn't wheedle Sir Alec into some dark alley and stab him with my nail file. I should bungle it, get caught, and Ruth would be left without a mother – if she were left alive at all. I can't take a hammer to the computer either. Only Sir Alec and I can get in here. He would know at once who did it.'

'So what do you have in mind?'

Bliss found it hard to hide the irony in his voice.

'Don't come the tolerant male, Hector, please. Listen and use your gumption.'

'You sound like Aunt Jane.'

'Well, maybe. I'm sure she would understand. Look – we have two things on our side. One is surprise; they don't know you know.'

'And even if they thought I did, they wouldn't care.'

'Exactly. Right now they are preening themselves at the Film Festival, having left you a quivering wreck slumped in your bedroom.'

'Max despises me – a definite advantage.'

'Our third asset, then, is our intelligence. I am not apologising any more for being clever. And you're no fool either. We are both certainly not going to make their mistake of underestimating the opposition.' She gestured at the screen. 'We have seen what they can do. They haven't seen what we can do.'

'We haven't done anything yet.'

'No, but between us we should think of something.'

'Judging by that, I should say you already have,' said Bliss.

'I'm half-way there,' said Connie.

She took out another cigarette.

'Consider,' she said, as she exhaled the first puff. 'From your own military experience, I'm sure you would agree that frontal attack is no good. We cannot go against the organisation. Nor is it wise to go against the head of it. Rather like the body of a chicken, there could be enough life left in the organisation after we had killed its head to dispose of us – even supposing we were capable of murder. I'm not – at any rate not yet – and I don't suppose you are. So what does that leave?'

'Sabotage,' said Bliss, catching her drift.

'Exactly,' said Connie. 'There is the means of his destruction, right in front of us.'

Bliss gazed at the screen.

'Is that the only one?'

'Yes. You don't think he'd duplicate all that, do you? Twice the security risk. At the moment, he and I are the only two human beings who can get in there. So I'm pretty indispensable. Although I say so myself, Cambridge Ph.D.'s who can create and run world crime syndicate computer programmes are rare. Honest ones, that is. And honest ones who are terrified of losing their only child are even rarer.'

'He could get a dishonest one.'

'I've no doubt. But that extends the risk. If the new man is dishonest, he's corruptible. Sooner or later he will either want a bigger share of the profits, or he will sell what's in there to someone else. Sir Alec is better off with the likes of me. And as he thinks I'm paralysed with fear, he's in a good position.'

'So I repeat – this time without the irony – what do you have in mind?'

'It should have occurred to you,' said Connie, 'that whoever has his name in that machine would give his eye teeth to get it out. So, if anything unfortunate should happen to it, nobody would shed any tears.'

'Except Sir Alec.'

'Except Sir Alec. That is why we go for the machine, the programmes, the system – not for him. Even supposing we could dispose of him, the computer would still be there, and some part of the organisation would come after me because of fear of what I might say about it, about what's in it.'

'But you said just now you wouldn't destroy it.'

'True. But if I could do it in such a way that I could not be suspected. If I could totally annihilate it. If the programmes – if the computer system were dealt with like that, who is going to chase after either of us and try and kill us when the computer's death has done them all a favour?'

'Sir Alec might still come after us.'

'Yes, but only Sir Alec.'

'I shouldn't be too free with the "only", if I were you. If he can show the contempt for human life that this evidence proves, he would be an uncomfortable person to have on one's tail.'

Connie looked very thoughtful.

'There may be a way to obviate that,' she said. 'Look.'

She extracted more discs from a file, and returned to her keyboard.

'Besides the secret information, Sir Alec keeps all sorts of routine material here – bills, accounts, the state of his ample cellar. See? – the claret and *rosé* supplies will soon need topping up. He can use this too to keep Mademoiselle Aline up to the mark. I tell you, there is nothing random about this man.'

'How does a set of household accounts help us?'

'It doesn't, so far as I can see. I'm just showing you the extent of the information he keeps in here. Now look at this programme.'

'What is it?' said Bliss, puzzled.

'Controls the air-conditioning. This one – does the same for the security – alarms, bells, electrification. And this one – this one relates to the fire precautions.

'You will have noticed, I'm sure, that this house has been built right away from the village and is surrounded on three sides by open heath and woods. Sir Alec presumably regarded its construction as a challenge; he wanted to snap his fingers at Nature by creating a miniature Kew Gardens and making his whole property impervious to fire.

'Timed switches control regular sprinklers to keep the grass fresh, right up to the perimeter wire. Beyond that, of course, he has no control over the scrub and forest. But there are also precautions for switching on special hoses should the temperature beyond the wire reach a certain level. All the fountains, streams, and pools can be tapped. There is an extra mains supply that can be called upon if necessary.'

'All computerised?'

'All computerised. Sherman Foster was very proud of it.'

'Who is Sherman Foster?'

'The man who put it in. Very proud of it, as I said. Very proud of his daughter too – Gina.'

Bliss looked at her.

'Adopted?'

'Of course. Remember – Sherman finished up in pieces in a lift in Marseilles.'

Bliss looked back at the screen, fighting down the nausea of revulsion.

'All automatic?'

'All automatic, except for emergency master switches under Sir Alec's desk. But – ' Connie paused significantly ' – if the computer programs were slightly – modified, that emergency control might not work.'

Bliss gazed at her.

'I got the idea in the church,' said Connie, 'when we lit the candles.'

'I thought there was something. So if the computer

appeared to break down, there would be no panic. Sir Alec would rush to his study and expect to save the situation with his master switches.'

'Only he wouldn't save the situation.'

'Be a surprise for him, wouldn't it? That would be the second surprise he got in his desk – my God!'

'What is it?' said Connie, alarmed.

'Dolly! She's gone, in case you didn't know.'

'No great loss,' said Connie, sniffing.

'No, you don't understand. She and Cass have gone back to England. Don't you see? She's turned him down. Rejected him.'

'I thought he'd cast her off.'

'He still wanted her around for – well, he still wanted her around. Max had even used pressure to get her to stay. She was furious. Now she's told them she doesn't care. Worse still, she put it in writing, and left it in Sir Alec's desk. And you can imagine that Dolly when cross is no diplomat. Don't you see? She's challenged him. She's taken him on. And she has no idea of the nature of the opposition.'

*   *   *   *   *   *

It was like having dinner off a coffin.

Sir Alec and Max both wore black armbands. Max stood up and announced that as a mark of respect there would no wine served that evening.

Julie lifted her eyes heavenwards and looked long-suffering. With no wrist to pat and no glass to raise, she pouted permanently and smoked ostentatiously between every course.

Mademoiselle Aline made chilly conversation with the guest journalist from *Time* magazine, who wished he

193

had gone to interview Prince Rainier instead.

For Bliss and Connie, the struggle was to show exactly the appropriate amount of regret. After all, what was Dolly to them? Or Cass?

*   *   *   *   *   *

'I'm still not sure I should have involved you, Aunt Jane.'

'Well, you have, and I should never have forgiven you if you hadn't.'

'The stakes are rising. We're not playing any more at guess the lady's secret with little coded riddles on the backs of envelopes. This is deadly.'

Aunt Jane put down her knitting and looked Bliss hard in the eye.

'Hector, I may be a bossy old woman who can never mind her own business, and I may have one foot in the grave, but I am a trained nurse who's seen more messy forms of death than you've had hot dinners. I've assisted at operations in the desert in Abyssinia and I've parachuted into occupied Yugoslavia to patch up Tito's partisans. My husband and son are dead. My brother – your father – and his family are all the kin I have. What better reason for living – or dying for that matter – could I have?'

If the gorgeous waiter with the tight black trousers had not been hovering, Bliss would have stood up and hugged her.

Aunt Jane used her knitting needle to wave away the touching remark that was trembling on his lips.

'Come on – business. Let's get to know the enemy. You've told me about Max. Now who is this awful creature Sherrif? I suppose it's not his real name either.'

'No, but Connie doesn't know what the real one is.

194

Understandably he doesn't keep a file on himself. From what she can piece together he may, like Max, have had an English mother. Father could have been Arab, Turk, Serb, Armenian – anything. Certainly some kind of adventurer – profiting by wars and revolutions, if not actually helping to start them. Master Alec popped up on the English scene as a brilliant undergraduate and took a first in Economics. He was already Alec Sherrif by that time.

'As you can imagine, he played down his obscure origins while he was building his niche in the English Establishment. A lot of his early career there is pretty common knowledge. His top-class degree, his charm, his capacity for hard work, and his ruthless efficiency proved an unstoppable combination. When he wasn't taking business rivals to the cleaners he was taking their wives to bed.

'He very soon discovered that an infallible way to stop people worrying about how you got your money is to give great chunks of it away. So alongside the image of Alec Sherrif the business giant grew the image of Alec Sherrif the philanthropist – cancer research, the arts, universities – you name it.

'The next rule he tumbled to was that everybody loves a sportsman. So, out went the millions on new clubs and stadiums and youth sponsorship. A string of racehorses soon appeared; so did the grey topper and the champagne in the royal enclosure.

'The third revelation came to him from the Vicar of Bray – be a good government man. So before long the fat industrial contracts began piling up in his "IN" tray.

'By the time you have added the frills – the private jet, the Riviera palace, the fabulous parties, the notorious wife dripping with diamonds – you get the feeling that the KBE came almost by public demand.'

'And the crime was going on all the time?'

'Apparently. Despite all that success piling legally, he couldn't resist going for even bigger fortunes illegally – and using the one to facilitate and to mask the other. Must have been his father coming out.'

'I wonder what is driving him?' said Aunt Jane.

'Just a criminal mentality? Won't that do?'

'No. There seems something obsessive about all this. If it were merely the desire for commercial power he would go on building and buying like the press barons and oil magnates; all his life would be consumed by it. If he were a master criminal pure and simple he would want more domination there. Yet he gives his subordinates and part-ners great freedom of movement, you say. It's as if both sides of his activities are calculated, balanced; as if both are intended to be complementary to each other. There's a reason, a pattern, a motivation behind it.'

'Well, I don't know about that. Our concern – Connie's and mine – is to stop him, not psychoanalyse him.'

'Maybe,' said Aunt Jane, 'but knowing what makes your enemy tick is most useful.'

'Not enough time. We have to do something, and soon. Sherman Foster is dead. Sarah is dead. Connie's husband is dead. And now Dolly and Cass. Connie is sick with fear. And do you think I can live with this threat over Pri and Parry and their families? To say nothing of Mum and Dad? A threat which we know he is all too capable of carrying out. My God – Sherrif is ticking all right – like a bomb.'

Aunt Jane put a hand on his wrist.

'I know, I know, Hector, and you must do what you

think best. I also appreciate that time could be short. Just remember what I say; bear it in mind. This terrible man seems to be completely in control and utterly assured of his progress to wherever he wants to go. You are contemplating challenging him; if you are successful you will have checkmated him. A man like that faced with sudden frustration or deeply-laid plans could react in the most extraordinary way. All I say is "be careful". And be warned.'

'You be careful too, Aunt Jane.'

'I'll be fine. I wouldn't have missed this for the world. Now get along to Connie and start your plotting. I'll get things going at this end.'

*　　*　　*　　*　　*　　*

Bliss replaced the book on the shelf.

'It is very kind of you to show me all this, Mademoiselle Aline. It helps me to get to know him.'

The still face registered goodwill if not actual pleasure.

'I keep his room exactly as he left it.'

Bliss decided he was on safe enough ground to venture a small joke.

'Surely not his socks on the floor?'

At last! A glimmer of a smile.

'No, of course not. But his toys and games and books are as he left them. I do not believe in keeping a child locked away in drawers and cupboards. Alan is away from his home a great deal. When he returns he needs to find familiar things in familiar places.'

'I understand,' said Bliss. 'You want him to be happy.'

'That above all else,' said Mademoiselle Aline with extraordinary fervour, quite out of keeping with the general tone of the previous conversation.

Then, as if she had said too much, she gestured awkwardly, and said, 'If there is anything else you would like to see . . . . '

'No, no, that's fine,' said Bliss hurriedly. 'That's been a great help. Given me a few ideas.'

Trying to put her at her ease, he said, 'I've seen you with some of the staff children, Mademoiselle. May I say that you have a gift in that direction.'

'Monsieur is too kind.'

The reply was perfunctory, but the pleasure registered in the face was genuine.

A bell rang somewhere.

'If Monsieur will excuse me; it may be the grocery deliveries for dinner.'

'May I stay for a while, Mademoiselle?'

'Certainly, Monsieur. And come in again whenever you wish.'

Bliss listened to her footsteps going down the stairs.

Well, she may be no potential ally, but at least she is no enemy. Not any more. And almost certainly she's no spy. We have nothing to fear from her.

There's depth there too, and power. She's worth a dozen Julie's.

He could have looked forward to working with her; she would understand what he wanted to do.

He idly picked up one of Alan's scrap books and turned the pages. The boy could draw. He had a good eye for detail.

He became aware of Aline's footsteps returning. She re-entered the room.

'Monsieur, do you know where I can find Dr. Marshall?'

'Right now? No. Why?'

'She has a visitor, downstairs in the hall.'

'A visitor?'
'Yes. Her daughter.'

Chapter Eight

' . . . . preparations for work are proceeding, though I must say that the word "work" seems incongruous in a delightful place like this. The tan is deepening and the waistline is expanding. For further news, see letter to Mum and Dad. Love to Thelma and the kids. Tor.'

Bliss addressed the card, stuck the stamp on it, and placed it with the one to Priam.

From the desk drawer he took out some sheets of embossed notepaper and began the letter.

'Dear Mum and Dad . . . . '

Chit-chat, gossip, details of planned timetables and activities with Alan. A few impressions of the members of the household. Put in dislike of Max – make it look genuine. Some comments on Connie; news of Ruth's arrival. Reference to the 'awful accident', but no details. If he made the account too innocent Max would smell a rat.

The letter had to be informative, but not emotional. No sign of danger must show; only the slightest trace of strain by the omission of details of unpleasant things. He was the dutiful son keeping his parents up to date, but telling them nothing that could cause worry or disturbance. It wasn't easy, and took longer than he had imagined.

He signed it, put all sheets together, and folded them in half. Before he slid them into the envelope, he turned over one corner of the top sheet. Then he stuck down the envelope, addressed, and stamped it.

Somewhere else in the house, if she was following his suggestion, Connie was doing the same.

'Dear Meg . . . . '

Her main topic would be easy – Ruth. She could go for Meg hammer and tongs for 'letting Ruth do something silly' without actually explaining why it was 'silly'. The surprise and strain could appear genuine. Max would buy that all right.

Bliss picked up the remaining sheets of notepaper and ran his finger over the embossed address.

Quite a girl, that Ruth. Connie had told him the story as soon as she got it out of her. A remarkable feat of organisation for a twelve-year-old.

It left Connie the prey to a wild variety of emotions. Delight in seeing her daughter, obviously. After the appropriate parental crossness had come pride; it was a considerable achievement to hoodwink a highly-educated and very fierce headmistress into delegating the school secretary to go into town and buy airline tickets, arrange taxis, escorts, and Heaven knows what else. Connie and Bliss shared a chuckle over the expression on Miss Crosby's face if she should ever find out.

All that was speedily followed by horror; Ruth was now under the very roof of the man who had ordered David's murder. Present too was the man who had more than once threatened Ruth's well-being, perhaps her life. Connie felt her insides go taut when Sir Alec beamed at the girl and showed her to a chair, or when Max patted her on the head.

'I can't stand it, Hector,' she said. 'If I sent her straight back, they'll think I'm planning to do something and want her out of harm's way. If I keep her here, these swines are right at her shoulder. What am I to do? What on earth am I to do?'

'Stop driving yourself mad, for a start,' said Bliss.

'It's all right for you. Sarah's dead; Ruth isn't.'

She hadn't meant it, of course, and she was all over him with apologies. But it was a sign of the strain she was under.

It took Bliss some time to convince her that Ruth's sudden arrival could be an advantage, not a disaster.

'If she were in England when they began making more threats, and you were tied hand and foot here, you'd be off your head with worry. Well, she's not; she's here. With you. Surely that must be a comfort. Neither Sir Alec nor Max will try anything under this roof. It's not their style. And they could never mask it unless they killed off half the household as well. No. Right here, she's safe. Move her, and there is danger."

'She can't stay here for ever.'

'She won't have to. Give me a little time, that's all. I can – I have something in mind. Now go and write those letters and do the other things we agreed.'

To Bliss' surprise, she did.

Bliss drummed with his fingers on the little pile of letters and postcards.

Planning, planning. Snatching advantages from near-hopeless situations. Ruth's arrival could be turned to their favour. If Connie kept her with them – 'Sir Alec asks me to tell you the child can stay as long as you wish, at no charge of course' – Max would assume that she was accepting the position.

After five years or more of regular visits to update his records and retrieval systems, Sir Alec had good reason to believe she was tame and obedient. Well, let him continue to think like that.

Max, after his revelations about Sarah, had equally good reason for assuming that Bliss was stricken and cowed.

Sir Alec and Max appeared to hold all the cards. That too could be turned to advantage; both of them, with total power and unbroken success, were the victims of arrogance. A lifetime of treading on people as if they were worms had made them incapable of respect for them, even those that turned. Like Dolly.

Dolly, with her heaving bosom and righteous rage, had thought that 'telling him where he got off' was the answer to everything.

Was that why she had been killed? Just for saying what she thought of him? Murdered – for a few South-London insults thrown over her suntanned shoulder?

Or was it the *News of the World* threat? Surely a man of Sir Alec's power and influence was not going to be intimidated by that. It was barely out of the 'I'll-tell-my-Dad-of-you' category. It was primary school playground stuff. Far more illustrious notables than Sir Alec Sherrif had survived innuendo from what a Palace secretary had once called the 'sewage press'.

A third possibility edged its way into Bliss' mind. Something to do with what had first made Dolly upset.

'All because I wouldn't chuck away me pills.'

Dolly, Bliss remembered, had told him what to do with his suggestion – 'stuff it'. Not the most appropriate choice of words, but her general meaning had been clear enough. Perhaps in her parting letter Dolly had expanded on this theme – told him how unsuitable he was for fatherhood. Had this been the taunt that strikes the vain man in a most sensitive area? Had dear diamond Julie said substantially the same? He had to take it from Julie, but he didn't have to take it from busty little wenches from Earlsfield.

In short, had Dolly died not from professional necessity but from sexual pique?

Had Dolly got near, albeit without knowing it, to what Aunt Jane was talking about? To what really made Sir Alec Sherrif tick? Surely not.

Bliss shook his head. Much too Freudian. What did the reason matter? Dolly was dead. Dead. A well-timed nudge from Albert's front wheel on the High Corniche, and that gorgeous body lay broken and grotesque, with parted lips and staring eyes, in a mass of tangled metal.

There would be no mourning here for Dolly, and none for her 'lovely' Cass, the only one who 'understood' her, who was 'a bit thick', like her.

Bliss sneered at the thought of the speed with which Julie would supply herself with a new dreamboat, a new wrist to pat. Twenty minutes on the beach anywhere between le Lavandou and Monte Carlo, and she would infallibly find something to fill the gap, something tanned and young and serviceable in white satin-gloss shorts.

Bliss pulled himself together. Let's stick to immediate problems.

He glanced at his watch. Max would be round soon to ask if he 'had any professional matters to discuss'. He would almost certainly look in if Bliss didn't answer the door. He would see the cards and letter on the desk, but would not take them, because Bliss had insisted more than once on posting his own mail.

'I respect your wishes in that matter, Mr. Bliss.'

Oh, no – Max was far too clever a cat to take them just like that.

Bliss smiled as he stood up. Well, Max, two can play at that game.

He left the two cards on the desk, and put the envelope in the inside pocket of his jacket in the wardrobe.

Then he went out to meet Connie in the garden.

*   *   *   *   *   *

'Are you sure this is the best place?' said Connie.

Bliss waved at the expanse of open lawn.

'Who can hear us? We are in full view of everyone who looks out of those windows, so we are clearly not making a bomb or anything. We are not rushing off to whisper in shady cafés or taking lonely rides along country roads, so we are obviously not plotting either. Ruth is sunbathing at the pool, isn't she?'

'Yes.'

'Good. Then, so far as they're concerned, we've accepted the situation and are taking consolation from each other. Perhaps even taking refuge in a forlorn flirtation.'

'Hector!'

Connie blushed.

Hector leaned forward and touched her hand. She did not pull it away, he noticed.

'Connie, I don't give a damn what they think, so long as they despise us. We are two more weaklings helpless in their masterful trap, fit only to be manipulated when the master decrees.'

He grinned mischievously.

'Besides, what's so outrageous about a flirtation? You could do a lot worse than me.'

The blush deepened.

'Hector!'

'All right, all right. Now – have you written some more cards and things?'

'Three cards, one letter.'

'Good. And you left them on the desk?'

'Yes.'

'Have you – er – adjusted the machinery?'

'The programs have been duly modified.'

'So when the alarm is raised . . . . '

Connie looked grim.

'The chief feature of the situation, I should say, will be the conspicuous absence of alarms.'

'What about the sprinklers, the sluices in the gravity feed, the reserve supply from – '

'Hector, listen. Sherman Foster may have designed the system and put it in, but I wrote the programs for its control. Believe me, I know exactly what I'm doing.'

'What you've done, I hope.'

'What I've done.'

Bliss nodded, reluctantly satisfied.

'Have you got the other stuff?'

Connie patted her dress pocket.

'Cassette. Here.'

'You picked out the worst?'

'Hector, they're all terrible. I picked out the ones I thought most easily traceable and provable in the space of one tape.'

'And in case something happens to it?'

Connie held up the newspaper she was carrying.

'Two sheets – names, places, dates, accounts – chapter and verse. I've stuck them between the theatre and sports pages.'

'Good – show me.'

'What?'

'Lay the paper out on the grass as if you're telling me about the weather or the latest sport. Go on – talk about it. Point at it.'

'Hector, is all this necessary?'

'Yes, it is. You know how many security men there are round the house. How do we know there isn't one right now, up in a tree with a pair of binoculars? After what Max told me about Sarah, he's bound to be wary to begin with. If I were Max, I'd certainly watch me.

'Max may think I'm pretty cowardly, but he'll watch for a bit to make sure. So let's give him plenty to get bored with. Turn over the pages and show me something else.'

Bliss leaned forward and put his head near hers.

'Good. Now take your handkerchief out of your pocket with the cassette inside it and wipe your nose. Keep your hand up. Now let me take your handkerchief and wipe your eyes – gently – like that.

'I'm consoling you, see? Now I'm going to be rather taken with your doleful beauty and I'm going to kiss you – like that. Don't move. That's fine. Just look still and woebegone. Restrain your natural impulse to fling your arms round my neck.'

'Hector, you're impossible.'

'Maybe, but I'm all you've got at the moment, so you'll have to make the best of it. There – now I shall give you back your handkerchief. Take my hand in both yours. That's it. Now, look grateful. That's fine. Don't overdo it. Now let me have my hand back. Good.'

'Where is it?'

'Where's what?'

'You know, the cassette.'

Bliss smiled.

'Well, if you didn't notice, Connie, I'm sure Hawkeye

up in the trees won't have seen it. He would have been too taken up by the – um – tenderness of the moment. Like you.'

'Hector Bliss, if you've done all this in order to take advantage of me – '

'Connie Marshall, if you don't trust me at a time like this, we're both finished and so is Ruth.'

'So it was all a show?'

Bliss tossed his head.

'Why is it that whatever the circumstances, women can always find time to wonder if they're being deceived? Hell, Connie, I don't know. We're both in the middle of the most desperate situation either of us has ever been in. I haven't got time to analyse what my feelings are; I'm too concerned with the preservation of our lives.'

Connie's lips tightened.

'All right then. I'll ask a practical question. Aren't you being a bit too cloak and dagger?'

'No, I don't think so. We shan't suffer from taking too many precautions; we shall certainly cop it if we take too few. We're amateurs, Connie, in this sort of thing; we can't afford to leave anything to chance. Ruth didn't. If a twelve-year-old can hatch a scheme like hers, I think we should take a leaf out of her book. If it turns out that we've been too cautious we can both have a laugh about it afterwards.'

'Hmmm.'

'Still not convinced? Right. We're going for a walk round the gardens, then we're going back to my room to pick up my mail and we're going to drive into Ste. Sophie to post it. Back just in time for dinner.'

'Can we take Ruth?'

'If you like. If you don't mind her hearing more proof of

what we're up against.'

'After what she's done to get here in order to help, I think she deserves to know.'

'So be it. On your feet. It's all right; I've got your newspaper. Now, hold my hand – we're flirting, remember?'

*   *   *   *   *   *

'Isn't it lovely and cool in here,' said Ruth.

'It is indeed,' said Bliss. 'Let us introduce you to the lady who helps to keep it cool. Come and meet Ste. Sophie herself.'

Ruth stood and looked up at the time-darkened picture.

'Does she really protect you from fire?'

Bliss gestured to the ranks of glowing candles.

'A lot of people seem to think so.'

'Are you going to burn that horrid man's house down?'

Bliss looked sharply at Connie.

'I told her,' said Connie. 'She came all this way to share my danger. She deserves to know what is at stake.'

'Very well. Let's sit down a minute.'

Bliss glanced over his shoulder, but every pew was empty. Nevertheless, he kept his voice low in an imitation of reverence.

'Now, young lady,' he said to Ruth, 'your mother thinks that I am either being over-cautious, or that I'm pretending we are involved in some cloak and dagger scheme that's half-way between James Bond and the Scarlet Pimpernel.'

He took his cards and letter out of his pocket.

'I wrote these in the belief that our friend Max would read them, and that he would not want me to know he had read them.'

'To lull him into a false sense of security.'

'Dead right. I see you've been studying all the right books.'

Ruth grinned.

'How do you know Max has been reading them?' said Connie.

'Because the cards had been lifted from the desk and put back again.'

'You couldn't be sure to the inch.'

'No. But when I put the stamps on, I purposely left one of those plain edge bits of stamp paper in between the cards. When Max picked them up, it fell out, but it was such a random, tiny, obvious piece of litter that he paid no attention to it. When I picked them up, it wasn't there. Someone had moved those cards.'

'All right,' said Connie, gazing up at Ste. Sophie, 'so he read the cards. But the letter was in your pocket. What can you prove from that?'

Ruth looked expectantly at Bliss.

'I can prove,' said Bliss, 'that Max was very clever, but not clever enough. The cards were easy meat, and were meant to be. I gave Max credit for expecting me to try and fool him. Hence the postcards laid out on the table, begging to be picked up and read.

'If he saw that as decoy, he would then start searching for the real thing. So I made him work a bit – inside a jacket, inside a wardrobe.'

Bliss took out the envelope and waved it.

'I can't prove he went to my wardrobe, and he couldn't leave fingerprints on my jacket pocket, but I know he read this.'

'How?' said Ruth, thoroughly engrossed.

'Because I've re-opened it and had a look.'

Bliss showed Ruth the reverse side of the envelope.

'I think that's been opened and stuck down again.'

Ruth peered.

'Because of that tiny blob of gum.'

'That's right.'

'Careless.'

Bliss smiled.

'I presume you did a better job.'

Ruth grinned broadly.

'Better than that one.'

'I agree. I'm sure Miss Crosby was right out of her depth with you. I should think one of Max's clerks was told to stick this back in a hurry. He deserves a detention for it.'

'You can't prove it,' said Connie.

'No,' admitted Bliss.

Ruth looked disappointed.

'But I haven't finished yet.'

Ruth perked up again.

Bliss carefully took out the three sheets of notepaper. Ruth recognised the embossed address.

'Look at this crease in the top right-hand corner of the first page,' said Bliss.

'What about it?'

'I put that crease there myself. In fact, I folded it right over before I put it in the envelope.'

'And the page was flat when you took it out,' said Ruth, jumping in.

'No,' said Bliss. 'It was still folded.'

'So you still haven't proved anything,' said Connie.

'Oh, yes I have. Max has been very observant and very thorough. Not only did he notice the fold when he took it out of the envelope; he replaced the fold when he put it back. The trouble is, the sheet was originally folded upwards; when Max put it back, he forgot, and folded it back underneath.'

'Well done, Mr. Bliss,' said Ruth.

'Not bad, eh?' said Bliss. 'Then how's this for an encore? Max, as I've said, is very thorough and very efficient. That makes him tidy-minded. When he put those three sheets away, he naturally put them away in the order in which they were written and in which he read them – pages 1,2,3. When I put them in the envelope I deliberately put them in the order 1,3,2. Max had to shuffle them to get the order right, and no doubt cursed the stupid Englishman for offending his tidy mind. Then he got so taken up with being clever over the fold that he forgot the bad order of the pages. He put them back in the right order – 1,2,3. He unconsciously corrected me – couldn't help it. So I've got him.'

'Mr. Bliss, I think that's terrific.'

Bliss shrugged modestly.

'One of my better efforts, I must admit.' He looked at Connie. 'Have I now satisfied the court that my correspondence has been interfered with?'

Connie said nothing.

'Oh, come on, Mummy, surely you agree.'

'I accept the argument,' said Connie at last. 'But I don't see where it gets us.'

'It puts us one jump ahead,' said Bliss. 'All we have in this game is the element of surprise and our own intelligence. I have used mine to make Max think that he knows something that we don't. It's his favourite state of mind. As long as he thinks he knows about our puny attempts to avoid his surveillance, he will continue to despise us. As long as he finds no evidence, even in the letter I try to hide, that I'm planning anything, he'll remain smugly confident. That is how we want him until – well – until, shall we say, the heat is on.'

'Mmm. I still think you're overdoing it.'

'Blame it on my military training,' said Bliss.

*   *   *   *   *   *

Bliss waited while the waiter poured the lager. Sunlight gleamed on glass and ice cubes. All around him, everything shone, sparkled, and dazzled – brass fittings, white paint, polished mahogany.

'Thank you, Rudi, that's all.'

The slim hips shimmered away.

'Aunt Jane, I think you overdo it sometimes.'

Aunt Jane looked the picture of surprised innocence.

'Now what have I done?'

Bliss put down his glass.

'I know you make private jokes to us about him "moving like Valentino". We understand you. But to share the joke with him. What on earth will he think?'

'I should think he'd be very flattered. But as a matter of fact, Mr. Prim-and-Proper, his name really is Rudi. So there.'

'I don't believe you.'

'No. I didn't think you would. That's why I never told you before. But it is.'

She waved a brisk hand in the air.

'Never mind my reputation. Don't worry; I won't shame the family. Have you got any more of the goods for me?'

'Couple of sheets. Here.'

'Right. I'll put those out this evening. For once there's no party on board tonight and no trip out.'

'Did you get the first lot through?'

'I spoke to Priam last night.'

'How did he take it?'

'Very reluctantly at first. He thought it was some escapade of mine. When I tied it up with you and Sarah he began to take it more seriously.'

'Did you stress the need for covert action?'

'I did. I told him all about you and Connie and Ruth. As he now knows about Sarah he'll understand the danger Ruth is in.'

'You didn't say anything about Max's threats to the family?'

Aunt Jane dropped her knitting to her lap.

'Hector, what do you take me for? I've told him everything you asked me to tell him and I've told him to instigate police inquiries without coming out into the open. He now understands the urgency of the matter and he's going to get moving right away. What more do you want?'

'Did you tell him the tape is on its way?'

'Yes.'

Bliss hesitated and took a swig of lager while he was making up his mind. Aunt Jane came to his rescue.

'If you want to know whether I sent it all right – yes, I did.'

She resumed work with the needles.

'I had a close call though.'

Bliss' heart missed a beat.

'What do you mean?'

'Well,' said Aunt Jane, 'I decided to carry out a little experiment like yours to see whether I'm being watched.'

'My God! Are you?'

'Oh, yes. It took me a while to find out, though. My

214

eyesight is none too good, as you know.'

She hitched her spectacles a millimetre up her nose.

'I wouldn't know anyone was following me unless he stood right behind me. So, like you, I made it easy for him.'

'Aunt Jane, what have you been up to?'

'Saving your bacon, that's what. Don't be so mistrustful. Anyone would think I was ga-ga, to hear you talk.'

'Sorry.'

'Right. Now – where was I?'

'Making it easy for them.'

A final warning gleam from the glasses.

'Ah, yes. Well. On the way to the Post Office I stopped for a cup of lemon tea at the marina café, and sat at a table beside the walkway. There's room for cyclists as well as pedestrians. I put my handbag on the table and pretended to be reading the newspaper.'

'Aunt Jane, really!'

'Now what? I suppose you think I was planning an ambush?'

'Well, not ex – '

'That I was going to wait for him to appear, and as soon as he made off with the bag, do a rugby tackle on him or on his bicycle?'

'Of course not.'

'Hmmm. Well, someone came along all right. He did it very well too. If I hadn't been watching out of the corner of my eye, I wouldn't have noticed it go.'

'What did you do then?'

'Let him get out of sight before raising the alarm.'

'Let him get out of sight?'

'Well, I didn't want him to get caught, did I?'

'Why not?'

'That would have made me too efficient. I thought the

whole idea of all this was to make them think we're a pushover.'

'Well, yes.'

'There you are then.'

'What about the cassette?'

'Why do you think I carry my knitting everywhere?'

'So they got nothing?'

'Nothing but an old bag which I've hated for years, full of old lady's junk. I'm glad to see the back of it.'

'I'm sorry, Aunt Jane.'

'What for?'

'For underestimating you.'

'If I can make you do it, I should have made them do it. So now what?'

'I'm going to try and get Connie to put another cassette together.'

'Gradually build up the weight of the evidence?'

'Yes. But it gets harder all the time. Connie's in a terrible state.'

'I'm not surprised.'

'Why do you say that? We're doing our best to fight back, which is what she wanted. We're protecting Ruth by not coming out into the open. Look at all the elaborate plans we've laid to put them off the scent. I know it's a strain. It's a strain for all of us. We could be in danger of our lives.'

'It's not the same, though, Hector.'

'What do you mean?'

Aunt Jane looked at him.

'This is going to hurt.'

'Well?'

'Sarah is dead and Ruth isn't.'

'That's what Connie said.'

'Well then.'

'She apologised afterwards.'

'Maybe. But she meant it. And it's true.'

'I can't help Sarah being dead and Ruth being alive. I'm doing my best.'

'Are you?'

'What is that supposed to mean?'

'Does it occur to you that it's Connie who has taken the biggest risks? It's her daughter up there, not yours or mine. She is the one who has betrayed the secrets; we are merely the messenger boys. She is the one who has tampered with the machinery.'

'It's an added precaution, that's all. That heath and forest surrounds the property on three sides. One day it's going to catch fire. When it does . . .'

'She has committed potential arson. All you have done is to say "what a good idea".'

'What do you suggest? That I do what Dolly did? Write him a rude letter and challenge him to pistols at dawn?'

'No. But you must do something to make her accept that you are as committed as she is.'

'Coming out into the open has no merit as far as I can see. It would be pure insanity. We could be swatted like flies.'

'I didn't say the answer was easy. Just think about it. I'll tell you this, though. I can't go on helping for much longer. My employers are off in a few days for a cruise. So you'd better come up with something.'

Bliss finished his drink.

'That reminds me. There is one favour you might ask from your employers for us. In the light of what you have just told me, it might fit very well.'

*　　*　　*　　*　　*　　*

Bliss lit a candle, and came to sit beside Connie in the pew.

'You haven't said a word in half an hour.'

Lips were pressed tighter.

'Connie, if you don't say something you'll burst.'

'I can't do it any more.'

'What?'

'What we're doing. Pushing out secrets in dribs and drabs.'

'It's what we agreed. You want to nail him, don't you?'

'I don't care if it's what we agreed. I can't do it any more. Not this way.'

'But it's working. I've got Pri assembling the evidence. He's got friends in C.I.D., Fraud Squad, Special Branch, and God knows what working on it.'

'That's just it,' said Connie. 'Sooner or later their inquiries are going to reach one of the men in Sir Alec's blackmail network, and they are going to warn him.'

'Connie, we have to take some chances.'

'Not "we". Me. I'm the one who does the breaking and entering. I'm the one he's going to come after. I'm the one giving away the secrets.'

'And I'm just the fence. I see.'

'I didn't mean that.'

'You haven't said what you really think. You still don't trust me, do you? I'm not committed enough, am I? It's what you said – Sarah's dead and Ruth isn't.'

Connie lowered her head.

'I'm sorry, Hector.'

Bliss fished a coin out of his pocket and placed it in her hand.

'All right, Dr. Marshall, have it your own way. Now – go and light that candle. And while you do, just think what you're going to be letting loose. At the moment we have the initiative, albeit a slender one. If we go ahead with what you have in mind, we shall be turning a beast loose, and there is no knowing how it will behave. We shall certainly have to run.

'And if we do, you place yourself and Ruth in my hands completely. I do have some experience of action out in the open. You don't. If you stay here, you know what you're about. Out there, you do as I say. It won't be calculation; it will be action. It'll be different, it'll be dangerous, and it'll be changing all the time. I can guarantee nothing.'

Connie stood up and walked to Ste. Sophie's little altar. She stood for a while very still.

At last she picked a fresh candle from the box and held it towards the flames. At the last minute she withdrew it and replaced it in the box.

She came back and returned the coin to Bliss' hand.

'Well?'

'I could hardly offer a candle to Ste. Sophie to ask for a house's protection from the flames – under the circumstances.'

*   *   *   *   *   *

'That's the last one I'm doing.'

'There won't be time for any more. Aunt Jane's yacht is sailing.'

'When?'

'Day after tomorrow.'

'Where to?'

'Elba and Capri. Ruth will enjoy it.'

'What?'

'You want action. You're going to get it.'

'You mean we escape by sea?'

219

'No. Ruth does. We go another way, and pull them after us – if necessary.'

'I can't leave Ruth on her own.'

'If you have her with us when the fire and brimstone descend she'll be in danger. Put her on the yacht and she's safe. Aunt Jane will arrange everything.'

'An old lady?'

'You forget. She has influential employers and her own private navy round her. To say nothing of infinite resource. And hundreds of miles of sea. Even if they guessed Ruth was there, they couldn't get near her.'

'I don't like it.'

'Look, Connie, put yourself in their position. If you have a low opinion of your cowardly enemies, you would expect them to cower away together. Well, we're going to split. It'll help us too; they'll be searching for a group of three people, not a duo.'

'So we'll be together?'

Bliss smiled.

'Got to keep you out of mischief somehow.'

Connie looked keenly at him.

'You've been working this out for some time, haven't you?'

'Like Churchill's funeral.'

'Pardon?'

'They called it "Operation Hope-Not". They knew the old boy was going to pop off some time or other, even though they didn't want him to. They also knew that they would have only a few days to mount a colossal exercise in funeral arrangements. So they did the common sense thing: they planned it all in advance, then put it in the drawer and forgot about it till it was needed.'

'This is hardly as big as Churchill's funeral.'

'It's a bloody sight more dangerous. Out of the two I think I'd rather have organised the funeral. As it is, I could well be setting in motion my own.'

Connie ignored the black humour.

'What else have you arranged?'

'Another false trail. As soon as you've finished talking to me you go into Cannes and you buy two sets of tickets – one for the airline, one for the train.'

'Where to?'

'Three air passages to London from Nice. Three train reservations to Paris, Boulogne, and London. Make inquires about Paris hotels; if it seems easy, book us in somewhere overnight.'

'Whereabouts? There are hundreds of hotels in Paris.'

'Thousands, I should imagine. There are plenty of reasonable small ones in the Marais – third or fourth *arrondissement*. Or up near the *Gard du Nord* – convenient for a quick getaway to Boulogne. I expect they'll know in the agency. Have you got enough money?'

'Yes.'

Bliss grunted.

'He pays you well too, eh?'

'He pays some of Ruth's school fees.'

'Bastard.'

Connie took the swear word in her stride – something she had rarely done before.

'What date shall I book?'

'At least two weeks from today.'

'Why so far ahead?'

'We intend them to find these tickets, don't we?'

'Yes – I presume so.'

'They will gloat over them, and sneer at our simplicity once more. They will note that our craven, futile flight will be planned for two weeks' time. They should not then be expecting any move at all from us in two *days'* time, much less a hostile one.'

'What do I do with these tickets?'

'Hide them. Put the airline ones in a fairly easy place. Make it look like a decoy. The others – '

Bliss pondered.

'Put them in Ruth's room. Stuff 'em into a pair of socks or something like that. If they don't find them they'll suspect nothing. If they do, they'll suspect even less because they'll be so sure of us.'

'Won't they arrest us or something?'

'Oh, no. Max will wait. He'll play cat and mouse. He'll enjoy that.'

'You have given this plenty of thought, haven't you?'

'I may not be up in the academic stratosphere like some people, but I'm not exactly a slouch, you know.'

Connie apologised.

'All right, I asked for that. What next?'

'That you can tell me.'

'How?'

'What do you know of Sir Alec's movements in the next few days?'

'Tomorrow I think there's a delegation due from Algeria. The day after that he's flying to England.'

'England!'

'Yes.' Connie's face was like stone. 'He's taking Dolly's body back for burial.'

Bliss stared.

'In person?'

'Oh, yes. The caring friend, the distraught host, the benevolent mourner. Guess who's paying the funeral expenses?'

Bliss felt sick. He could see the solemn features, the black armband, the crossed-over hands, the bowed head.

'Poor Dad.'

'What?'

'I said "poor Dad". On the grass outside Earlsfield crematorium, a lonely widower is going to gaze at a colossal floral tribute from a man he's never seen before and will never see again, and wonder how his only daughter got mixed up with him.'

'I see what you mean.'

'From bed to hearse,' muttered Bliss to himself. 'Poor kid.'

'What did you say?'

'Nothing.'

Bliss sneered.

'And what will the dutiful Max be doing? Telling the rest of the family how "full of life" she was?'

'No.' Connie's voice went hard again. 'He'll be flying to Cracow with Cass' body.'

'My God.'

There was silence for a while.

'It does leave the coast clear,' said Connie, breaking it.

'Yes, it does,' said Bliss, pulling himself together. 'And don't the staff have the day off then?'

'Yes, except Aline.'

'Right. Tomorrow, I'm going to take Aline shopping.'

'Oh?'

'Yes. We're going to buy some gear for a camping trip with Alan. Tent, rucksacks, sleeping bags, stove – that sort of thing.'

'What do I do?'

'You go shopping too. Take Ruth. Get some good shoes, thick socks, shorts, surgical spirit, sunburn lotion, and tanning cream. Make it look as if you're buying for both of you. If you can stand the shock, choose some hair dye. If you can't face that, get a pair of barber's scissors.'

'I take it this is the real plan?'

'Yes. Let's hope it can fool them.'

'It won't for long.'

'Maybe not. But we don't need long.'

'Why?'

Bliss considered.

'If our first plan works, all this will prove unnecessary. The police will digest our information, and will sooner or later arrest him.'

'He could still order our execution even as they do it. The computer records have a thousand slaves to carry out his orders.'

'True. But if your second plan works, the records will be destroyed. What we are preparing is bound to get into the paper, and all those slaves you spoke about will put two and two together and realise that they are slaves no longer. Sir Alec will retain his power for only a few days.'

'Then the Sherrif's posse will disperse. The professionals – the wolves – will all split up and look for another pack to join. All we have to do is stay out of the way for half a week. We simply disappear.'

'Just like that.'

'Not quite. I've thought about this too. If we are lucky, they won't suspect us at all. They'll simply blame the weather, or terrorists. If they do blame us, they'll expect us to try and get to England.'

'So?'

'So – we stay in France. Secondly, they'll expect us to stay together. So – we pack Ruth off to Elba with Aunt Jane. Even if they tumble to it, it'll take time. Thirdly,

224

they'll expect us to run. So – we walk. They will be looking for a middle-aged schoolmaster and a pale-faced university egghead.'

'And we, I presume, shall be striding out across Provence – '

' – a bronzed and healthy couple of outdoor fiends. Thank God it's June. If it were August, we'd stand out a mile.'

'Why?'

'Walking in the high summer sun – in Provence? We'd look as barmy as Van Gogh. Probably get run in.'

'Where do we walk to?'

'Nowhere in particular, though I've one or two ideas. Don't you see? All we do is use up time, keep away from towns and officials – anyone who could be a tool of Sir Alec. We keep out eyes on the newspapers and wait for the news to break.'

'Is that all? Is it really that easy?'

'No, of course it isn't. That's only the plan. What happens when you put the plan into operation is a different matter entirely. Ask any soldier who has seen any action.'

'What will happen then?'

'I haven't the faintest idea. You wanted action; you're getting it. I can't promise you'll like it. But I don't think it will be dull. You can still pull back now if you want do.'

Connie swallowed.

'No, no. We'll go on. So I cut my hair tonight?'

'Good God, no. Not till just before zero hour. Same with the tanning cream. You can start rubbing surgical spirit in your feet though. And practise getting all you need into a single overnight bag. Then it'll fit into a ruck-sack easily enough and leave room for food.'

225

Connie looked a little mournful.

'I'm not very good at this sort of thing, am I?'

Bliss patted her hand.

'For someone who's never committed crimes before, you're not a bad criminal.'

'What about being a fugitive?'

'There are no colleges and diplomas for that, I'm afraid. Most practitioners have to pick it up as they go along. Don't worry; you'll be all right.'

Connie nodded hopefully.

'I don't suppose you've ever committed arson before.'

'As a matter of fact, I have. The difference was, the Government was paying me to do it then. And I did have a platoon of men to hold my hand and get me out of trouble if I made a b – if I made a mess of it.'

*　　*　　*　　*　　*　　*

Bliss packed and re-packed the rucksack until he was satisfied, then he emptied it and stood it in a corner.

He went over the coming arrangements in his mind for the umpteenth time. Enough was enough. If he wasn't ready now, it was just too bad.

There remained one more job to do. One last precaution – a sort of insurance policy.

He went to the desk and sat down. From the note case in his hip pocket he took a slip of paper.

He read it through once more. It was a detail from Sir Alec's records. He had asked Connie to extract it for him from the computer.

He took out one of the embossed sheets of notepaper – 'Ste. Sophie-les-Mimosas'. He picked up his pen, thought for a moment, and began to write . . . .

'*Mon cher Joseph* . . . .'

Chapter Nine

CONNIE HAD NEVER seen anything like it. One minute, it seemed, she was gazing anxiously out of the window and seeing nothing. The next, after a glance in the mirror at her new haircut, she looked again and saw walls of black smoke.

For a moment she stood paralysed with shock. This was it. They had loosed the beast. Oh God – now what?

From her window she saw security guards rushing to and fro. Others ran in from the perimeter bawling their heads off.

'They've seized up; they're not working.'

You should be more observant; they haven't been working for nearly a week. Serve you right for taking time off when the boss wasn't looking.

Now that she could see signs of her handiwork, Connie felt more settled, more calculating.

When more men dashed about dragging great lengths of empty hose, she smiled grimly. On the edge of one of the lawns, someone opened the top of a hydrant. Even from the distance of her upper window Connie could see the tenseness and urgency in the set of the man's shoulders; she could sense the frustration as he banged impotently on the ground with his hand.

You won't get anything there either.

Connie looked back at the smoke, and gasped. The height of it was awe-inspiring. Lower down she could now see sinister gleams of red and orange. On the ground the chaos was getting worse. Puny efforts were being made with hand-pumps at the swimming pool. Gardeners' sheds were being ransacked for buckets. Guard dogs abandoned by panicking handlers were barking and jumping at anything that moved.

Connie smiled again, then stopped. It suddenly struck her that this was power, or rather the intoxication of it. She had done this.

True, Hector had started the fire, but it was her brain that was responsible for the bafflement and confusion below. As she watched those men run from one device to another, trying to follow drills and practices they had been through so often, she knew in advance that nothing would work. Because she had seen to it that nothing would work.

Of all the people in that household, she alone had the knowledge and skill to make sure that the hugely expensive, vastly complicated, infinitely sophisticated, ultra-modern system would not work. Sherman Foster's pride and joy – 'the whole Coat d'Azooer can go up in flames and that shack of his will be safe' – was not going to work. Because it all depended, ultimately, on electronic impulses which she could create, control, manipulate – or cancel.

This was power. This was the heady effect it had. This was the faster heartbeat, the gleam of the eye, the lick of the lips. Connie had stopped smiling because she suddenly realised that this was the breath of life to people like Max. She now knew how Max felt.

It was terrifying.

She tore her eyes away from the window and went to the mirror above the dressing table.

A strange tanned face peered out at her. The bob

cut looked an awful mess, but at least it was different. She had also put on some heavy pencil to darken her eyebrows, and Ruth had suggested some purple lipstick.

The bush jacket sleeves were rolled up from brown forearms. The leather belt was drawn in tightly. The khaki shorts were quite natty, and, though she said so herself, she didn't have a bad pair of legs, especially now that they looked so dark. The white ankle socks and shoes reminded her of something out of an American film of college life a generation before.

She picked up her rucksack, hoisted it over one shoulder, and looked again.

She felt almost sick with fear and excitement; she felt half naked with such short hair; she felt as if the whole world was going to laugh at her shorts and ankle socks. Yet it was difficult to escape the impression that she was leaving behind in this room something she had never particularly wanted.

As she put out her hand to open the door, a fist hammered urgently on the outside.

Before she could say 'Come in' Aline had pushed it open.

'Oh, Madame. You must come quickly. The switches – you must see to them.'

She looked at Connie, her eyes taking in all the new details – clothes, skin, hair, make-up.

'Please, Madame, there is little time.'

Where was Hector? Oh, dear. What now?

'Very well, Mademoiselle Aline. I will do what I can. Let me get my keys.'

Aline fidgeted and fretted while Connie found the keys to the computer room. She still noticed, though, that Connie kept her rucksack on her shoulder.

Why doesn't she comment, thought Connie. Why doesn't she ask me why I'm got up like this? What is she thinking?'

Aline practically dragged her downstairs, where they bumped into Julie rushing in through the front door.

'What's gone wrong, for Christ's sake?'

'We do not know, Madame. Dr. Marshall and I are going to find out.'

'It's reached the gardens, dammit. Why aren't the Fire Brigade here?'

'Perhaps the alarm system has broken down too,' Connie heard herself saying. 'Or they are still at Fréjus.'

'You should not stay in the house, Madame,' said Aline.

'Don't worry; I won't,' said Julie. 'Not when I've got what I came for. Jurgen? Get in here.'

A dark vision of Aryan beauty bounded through the door and followed her up the stairs.

Aline tugged at Connie's sleeve.

'Madame, please!'

Dear God – where was Hector?

Connie followed Aline across a courtyard to the computer room in the office wing. She unlocked the door and went in.

Now what? She stood in front of one of the screens.

'Can you not do anything, Madame?'

Connie went through the motions of turning things on. This was ridiculous. They were half-way through burning the whole place down; they had their escape gear and plans were all ready; the security staff was in shreds; and here she was dithering over switches which she knew would do nothing – all because she couldn't bring herself to tell her arch-enemy's housekeeper to go to Hell.

Hector – please – where are you?

Connie peered at random images and figures she had conjured up on a screen.

'It's no good, Mademoiselle Aline – the whole system has broken down. The programs have been tampered with. I can do nothing.'

Might as well tell the truth; it's easier.

Instead of becoming more agitated, Aline leaned forward intently.

'Are you quite sure, Madame? The breakdown, you say, is complete?'

'Total.'

I should know.

'Is there no other way?' said Aline.

'There are emergency switches in Sir Alec's private office,' said Connie.

If she dashes off there, I can lose her.

Aline looked at her keenly.

'If they do not work – am I right? – nothing can save the house.'

'Not unless the Brigade gets here. The public alarm circuit is jammed too. Depends on how soon they notice the smoke and locate it. And if they arrived they'd only have the water in the pool – nothing else.'

Aline looked out at the darkening sky, looked round the room at the hardware, then looked again at Connie, raking her with her eyes from head to foot. She put out her hand.

'Come with me, Madame. We must try.'

Puzzled and uncertain, Connie followed her, more to fill in the time till Hector appeared than for any other reason.

Out in the courtyard, they could hear the fire now.

The air was getting thicker. Black smuts were falling everywhere. There were fewer security guards around. They heard a car start up and zoom towards the front gate. Dogs were running with lowered tails.

Outside Sir Alec's study, two or three guards hovered indecisively.

'Go in,' shouted Aline.

They stayed still.

'Nobody is allowed in there, Mademoiselle, except Mr. Bowman.'

In the height of the crisis, with his employer aloft in his private jet, the man was still paralysed with fear.

Aline drew herself up.

'Open it.'

'It is locked, Mademoiselle.'

'Give me your gun.'

Deprived of will-power, the man obeyed.

Aline released the safety catch, pointed the weapon, and fired three times, blinking and grimacing. Expensive polished splinters flew about.

Connie followed her in. Aline went unerringly to the spot behind and under the desk.

'Come and see what you can do, Madame.'

Connie tried. Nothing responded. She would have got a shock if it had.

'It's no good, Mademoiselle.'

'Are you quite sure?'

Connie felt annoyed at the insistence; it was as if her intelligence were being questioned.

She put her head down and looked again.

'Of course I'm sure,' she called out. 'It's hopeless. You'll have to evacuate. There's nothing we – '

She came up again. Aline was gone. So were the

security guards.

Connie went back into the hall. She could smell the fire now, even indoors. She looked round. In a short while, this gorgeous furniture, these rich rugs, the paintings, the panelling – everything would be consumed.

Everything? Was there a chance in a million that the office wing would survive? Surely not.

Smitten by sudden doubt, Connie turned to go outside and bumped into Julie coming down the stairs.

Without a glance in her direction, Julie went into her husband's study. Connie followed her, and saw her fiddling with some false book spines on a shelf.

She banged them in annoyance.

'If you're trying to get into the safe, you're wasting your time. The circuits are jammed.'

It was not the sort of technical language she would have normally used, but she had to get the truth across quickly to this hard-faced adventuress – namely, that she couldn't get her hands on any spare cash, bonds, or share certificates.

Julie shrugged.

'I guess you should know. Anyway, what the Hell? I've got enough.'

She waved a small leather pouch. The contents rattled.

'Girl's best friend, dearie. Can't beat an old-fashioned box under the bed with an old-fashioned lock and key.'

'Are you leaving him?'

'Had it in mind for months. Now is as good a time as any. Excuse me.'

She pushed past Connie and called up the stairs.

'Jurgen? Come on, for God's sake. What are you – some kind of weakling?'

Jurgen appeared at the top of the stairs, with his arms

full of expensive dresses. As he began to totter down the stairs, Connie came out of the study.

'Aren't you afraid?'

Julie turned in genuine surprise.

'Afraid? What of? I'm part of what he shows to the world, not what he hides. I'm sorry for you, though.'

Jurgen reached the foot of the stairs.

Julie looked at his bundle.

'That'll do. Put it in the trunk and let's go. This is Jurgen,' she added to Connie. 'Jurgen – this is Dr. Marshall.'

Jurgen managed a mockery of a military bow with his arms full.

'How do you do, Doktor Marshall?'

'You see?' said Julie. 'Perfect gentleman. Now if you'll take my advice, honey, you'll get out of here. Alec won't be liveable with when he gets back and sees this.'

'Where are you going?'

'Back to the States, I guess. If he wants me, he'll come after me. If the price is right, I'll come. If the other price is right, he can divorce me. 'Bye.'

She reappeared momentarily at the door.

'You look cute in those shorts. Kick Max up the ass for me.'

Hector, Hector, where have you got to?

And where did Aline go?

And what were you doing when you bumped into Julie?

The computer room.

In the courtyard, it was getting gloomy. Connie thought the air felt hotter. There couldn't be much more time.

Even so, leave nothing to chance. What did Hector

say? Take a leaf out of Ruth's book. She reached the records room.

Was there a chance that they might survive inside the steel cabinets? Get them open. Tip everything on the floor.

Connie paused in alarm. Somebody was smashing something next door.

Hector! At last.

Connie rushed through.

Aline was using a hammer to smash screens, terminals, anything within reach.

Both women stood still, dumbfounded.

Connie looked at Aline – panting, dishevelled, but triumphant.

Aline surveyed Connie – in her suntan and shorts, with her arms spilling discs and tapes, and the rucksack slipping off her shoulder.

At that moment Bliss burst in.

'God, I didn't think it would move so fast. Are you ready to – '

He caught sight of Aline and her hammer. The fact that her damage was futile in no way detracted from her grim dignity.

Aline saw him also dressed in walking gear. Outside, the noise of the fire grew stronger.

Bliss walked slowly across and took the hammer from Aline's hand.

'That will not be necessary, Mademoiselle. Dr. Marshall has already done more than enough. The fire will do the rest.'

He touched her arm.

'Come. It is now getting dangerous.'

At the door Aline hesitated.

'Have I time for one thing? In the house? One minute only?'

'One minute only. We will wait at the foot of the stairs.'

When Aline reappeared she was carrying two things – a studio photograph of Alan as a baby, and a teddy bear.

Bliss hustled them both out of the house and towards the gardens that lay away from the fire. Somewhere at the back a mower's engine exploded.

'Keep going,' said Bliss. 'That's nothing to what you'll hear when it reaches the winter supply of oil.'

Sirens could be heard in the distance.

They came through a clump of mimosa and reached a bend in the main drive.

Bliss paused to rub a black smut out of his eye. A faint noise of crunching gravel made him turn round.

It was coming straight for them, and accelerating. It could almost have been lying in wait.

Bliss whirled round and flung himself in a rugby tackle at the two women in front of him. As they all collapsed in a tangle of screams and limbs the wheels went past their noses. Dust and gravel were thrown into their faces, partially obscuring the deep red of the bodywork.

'Albert!'

Aline spat.

'Do you think he knows?' said Connie.

'How could he possibly?' said Bliss.

A new noise now made itself heard, above.

A small aeroplane was circling. As they watched, it came lower.

'Spotter plane, I expect,' said Connie. 'Police.'

'That's an executive jet,' said Bliss, his mouth going dry.

'It is Sir Alec,' said Aline.

'Are you sure?' said Bliss, fearing the worst.

'Yes. I am certain. I know the markings. He often circles before he lands at Nice.'

'How could he know?' wailed Connie. 'It's impossible.'

'He didn't,' said Bliss. 'He just circled as usual – this time on his way out instead of back. Then he saw the smoke. Perhaps it was the smoke that attracted him first. Damn and blast.'

'Albert saw him too,' said Aline. 'He has guessed that he will return and is driving to the airport to meet him.'

'Killing us on the way,' said Connie. 'Convenient.'

'We don't know that for sure,' said Bliss. 'We do know, however, that our wonderful plan has lasted about five minutes. Sir Alec is on his way back and Albert has seen our get-up. So we've lost our start and we've lost our cover.'

'And we've gained an ally,' said Connie, nodding towards Aline.

Bliss turned towards Aline.

'Mademoiselle, you cannot stay here.'

Aline drew herself up. In the dust and the black smuts and the gloom; amid the noises of engines and firemen's distant voices and sirens and crunching gravel, she contrived to look deathly still.

'It is what I have waited for these many years. It was I who called him back.'

Bliss stared.

'You?'

'Yes. When I knew – knew for sure that the house could not be saved – I left Dr. Marshall in the study.'

Bliss glanced at Connie, who confirmed it.

'I wondered where she had gone.'

'I knew where Max had a radio transmitter which he used for contact to the aeroplane. I called him, and told him.'

Aline's face settled into an expression of deep composure.

'I wanted him to see the fire. I shall be here when he arrives. I want to see his face.'

Bliss was dying to ask why, but it hardly seemed the time and place for lengthy explanations. He looked round anxiously.

'Mademoiselle, I urge you not to stay here. If Sir Alec finds you waiting like this, he will think you did it.'

'That is what I intend.'

'He could kill you.'

Aline shook her head.

'He cannot kill someone who is already dead.'

Bliss looked in desperation at Connie.

Before Connie could think of anything to say, Aline grasped Bliss' arm.

'I can help you. Listen to me. If I can convince Sir Alec that I am responsible, you will have more time to get away.'

'Why do you do this for us, Mademoiselle?' said Connie.

'It was a brave thing you did, Madame, with a daughter in such great danger. Believe me, I understand.'

'Mr. Bliss helped.'

'I know, and I want him to help me in return. When you go back to England, will you give me your word to look after Alain?'

'Alain?'

'She means Alan,' said Connie. 'I begin to understand.'

'You mean Sir Alec's son?' said Bliss.

'Sir Alec is not his father.'

'But you are his mother,' said Connie.

Bliss passed a hand over his brow.

'Look, all this is a bit too much for me. Whatever we have to say, can we please say it later on and somewhere else?'

There was a colossal thump and roar.

'That's the oil going up. Mademoiselle, we must move a little distance at least.'

They scrambled to their feet and made their way to the edge of the property. An artificial grotto opened before them, bedecked with coloured shells and numerous fauns and satyrs. Stone seats in leafy alcoves looked the perfect settings for lovers' trysts.

'Looks as if it should have fountains playing in it,' said Bliss.

'It does, usually,' said Connie. 'Thorough, see?'

They sat down.

Aline still hugged the photograph and the teddy bear.

'Now,' said Bliss. 'We are safe, but only for a few minutes. Mademoiselle, what did you mean?'

'I mean what I say. Will you look after Alain?'

Bliss opened his mouth to say something, but nothing came out.

'Of course he will,' said Connie. 'He will be honoured by your trust.'

A great weight seemed to be lifted off Aline's shoulders.

'Now it will be easy.'

'Easy?'

'To kill him.'

'Kill him? Why?'

'He killed Alain's father.'

'Mademoiselle, you are losing me again.'

'Perhaps if you went back a bit, Mademoiselle,' said Connie, 'to your marriage with Sir Alec.'

'Marriage?'

'Hector, stop repeating things and listen.'

'Madame is right,' said Aline. 'I married Alec eighteen years ago. At first I was happy, very happy. He was rich, powerful, influential. But I committed one great sin. I failed to have any children. He blamed me. Not just with words, but with blows, with humiliation. I came to hate him.'

'Why did you not divorce him?'

'He would not agree. The shame, you understand. His pride would not allow it. People would whisper about infertility, or worse. Moreover, he struck great fear in me. I was afraid to challenge him.'

'So you took a lover,' said Connie.

'In my misery, yes. And I became pregnant.'

'And he found out.'

'I told him. I thought it would make him release me. But I reckoned without two things.'

'What were they?'

'One was the shock. You see, to a man like him, that sort of thing is greatly important. He went grey almost over-night, and he lost the power of speech. There is nothing wrong with his vocal chords. It is all psychological.'

Aline shuddered.

'His silence was terrible.'

'And the other?'

'The other is his great appetite for revenge. He was not content with refusing a divorce. He had my lover murdered.'

'Oh, Aline!'

Connie put a hand impulsively on her arm.

'Then,' said Aline, 'he took me away to a hospital, where I had the baby. He told me that the baby would be reared as his own son. Not our son. *His* son.'

Bliss recalled a remark of Julie's. Alan was only 'Sir Alec's heir'.

'I was to stand by,' said Aline. 'and watch while he had the boy raised in his own image. He would take especial care of his education so that he grew like his father – his "official" father. Alec had great plans for him. His revenge was for me to watch him get further away each day.'

Connie's blood ran cold.

'But you had him till he was five,' said Bliss.

Aline gave a twisted smile.

'He made it into a contest. I was allowed to choose his name, and I was to have him for the first five years. Alec after that. We were to see whose methods would triumph. And just to make it "interesting", he said, Alain's mother was to "die".'

'The mining accident in Brazil,' said Connie.

'Yes. There is no wife under that mountain.'

Bliss stared.

'You mean, he had dozens of miners killed – for a hoax?'

'He is capable of anything, Monsieur, anything.'

'What happened to you?'

'I was taken to another hospital and put to sleep. When I awoke, they had changed my face. And they had made sure that I had no more babies.'

Connie looked agonised at Bliss.

'Why did you not try to run away with the baby?'

'For the same reason that Madame has never tried to run away. She understands.'

Connie held Aline's hand. It was all she could do.

'So,' said Aline, 'that was his revenge. I was to be

"Mademoiselle Aline" and I was to keep silent if I wanted Alain alive. I was to watch while my son and my lover's son was turned into a copy of Alec Sherrif.'

Aline smiled at Bliss.

'But you began to change that, Monsieur. And then today, when I saw Madame's bravery, I knew there was a chance. Madame has destroyed his evil system. All that remains now is the man. That is easy. So I ask you again – do I have your word about Alain?'

Bliss swallowed.

'You do, Aline. I promise.'

Connie squeezed his hand.

'Aline, is it really worth it, just for revenge?'

Aline turned slowly and looked her full in the face.

'Yes.'

Bliss scratched his neck.

'I'm sorry to be practical, Mademoiselle, but how are you going to do it?'

'You haven't seen this,' said Aline.

From behind the photograph, she took the gun she had seized from the security guard.

'If you have not suspected, neither will he.'

Bliss stood up.

'In that case, Mademoiselle,' he said, 'we must be on our way.'

'How will you manage?' said Aline.

'The police know about him, thanks to Madame,' said Bliss. 'If you don't get him, Scotland Yard or the French police will. It is only a matter of a few days.'

'Take the greatest care,' said Aline. 'There is still Max, and there is still Albert.'

'Max is in Poland.'

'He will return. He is another who does not easily

forget an injury.'

'We shall be careful.'

Connie kissed her.

'Goodbye, Aline.'

'Goodbye, Madame.'

She held out the teddy bear.

'Give this to Alain. Tell him – tell him I think of him.'

Bliss took it and kissed her hand.

'I'll tell him, Mademoiselle.'

*   *   *   *   *   *

Bliss twiddled the knobs on the binoculars.

'Are you sure we're safe here?' said Connie.

'The breeze isn't blowing this way. We've enough time for my purposes.'

'What are they?'

Bliss focussed on the inferno below.

'Just making sure the object of the exercise is achieved.'

There drifted up to them the sound of a string of small detonations.

'Ah!' said Bliss. 'That should do the trick.'

'What's that?'

'I found some jerrycans full of petrol near Albert's workshop. So I borrowed them. Put them behind the office wing. The heat's just set them off.'

'Was that why you were so long?'

Bliss nodded.

'Sorry, but we had to make sure. Thorough, see?'

Connie smiled.

'All right. *Touché.*'

Bliss put away the binoculars.

'It's beyond saving now. Stage One therefore complete. Did you get Ruth on board?'

'First thing. No trouble. I told them we were going for a dip in the sea – a change from the eternal pool.'

'And they bought it?'

'Seemed to.'

Bliss grunted.

'How did Ruth take it?'

'Hard at first.'

'She would. That's a brave daughter you've got there.'

'Thank you. And an intelligent one, fortunately. She wouldn't accept being shunted away just for her own safety. So I appealed to her brains. This was another one of Mr. Bliss' subtle bluffs, I said. I explained about the use of the unexpected and the strategy of splitting. When I told her that her presence on the yacht was the key to the whole of your plan, she went like a lamb. You come high in her estimation, you know.'

Bliss made a face.

'That's something then. Did you get the grub?'

Connie patted the rucksack.

'Good,' said Bliss. 'Keep it. I'll keep the tent. Take this sleeping bag. It's as well you should carry your own in case we are separated.'

'What about the tent?'

'It's heavier. I'll take that.'

'So if we're separated, you'll have the roof.'

'Carry it if you like. It's less for me then.'

Connie backed down hastily.

'I'm sorry, Hector. I'm not very used to this sort of thing.'

Bliss smiled reassuringly.

'Don't worry. Neither am I. I've never been a fugitive before. Not a real one.'

'What do you mean – not a real one?'

'Oh, we used to have exercises in the Army – you know, pretending to be escaped prisoners and the hillsides swarming with horrid Nazis and we had to get to a prearranged rendezvous. And we weren't allowed to thumb lifts.'

'What did you do?'

'We thumbed lifts.'

Bliss tugged a water bottle out of his rucksack.

'And that's what we're going to do now.'

'I thought you said we were going to walk.'

'We are, till we get a lift. Look, Connie – Stage One is fine; the house is a cinder, or soon will be. Stage Two – Ruth is on her way to Elba. Also fine.'

'Stage Three – Aline is going to take care of Sir Alec.'

'That's a bonus, I agree. But only a possible bonus. I wouldn't bank on it. She's got Albert to deal with as well. And Max is coming back tomorrow.'

'Poor Aline.'

'Well, maybe it's "poor Aline" and maybe not. I certainly wasn't going to stand in the way of a revenge like that. Right now, we have ourselves to consider. And I'm sorry to have to say that nearly everything else in the Bliss master plan has misfired.' He grunted. 'Just like Biggles.'

'Pardon?'

'When I was a lad, I used to read Biggles. Do you know who Biggles was?

Connie smiled. 'Oh, yes. The airman. My brother used to read him.'

'It's great stuff. One of the things that impressed me about Biggles was not that he could always cook up a plan to deal with anything, but that he fully expected his plan to go wrong. And sure as eggs it always did.'

'I think you've done very well so far.'

'Well, I don't. We have far less time now that Sir Alec is on his way back. If Aline doesn't bump him off, we shall have him on our tail within a couple of hours.'

'How does he know we're responsible?'

'If we're not around, he'll put two and two together. And there's Albert, remember. He saw us, and in this rig-out. He'll tell the boss.'

And Ruth wasn't with us. I hope to God Albert didn't notice that.

'None of it was your fault,' said Connie.

'That's never any use,' said Bliss. 'It doesn't matter a damn whose fault it is; we're not off to a good start.'

'What do we do then?'

'We get away from here. We daren't go back towards Cannes; we don't know how many of Sir Alec's victims, or his security guards, are around there.

'We can't go east towards Nice because of the airline tickets. He'll be watching the false trail we laid. We don't go west to Fréjus because of the railway tickets.'

'So it's north then?'

'Yes. I was going to stay fairly close to the coast, because that would be the last place they'd expect us to be. But now that they probably know what we look like, we must move. We'll cross the autoroute and head north, and try to get a lift to Pégomas and Grasse. If it looks safe we might take a bus from there. If not, we'll hitch-hike again.'

'Of course all this may be unnecessary.'

Bliss held out the water bottle.

'Would you care to sit around and find out? I'd rather feel foolish than dead.'

'Sorry.'

'Have you a skirt in there?'

Connie blushed.

'I hope you don't mind. I thought just one wouldn't matter.'

'Put it on.'

'What about my shorts?'

'Take 'em off.'

Connie screwed the top back on the water bottle.

'I was just beginning to enjoy them.'

'Hard luck, I'm afraid. If you don't do as I say, you may not live to enjoy much more.'

Connie did as she was told, while Bliss changed into a pair of lightweight slacks, and shoved the water bottle back into the rucksack.

'Have you got a hat?' said Bliss.

'No,' said Connie, feeling inadequate.

'Here. Put this on.'

'But it'll hide my new haircut.'

'That's the idea. We don't want you passing out with sunstroke either. It's my fault; I should have thought to tell you.'

Connie put it on reluctantly; it was little more than a cheap canvas pimple. She looked down at herself, at the ankle socks and heavy shoes below the skirt. She fished a handmirror out of a pocket and peered at herself.

'Hector, I look awful.'

'Oh, I don't know.'

'I look like some eager secretary of a ladies' bowls club.'

'Do you want high fashion or survival?' said Bliss, as he knotted a white handkerchief and put it on his head.

Suddenly they heard an engine.

'Helicopter!' said Bliss. 'Quick!'

247

He looked around.

'Blast!'

'What is it?'

'No cover.'

'What do we do?'

'This.'

Bliss threw her to the ground, rolled her over on to her back, and flung himself on top of her.

Connie screamed in shock.

'Shut up,' said Bliss. 'Put your arms round my neck. Look as if you're enjoying it.'

They heard the blades rattle past.

'What are they doing?' said Bliss.

Connie looked.

'Oh, dear, they're turning. Coming back for a second look.'

Bliss remained sprawled across her.

'I've got an idea,' said Connie, moving slightly.

'What are you doing?' said Bliss, horrified.

'Waving.'

'What?'

'Waving. They waved back.'

'Thank God for that.'

Bliss heaved himself away as the helicopter clattered into the distance. He grinned.

'Perhaps you were enjoying it after all.'

Connie dusted her clothes.

'Don't fool yourself, Hector.'

'And don't you fool yourself. That chopper could have belonged to Sir Alec. The sooner we get a lift the better.'

They stood up and saw the great billows of smoke. The sunlight behind and the flames beneath turned it into a hundred sinister shades of vermilion and crimson.

A surrealist flat scarlet disk showed through like a plate on a dirty wall.

'I've never seen the sun like that before,' said Connie.

'Blood on the sun,' muttered Bliss.

'What?'

'An old James Cagney film,' he explained. 'Can't remember the plot. But I bet I know what the hero would have said to the heroine at this stage.'

'What?'

' "Let's get outta here." Come on.'

*　　*　　*　　*　　*　　*

'Have you got that, Pri? . . . . Now read it all back . . . . To Hell with the bloody cost . . . . I want to make sure you've got it right . . . . that's it . . . . and the address . . . . the number you'll have to look up. Now get on to your tame chief inspector and have the boy taken away . . . . I don't care. Don't you understand? His father is capable of anything, especially now that he isn't – oh, never mind. Just do as I ask . . . . Take it from me – I am responsible for the child's safety . . . . All right, all right, but will you do it? . . . . I don't know. Think of something. Tell your inspector I've unearthed evidence of a rival gang who want to get at him through Alan; say there's a kidnap in the offing. Dammit – they'll know from the fire that something's up. Tell him whatever you like, but make him get the boy away from school. Take him to Parry if you can't think of anything. But don't let anyone know. And get a police guard put on the house. Thelma will look after him . . . . He's a bright enough lad; he must know about kidnaps and ransoms in his position. I'm sure he'll understand . . . . Well, of course it may not be, but I can't be sure, can I? He may

249

have turned the tables on her. In which case he and Albert will be after us . . . . Oh, we'll manage . . . . No, I can't; there's nowhere we can go. There's nobody we can be sure of. How do we know who's on his payroll or his blackmail list? We haven't got Connie's records in front of us, and there may be more for all we know. He's got dozens of officials under his thumb. We could stick a pin in the atlas, give ourselves up, and we'd pick the one rotten apple in the barrel . . . . No, we're staying out . . . . Yes. Well, if your snoopers in Special Branch got a bloody move on and started some arrests, Connie and I wouldn't be skulking round the countryside like prisoners out of Colditz . . . . I'm sorry, but you're not here . . . . Oh, from hand to mouth, I suppose. We'll keep an eye on the newspapers. The story will break tomorrow, I expect . . . . On a farm. I didn't want to use the official sites if I could help it. He's quite a nice bloke. His wife has given us some cheese and some fruit. She's making a great fuss of Connie . . . . Because I told her we're on a second honeymoon. Connie's furious . . . . Yes. Yes. All right. I will . . . . I'll ring when I can. 'Bye.'

Inside the glass booth, even though it was getting on towards evening, the sweat was pouring off him. He pushed open the door , sat on a wall, and mopped his brow.

Nowhere to go . . . . Nobody we can be sure of . . . . Well, perhaps . . . . But it was no good telling Pri; he would only worry.

Bliss walked back to the farm and found Connie sitting outside the tent trying to make a better job of her hair. She was very glad to see him.

He told her about his call to Priam.

'I also rang a newspaper. Told them the fire was the

work of the Basque terrorists.'

'Don't you think that's overdoing it?'

'Can't do any harm. It might might make them look for a different type of person from us. Besides, Sir Alec blamed terrorists and was believed. I feel there's a certain poetic justice in our doing the same.'

'Isn't it possible that Sir Alec – if he's still alive – will tell the police it's us?'

Bliss shook his head.

'No. It would be bad for his image to admit that two of his own employees burned his house down. People might think he asked for it somehow. Blaming the terrorists makes him the respected victim of the enemies of society. And I think there's a better reason still.'

'What's that?'

'Something Aline said. "His great appetite for revenge." If he is alive and if he believes we were the ones who destroyed his system, he won't want the police interfering with what he wants to do to us. He'll come after us himself.'

'The personal vendetta?'

'Something like that. You wait and see.'

'You speak as if you were looking forward to it.'

Bliss shook his head.

'Not looking forward. Just foreseeing. There's a big difference.'

Connie narrowed her eyes.

'Are you planning something?'

Bliss looked blank.

'Yes. I am planning to eat. What have you got for our supper, Mrs. Bliss?'

Connie opened a penknife and spread butter on a chunk of bread.

'Yes, that reminds me. I'll murder you when we get out of this.'

'If Sir Alec doesn't beat you to it. I can always leave you now if you like and you can divorce me.'

Connie shook her head in alarm.

'No, no! No separations now. I was even frightened when you went to the 'phone. I wish you'd let me come.'

'What? And deprive you of the opportunity of preparing your husband's honeymoon supper? Where's your sense of romance?'

It had also meant that a call could be put through to Joseph with no explanations being needed.

Chapter Ten

CONNIE'S HANDMIRROR SLIPPED.

Bliss put out a hand and balanced the tiny piece of glass once more against a loose stone on top of the crumbling wall.

Stooping, peering, and grimacing, he finished shaving. Already the morning sun was hot on the back of his neck.

He mopped his cheeks, combed his hair, and put on his shirt. Then he picked his way through the long grass, brambles, and old rubber tyres to rinse out the aluminium bowl under the cold water tap behind the barn.

As he shook the remaining water drops out of the bowl, he looked up at the sky. It was a perfect morning. He took a huge breath and exhaled with great satisfaction. There was nothing like a bright early morning for raising the spirits. At that precise moment, the problem of staying out of harm's way for two or three days seemed child's play.

He went back to the tent, knelt down in the unzipped entrance, and shook Connie's shoulder under the material of the sleeping bag.

'Wakey, wakey, Mrs. Bliss!'

Connie stirred unwillingly.

Bliss shook her again. She opened her eyes.

'What's the time?'

'Time for honeymooners to rise and shine. There's a cold tap behind the barn and an outside loo at the end of the house behind the kitchen. If you look forlorn enough,

Madame might let you use the bathroom.'

Connie groaned.

'I certainly feel it.'

'I'll have breakfast ready when you get back.'

Connie struggled out of the sleeping bag. She collected a few bits and pieces, and edged on hands and knees towards the door of the tent.

'It's a beautiful morning,' said Bliss.

'Hmmm.'

Connie stood painfully.

'God – I ache all over.'

Bliss fiddled with the tiny Camping Gaz stove.

'I shouldn't tell that to Monsieur; he'll wonder what we've been up to all night.'

'Oh, shut up!'

She felt much better by the time she came back, and tackled breakfast with a will.

'Where to this morning, Captain?'

Bliss smiled. It was amazing what fresh air, warm sun, cold water, hot coffee, and a chunk of bread could do to the spirits.

'I'm going to see Monsieur to cadge a lift. He said something last night about going to market today. He might also have a morning paper delivered. My friend Joseph always does.'

He stood up and dusted the crumbs from his trousers.

'You can do the washing-up while I'm gone.'

'Thanks.'

'Beginners always do the washing-up. Old camping tradition.'

'I'm sure.'

'Get the sleeping bags out, turn them inside out and air them on the wall.'

'Anything else – sir?'

'Yes – put a face on. Plenty of that hideous purple lipstick. And wear your sunglasses in town.'

'Here – wait a minute.'

'What?'

Connie peered up.

'You've shaved off your moustache.'

Bliss put a hand to his naked upper lip.

'Took you long enough to notice.'

Connie squinted in the sun.

'It's an improvement.'

'Oh, thanks. Max gave me the idea.'

'Max!'

'Yes. He once made the sensible point that the best disguises are where you take things away; you don't add. That's why I suggested cutting your hair and not wearing a wig.'

'I'd have melted in the sun.'

'Probably. Yours is an improvement too.'

'My, my! Aren't we both being gallant this morning.'

Bliss grinned.

'Yes. Now get on with the washing-up.'

It was different when he returned. Connie could tell by his face.

'What is it?'

Bliss sat down and heaved a colossal sigh.

'I've been looking at Monsieur's paper. Aline is dead.'

'Oh, God!'

Bliss tugged mindlessly at some grass between his sprawled legs.

'It was right across the front page. Pictures and everything. The whole place is gutted. . . . so you did what you set out to do.'

'But Aline didn't?'

'Apparently not. The report says her body was found in the ruins, almost unrecognisable. Guess who identified it.'

Connie gaped in incredulity.

'To kill her, and then – '

'I know. Just like Dolly. Oh – and Max is back too. Sir Alec must have summoned him hot-foot from darkest Poland.'

'Did it mention us?'

'No. Only negatively, saying that no other bodies were found, but various people are missing. There was no mention of us by name – or Julie.'

'Keeping the skeletons locked up in the cupboard.'

'Looks like it. There was the usual journalistic speculation about terrorists. They referred to my 'phone call.'

Connie put away her lipstick.

'So it's Sir Alec and Max together again – after us.'

'Plus Albert and his bloody great red Rolls.'

'Thank Heaven Ruth isn't here.'

Bliss patted her hand.

'You sound like Ben Gunn with Captain Flint after him. We're not "as good as pork" yet, not by a long chalk. They've got to find us first.'

'With that blackmail list? How do we even know if we get spotted?'

Bliss looked sternly at her.

'We knew about these chances when we started. I warned you. However, it's not as bad as you think. Ruth is out of the way and they'll still be looking for three people, not two. You don't look much like Dr. Constance Marshall, Ph.D., and with my well-oiled hair and bare lip, I could pass for Cary Grant.'

Connie smiled.

'That's better,' said Bliss. 'Remember, optimism is everything.'

'What about realism?'

'The realism,' said Bliss, 'tells us that it's now a race. If they guess what you've done, and they will, they will also guess that you've shopped them. If we are only one jump ahead of them, they are now only one jump ahead of Fabian of the Yard or Chief Inspector Maigret, and they know it. They also know that their organisation is collapsing at this very minute. The professionals will lie low; the hatchet men will simply look for another boss; and all over France his blackmail victims are going to see that picture of his ruined house and they're going to put two and two together. His power won't last more than a few days. So, I repeat, it's a race. They've got to find us before the police find them.'

'Will they bother?'

'They'll bother all right. Remember what Aline said about his "capacity for revenge"? Right now it's the only thing keeping him going. Max, too, I shouldn't wonder.'

'How do they know where to look?'

'I don't know; I'm not Max. But how many times have I said – don't underestimate them.'

'What else did the paper say?'

'Not much. I couldn't devour the whole page; I'd only asked Monsieur if I could see the weather forecast. Now pack your bags and we'll get this tent down.'

That'll stop you worrying for a bit, learning how to pack sleeping bags and fold up tents. Let me do the worrying . . . .

Why had Max issued a statement about the terrorists, and suggested check-points and roadblocks in so many specified directions? North towards England; east towards Italy; north-east towards Switzerland; south-west towards Spain. Why not due west into mainland France? Max knew that Bliss would read the papers; he was an intelligent man. Was he trying to tell Bliss something?

And there was another funny thing, though he could not be sure. Several times, the article had referred to remarks that Sir Alec had made. Not Max. Sir Alec. Odd, that.

∗ ∗ ∗ ∗ ∗ ∗

'Hallo, Pri? . . . . So far, so good . . . . Have you read the reports from Ste. Sophie? . . . . Yes, pretty thorough, I thought . . . . They had pictures in the French papers . . . . Yes, I know .. . . And Aline's dead . . . . Aline, the house-keeper . . . . Murdered . . . . No, murdered . . . . Sir Alec, of course . . . . Never mind how I know. Take it from me he did . . . . Yes. And Max. He's back from Poland . . . . And Albert of course . . . . No. We're keeping one jump ahead. If your wretched policemen move faster, they can get a call out on his car. Surely they can spot a red Rolls . . . . That's all very well. Damn the *Entente Cordiale*! We're the ones being chased . . . . All right, now what about Alan? Have you got him away? . . . . Good. Tell Thelma I'm sorry and I'll explain everything when I get back . . . . What? . . . . When? . . . . And the headmaster let him in? Didn't he ask to see the man's credentials? . . . . Ah, I see . . . . Very clever of him . . . . Good . . . . Well, tell them to hold him until you've picked up Sir Alec . . . . Damn the regulations . . . . Tell them to get a bloody move on . . . . Now? . . . . In a small town not far from Avignon . . . . Yes – good guess . . . . Oh – local cars and lorries mostly. I don't think Connie likes the rural smells very much . . . . I've left her by the fountain in the square. The less we're seen together in towns the better . . . . Well, she'll have to learn . . . . I'm not. She'll thank me when it's over . . . . Try and get a bus to Avignon, I expect . . . . Yes, it is. But nobody's challenged us yet, so perhaps I'm worrying too much. You know me – always seeing too many snags. What about Aunt Jane? Has she – ? . . . . Good, good . . . . Yes, I know. She's had more fun out of this than anybody . . . . Yes, I'll tell her . . . . And ask Aunt Jane to tell Ruth from me that Mummy says she's fine and she's enjoying the camping . . . . Enjoying the camping: thinks it's terrific . . . . Yes . . . . O.K. . . . . I will . . . . Till next time . . . . Cheerio, Pri.'

*   *   *   *   *   *

The driver lit another cigarette as he came out on to the autoroute.

Bliss opened his eyes when he felt Connie fidget.

'Don't worry; everything's fine.'

Connie lit a cigarette too.

'At least Ruth's all right,' she muttered.

'How could she be otherwise, with Aunt Jane in command?' said Bliss cheerily. 'Heaven help Max and Sir Alec if they ever catch up with my Aunt Jane.'

Connie forced a smile.

'And you said that we – '

'I told you. I said to Pri, "Tell them that we're having a super time and that Mummy is loving the camping – " '

'Hmmm.'

' " – and that Mr. Bliss is very nice." '

Connie gave him a steely look.

'I can see why you were a good officer.'

'Oh? Why?'

'Because you're so damned conceited that you would never conceive the prospect of defeat.'

Bliss grinned broadly.

'Optimism, madam, that's all – the basis of good morale. That's why we won the War, you know – combination of optimism and stupidity. There was once an official army order issued by the German High Command in which Marshal Keitel said –' Bliss imitated a Hollywood German accent ' – "Although ze British military position is hopeless they show not ze slightest sign of giving in." '

Connie did grin a little more easily that time, settled back, and looked out at Provence whizzing by.

The driver tooted his horn at a group of children waving from the middle of a footbridge.

Bliss shut his eyes again. At least he had put one mind at rest for the time being.

His own tried to conjure up a picture of the man Connie had described at the bus terminal.

'How do you know he was watching you?'

'He kept looking in my direction.'

'All the time?'

'No – not exactly. He turned away if I looked at him.'

'Did he appear to be watching anybody else?'

'He didn't *appear* to be doing anything much.'

'So he could have been just standing there.'

'People don't just "stand there".'

Bliss allowed a trace of irony to show.

'He could have been waiting for a bus, you know. It was a bus terminal.'

'He didn't look like someone waiting for a bus.'

'Did you try walking away to see if he followed?'

'No. You told me to stay put. If you'd come back and I wasn't there, you might have gone rushing off, and when

I came back – '

'Yes, yes, yes. All right, all right.'

This wasn't getting them very far. Bliss tried another tack.

'What did he look like?'

Connie shrugged.

'I don't know . . . . like a Frenchman. What was he supposed to look like?'

'Tall, short? Young, old? Fat, thin?'

'Oh . . . . youngish, I think. Not fat. Looked pretty fit. I couldn't see his face; he was wearing sunglasses.'

'How was he dressed?'

'In a suit. Dark tie.'

'Did he look like a policeman?'

Connie spread her hands.

'What are plain-clothes policemen supposed to look like? I don't know. The only ones I've seen have been on the television.'

'Well, did he look like a television plain-clothes policeman?'

Connie nodded.

'Yes – sort of.'

Bliss let his head roll with the movement of the bus. He could smell Connie's cigarette.

Was there any point in reacting to a possible sight of a man at a bus terminal who 'scrt of' looked like a television plain-clothes policeman, who might have been watching Connie because he wasn't 'just standing there'?

Was it possible that, by some twist of depraved sense of humour from a malign Fate, they had been on the run through the territory of some *sous-préfet* or *commissaire* who was under orders from Sir Alec or Max? Was this poor official so terrorised by the blackmail machine in which they had gripped him that, even twenty-four hours after the news of the fire, he was afraid to throw off the shackles? Did he therefore have his men out on patrol at every railway station and bus terminal?

Or – worse, perhaps – could it be that the police themselves wanted to find them? Either simply to account for them after the fire or to ask them some questions about it. The paper had said 'terrorists', but the police could have arranged that.

There you go, Hector – just as you told Pri – 'always seeing too many snags'.

He forced his mind to stop racing by thinking about introducing Connie to Priam and Paris. How would Joan and Thelma react? How would they compare her to Joy?

He soon dozed off.

*   *   *   *   *   *

They changed buses at Nîmes.

'There he is,' said Connie. 'There's another one.'

Bliss glanced over his shoulder.

'Sunglasses and all. But he's not following. Let's give him something to think about. You stay here, and I'll – '

'Hector, no!'

'Connie – yes! If he is what we think, the other one would have picked you up. It could be they're only watching. Let's find out which one he wants to watch more.'

'But what do I do if he comes near me?'

'Scream and say he attacked you. If he's one of Sir Alec's nasties, he'll run. If he really is the police, at least you're safe. But don't worry; nothing will happen, and I shan't be long. Just going to pick up some news. Now, stay here.'

The suit and the sunglasses did not follow. So was it worry for nothing? Bliss still could not be sure.

He found a busy café-restaurant with a television set switched on. He sat down where he could see the screen and ordered a beer.

When he rejoined Connie she looked a little better.

'I think he's gone. I can't see him any more.'

'He didn't follow me. Anyway, I've got the latest bulletin – TV News. Apparently Sir Alec has "mysteriously disappeared". So has Max. The newsmen are naturally tying it in with the fire and speculating like mad.'

'Have they mentioned us?'

'No. But there was another interesting little titbit. Sir Alec's car has been found.'

'The red Rolls?'

'The red Rolls. Guess where?'

'Where?'

'Just outside Tarascon.'

'Where's Tarascon?'

'Between Cannes and here; in fact between Avignon and here, very roughly.'

'Oh, my God.'

'Now, stop looking like Ben Gunn again. If he's abandoned the Rolls it must be for a reason. It certainly can't have broken down; Rollses don't break down.'

'Well then?'

'It means that a red Rolls has become too conspicuous. And why would Sir Alec not want to be conspicuous any more?'

'Because the police are after him.'

'Could well be. That news item about being missing could mean that the police are not concerned for his welfare but eager to ask him some questions. At any rate he can't afford to take chances. He's now in the same league as we are.'

'He's on the run too.'

'I sincerely hope so.'

'But why Tarascon? Why so close behind us? How could he know?'

'He's got to run somewhere,' said Bliss.

Connie looked stern.

'Hector, you don't believe that.'

'I have no evidence for believing it or for disbelieving it. "It is a cardinal error, Watson, to theorise in default of the facts." '

'That man with the glasses could have told him. He has a radio in the Rolls.'

'Connie, a dozen little men in sunglasses *could* have told him. But we don't know for sure.'

'So we're just as badly off?'

'Oh, no, far from it. We're better off.'

'How?'

'In two ways. One – we know roughly where he is. Two – we know he doesn't have radio contact any more. The organisation is crumbling. The race is going our way.'

'So long as we keep ahead.'

'That's right. So go and spend your penny and we'll take you for another ride.'

'Where to this time?'

'Montpellier. If we see any other men there in dark glasses, we'll think of something else.'

'Hitch-hiking again?'

'If necessary. We might even risk a proper camp site and get a shower.'

* * * * * *

The launch drew alongside and made fast.

The officer presented his credentials to the yacht's owner.

'I regret to cause inconvenience, Signor Baker, but I have reason to believe that you have on board someone who is being kept here against their will.'

Before Howard Baker could answer, an elderly lady pushed in between them.

'Ah, captain, you received my message, then?'

The officer blinked.

'Signora?'

The lady drew herself up and examined him through heavy spectacles.

'You are Captain Orlando, are you not?'

'No, Signora, I am Officer Cantelli, and I am here to – '

The lady waved a knitting needle in annoyance.

'Well, it doesn't matter who you are, so long as they sent somebody. I take it you speak good English? I specifically asked for a good English speaker.'

Officer Cantelli could not resist saying that he had perfected his command of English by spending two years in the London 'province of Cheesic'.

The lady raised her eyebrows.

'Really? I suppose that will have to do. Well, do your duty. I want this ship impounded, or confiscated, or whatever it is you do.'

'Signora?'

Officer Cantelli had shrunk a little behind his moustache.

'Get out your pencil and paper and take down my complaint. That's what you came about, isn't it?'

Officer Cantelli frowned.

'You are the one who is being kept against her will?'

'Don't be ridiculous. I complained of being hired under false pretences, not of being kidnapped. As usual, your silly girls on the telephone exchange went and got it wrong. You really don't think this pompous mid-western buffoon could keep me here against my will, do you? I am a British citizen. I am also an American citizen. I therefore hold two passports – a conclusion at which you have doubtless already arrived, since you are obviously an officer of considerable perception, who should go far in his chosen profession.'

Officer Cantelli's eyes began to glaze, though he brightened a little towards the end as he caught the vague drift of a compliment. He looked for guidance over the lady's shoulder towards Mr. Baker, who at last managed to get a word in.

'You will have gathered, officer, that this lady is a considerable nuisance to us. Far from keeping her here against her will, I should be only too grateful if you would take her away with you.'

Officer Cantelli got as far as opening his mouth.

'You see what I mean, sergeant-major. I am reviled at every turn. I am not being treated with the courtesy which is my due. I was hired as companion to this – this *gentleman*'s mother, on the understanding that she was an amenable, kindly lady well able to care for herself. Imagine my chagrin when I discover that on the contrary she is awkward, argumentative, cantankerous, and semi-bedridden. Although it is my private opinion that the old crone is thoroughly spoilt and bone idle.'

Officer Cantelli was retreating before the onset of each adjective.

'How dare you say that about Mother!' said Howard Baker, raising his voice. 'You have done nothing but cause trouble since you arrived on board. If I were not a gentleman I should have torn up your contract long ago.' He puffed out his chest. 'But I happen to be person of my word.'

'There he goes again, captain,' said the lady. 'I hope you're getting all this down. I want you to take a deposition to the British Consul in Livorno or the American *chargé d'affaires* or whatever they call him in San Remo. I intend to complete this cruise and I intend to get my due. When this scandal becomes public, I shall either compel or shame this wretched man into fulfilling his obligations.'

Officer Cantelli's back was now against the rail. He looked behind him. Two of his crew were smirking to each other.

'I regret, Signora, that I cannot act as go-between in private disputes.'

The lady gazed in consternation.

'Do you mean to tell me that you are not going to do as I say?'

Officer Cantelli smoothed the front of his jacket and adjusted his tie.

'I am not a messenger boy, Signora.'

The lady advanced on him.

'Do you not see how I am victimised and ridiculed and persecuted. Come with me.'

Grabbing him by the gold braid on his cuff, she dragged him to a small table, where a dark young member of the crew was setting out drinks.

'Look, look at this. Alcohol! Always alcohol. When I remind him of the terms of the contract – pure fruit juices – they laugh. They throw meat at me when they know I am a vegetarian. Well, I tell you this, Colonel Mantilla, I do not intend to tolerate it.'

Officer Cantelli spread his hands and looked over his shoulder at Howard Baker, who shrugged.

The lady seized him again by the arm.

'Look at that waiter. That lackey! Laughing at me. I will not have it.'

She grasped a parasol, and set about the young crewman, who screamed and wailed, and backed towards the rail.

The lady gave him no mercy, and before Officer Cantelli could intervene, had despatched him over the rail with one final deadly thrust.

The scream as he fell was blood-curdling.

Howard Baker rushed forward and flung a line. Two or three crew members hurled lifebelts and finally hauled him in.

He stood again on deck, quivering in pathetic terror.

Howard Baker took Officer Cantelli by the arm. Everybody seemed to be taking him by the arm.

'I'm afraid it isn't the first time this has happened, officer. You can see that it is most embarrassing for all concerned, and very distressing for my mother. I personally think the sun has something to do with it; she will never use the parasol.'

Officer Cantelli glanced at the lady's weapon. Baker followed his eyes.

'At least, not for the proper purposes. But she is elderly, and we do not wish to provoke a crisis if we can help it. We try to make allowances for her fads and fancies.' He made a wide gesture. 'When one is old – you understand . . . .'

'*Si, si, si.*'

The moustache now bristled with more confidence.

Howard Baker nodded towards a crewman, who approached with two bottles of malt whisky.

'If this would go some way to make up for all the trouble we have caused you.'

'It is not you, Signor.'

'I know, but I feel kind of responsible. After all, I did hire her – for better, for worse. You know what I mean?'

Officer Cantelli nodded vigorously, as he clasped the bottles.

'You are a gentleman, Signor.'

'Then we will say no more?'

'Do not disturb yourself, Signor. I know how to keep the Mum, as you say.'

He swung his legs over the rail and jumped on to the launch.

He slipped, and nearly dropped a bottle. One of his crew laughed.

Officer Cantelli swore at him, gave orders to cast off, and turned to salute with the bottles still in his hand.

Out of sight from his launch, on the foredeck, everyone was congratulating everyone else.

'Aunt Jane, you were marvellous.'

Ruth flung her arms round her neck and kissed her.

Howard Baker wrung her hand.

'My dear, that's the finest performance I've seen since Scarlett O'Hara.'

'It was brave and generous of you to permit it to be staged, Mr. Baker.'

'Nonsense. I wouldn't have missed it for the world. I can dine out on this story for months.'

Aunt Jane turned anxiously to the soaking crewman.

'I didn't hurt you, dear, did I?'

Rudi grinned broadly.

'No, Madame. I had to scream to stop laughing.'

'You were wonderful, Rudi. You should be in films.'

∗   ∗   ∗   ∗   ∗   ∗

Bliss stretched out his legs and put his hands behind his head.

'Feel better now?'

Connie groped for her cigarettes.

'Much. That was a splendid meal out of two metal cans.'

Bliss waved airily.

'A minor miracle. You should see me when the spirit really moves. Another snifter?'

'Please.'

Connie took a swig from the bottle, and handed it back.

'Two days ago I could not have imagined myself doing that.'

Bliss drank too and wiped his mouth.

'Circumstances can be a great educator,' he observed. 'I don't suppose you've ever hitch-hiked either.'

Connie put her hands over ears and winced.

'Don't! Those metal bins. I can hear them rattling now.'

Bliss laughed.

'Teaches you to be adaptable – hitch-hiking. You can be in the back of a haycart one minute, and whizzing along in a Mercedes the next. Careful with that match. Put it in the rubbish bag.'

'Sorry. And the drivers! What about the old boy who hardly ever dropped out of top gear? And turning round to gesticulate all the time.'

She chuckled at the memory.

'You quite enjoyed it, didn't you?' said Bliss.

270

Connie thought.

'Yes, I suppose I must have done.'

'They say it was like this in the War,' said Bliss. 'You know – ordinary people, thrown together by chance, taking lots of pleasure out of tiny things, even though great threats hung over their shoulder.'

'I wouldn't call you ordinary, Hector.'

Bliss turned, but could not see her face clearly in the dark. He thought he noticed a catch in her voice though.

He made a small noise in his throat.

'I think you're quite a girl yourself. After what you did.'

'I couldn't have done it without you.'

'So you trust me now, eh – at last?'

'Yes.'

' 'Bout time too.'

Connie's cigarette glowed.

'And I want you to know – whatever happens – that – well – that I don't think anyone could have done better. I have no regrets for what we did. We could have done it no other way.'

'Thanks.'

They lay in a silence that neither could break nor particularly wished to break.

In the darkness the piping voices of children at play could still be heard.

'They shouldn't allow children up so late,' said Connie at last. 'They're not even of school age.'

In the shadowed play area, they could see black silhouettes against the dark sky as persistent infants still worked the swings.

'The French are late birds on holiday,' said Bliss. 'They don't get up early either. We shall probably beat them all to it.'

'Mmmm.'

Connie took another puff on her cigarette.

'Tell me about Sarah.'

'Nothing much to tell, really. We adopted her in Africa when she was a few months old. She lived fifteen years. She was killed in a car crash – or rather murdered. That's it.'

'Come on, Hector. You can do better than that. That's what you say to me.'

'It's difficult to sum it up. I don't know where to start.'

'Anywhere.'

'We wanted her so badly. A burning mission station in the middle of Africa is hardly the best place to adopt a child. But there she was, and there was Max . . . . anyway, you know all about that.'

'I do. Was Joy with you in Africa then?'

'Yes. She usually followed my postings. I liked having her with me, but she didn't take easily to Army life. It was one of the reasons I packed it in . . . . '

'About Sarah,' prompted Connie.

'Ah, yes. Well, we knew Joy couldn't have children, and it was driving us apart. I think she thought I blamed her, but I didn't. Really I didn't.'

'Go on.'

'We poured five years of frustrated parental affection into Sarah, and I suppose we overdid it. She was so pretty too, especially when she was tiny. Glowing eyes, masses of glossy dark hair. Not unlike Ruth. Just looking at her made you want to pet her. Looking back, I guess she couldn't take it all. She burst.'

'Was it really as simple as that? Surely it wasn't *all* your fault?'

'That's what I've been asking myself ever since. She

never responded like ordinary children. There always seemed to be some kind of distance between us. It wasn't just me; it was the same with Joy, though perhaps I went over the top more than she did. They say fathers can be like that with daughters.'

'I'm sure you were an ordinary loving father.'

'Well, I certainly tried to be. But she was – well, like a cat. You know how you can pet a cat and it will jump out of your arms as if you're just not there. Sarah was like that. As she grew older it got worse.

'And there was a sort of knowingness about her, as if she was receiving things on a completely different wavelength from yours. I often wondered whether there was any kind of inherited mental imbalance. In the old days they would have called it a "kink". My mother still does.'

Bliss showed signs of drying up, so Connie prompted him again.

'And then she started getting into trouble.'

'Yes. Again, looking back, she seemed to resent everything so much, I suppose it was only a matter of time before she got fed up with arguing against the rules and just threw them out of the window. It didn't seem to make her any happier. The boy who got her pregnant – nice lad, funnily enough, and terribly upset about the whole business – he told me once she frightened him! Yes – frightened him.

'She drove Joy to rage and despair, and it drove Joy and me further apart again, because she thought I made too many allowances. She used to say that I spent so much time seeing the other side of the picture that I missed the picture right in front of me. Perhaps she was right.'

'I don't know. You seem pretty understanding to me.'

Bliss sighed.

'Anyway, it was one damned crisis and scandal after another, until – well, you heard Max. One of his creatures obviously filled this kid up with Scotch. Out they go on a lonely road late at night – this kid no doubt showing off like mad, and Sarah with her jaw set and her eyes gleaming as they always did when she knew she was behaving badly. A nudge from Albert, and over they go.

'The boy was killed outright. Sarah lingered on a life-support machine for about a fortnight.'

Bliss swallowed.

'I was the one who took the decision to have it switched off. Joy had been going mad with the tension. They told me there was absolutely no hope; if she woke up she'd be subnormal. So I gave the word.

'Joy's never forgiven me. Said I should have given her longer. But I'd seen Sarah; I'd seen Joy going round the bend; I was pretty far gone myself. I knew there was no future. I knew, Connie, I knew.'

'I'm sure you did.'

'I'd seen it before. One of my men was in a terrible accident on a big exercise in Germany. I helped his mother to make the same decision. Believe me, I knew.'

'You did the right thing, Hector.'

'People outside don't know. They think it's easy. "After all," they say. "Common sense," they say. "Logic," they say. "The only thing to do. For everyone's sake." Well, it bloody well isn't easy – to take a cold-blooded decision to cut off a human life. There's a damn sight more to it than logic and common sense.'

Bliss turned towards Connie.

'And do you know what the worst thing is? It's not Sarah being gone. It's not Joy going for me. It's me. I say to myself "are you relieved she's not there?" and I'm forced to admit the answer is "yes", because there's no more scandal or rage or humiliation or pain or deceit or bitterness. So I say, "Perhaps that influenced your decision to switch off." '

'You mustn't do that, Hector.'

'That's easy to say.'

'I know, but it's true. So far as I can see, you were a good parent, and I've no doubt Joy was too. You had no idea what Sarah's true parents were like.'

'Ruth has turned out all right.'

'We were just luckier, that's all.'

'Hmm.'

'Hector, you would not have been attracted to teaching if you were not interested in children.'

'Teachers don't always make the best parents.'

'I know that old chestnut too. Believe me, you're all right. Aunt Jane agrees with me. Surely you respect her opinion.'

'Well . . . . '

'And soon you're going to do your best for Alan.'

'I owe it to Aline.'

'Even so. He's a lucky lad, with you on his side.'

'Thanks. If Sir Alec doesn't get to him first.'

'You don't think he would harm the boy, do you?'

'Hard to say. We don't know what Aline said to him before he killed her. She could have told him that the secret is out, that we know Alan is not his son. Besides, with Aline dead, half the reason for keeping Alan has gone. And there's something else too.'

'What?'

'Something Aunt Jane said. She thinks Sir Alec is obsessive about something, that he has very deeply-laid plans, of which Alan may or may not be a part. We have now frustrated those plans. Aunt Jane reckons that a man like Sir Alec, in such a situation of sudden checkmate, could react in the most extraordinary way. Even unbalanced.'

'Like coming after us.'

'Oh, that's quite understandable, under the circumstances. No, I was thinking of Alan. We just don't know what he will do, so we take no chances.'

'You've arranged something, haven't you?'

'I've got Priam to take the boy away from school.'

'Where to?'

'Never mind.'

'So *you* don't trust *me* now?'

'It's not that, Connie. It's just better that you don't know for the time being.'

Connie thought for a moment.

'You are a thorough man, and no mistake.'

'We've survived this far.'

Connie stood up and yawned.

'God, I'm exhausted! I'm going to clean my teeth, then I'm going to sleep.'

She rummaged for a toothbrush.

'Thanks, Connie,' said Bliss.

'What for?'

'Listening.'

After Connie had crawled into her sleeping bag, Bliss lay for a while looking at the stars . . . .

A burning mission station in Africa . . . . a collapsed hotel in Spain. What was it Dolly had said about Sir Alec owning 'about a million' hotels in Spain? A pardonable exaggeration, but there was a basic truth in it too. And then there was Sherman Foster and his wife, who, according to Connie, had acquired their daughter when the child's mother had been killed in a bus crash. Was it odd that all these infants should have become available as the result of chance disaster? Had there been other such chance disasters on Max's adoption files?

Was the creature capable of manufacturing disasters to order? Would he have whole families murdered by hired black terrorists? Would he destroy one of his own hotels? Would he have a coachload of people driven off the corniche into the sea? Was he that callous in his disregard of human life?

If Aline was right, the answer was most definitely 'yes'. He had, after all, blown up a whole mountainful of miners in order to mask a death that had not even taken place. To say nothing of two lifts full of innocent people.

Sir Alec's glowing, intent eyes came before him. He could see the gleaming smile as the hand was extended to let him take precedence through the door.

It made the flesh creep. Aunt Jane was right, but possibly for the wrong reason. This man was mad all right. He was a totally unhinged homicidal maniac.

Each time Bliss thought about him he came to more horrific conclusions.

There was yet another which he dared not face. He fought to control his mind and get off to sleep. By one o'clock he had succeeded.

*　*　×　*　*　*

At half-past three Bliss awakened by shouts and sirens. Connie was already coughing.

He put his face to the half-open door of the tent. It was a nightmare of red, yellow, and black; of roaring and screaming; of clattering property and thudding feet; dashing figures and desperate gestures; of worry and anguish and panic.

Bliss fell back into the tent.

'Put something on your feet – quick. We've got about thirty seconds – a minute at most. Just ram everything in. Leave your sleeping bag out.'

Connie did as she was told. Bliss finished first and crawled outside.

'Come on out. Bring the bags with you.'

When Connie got outside and stood up, Bliss started yanking at pegs and screwing the tent into a shapeless ball.

A fireman rushed past.

'*Vite, Monsieur, vite!*'

Bliss picked up his rucksack and stuffed in the flysheet. He tossed the inner half of the tent to Connie.

'Get that in. Right. Get it on your shoulders.'

'What about the bags?'

'Keep them open. Give me mine.'

Bliss yanked on his misshapen rucksack.

'Right. Come on!'

'Why are you going that way? Everyone's going towards the main gate.'

'Exactly. There's a small footbridge over the river at the back. The flames haven't reached the bank yet. Put the bag over your head and keep as much smoke away as possible. Now – run!'

Nobody tried to stop them; they were too busy. One fireman shouted after them, but did not pursue; he had his hands too full with campers running in the right direction.

Connie stumbled along behind, nearly slipped down the bank, wobbled and wailed on the bridge, and tripped at the far end, but she made it.

'Quick!' said Bliss. 'Into these bushes.'

'Shouldn't we go a bit further?'

'The flames won't cross the water – not yet anyway. There is little wind to carry the sparks. We've got a few minutes at least.'

'Can I put a skirt on?'

'Yes. We'll both get decent, and repack too.'

'How did you know this bridge was here?' said Connie.

'Because I made a point of looking yesterday evening, when you were having a shower.'

'You didn't tell me.'

'There was no point in worrying you.'

'Worrying me! Hector, I'm scared half to death.'

'There was no point in worrying you *in advance*. I just thought it as well to have a second exit. We were lucky; these places are usually wired or fenced right round.'

Connie rammed the sleeping bag back into its stuff sac.

'So you think this is Sir Alec's work?'

'It's his style, you must agree. Burn a lot to catch one – or rather two. At the very least, it's one hell of a coincidence. It's a bit like catching rabbits with ferrets and nets, isn't it? If the fire doesn't get us, Albert would break our necks as we dashed out of the front gate. In all that darkness and panic, they'd get away with murder – literally.'

They finished packing and strapped the rucksacks.

'I can't find my mirror,' said Connie.

Bliss glanced at her face, lit up by the flames.

'You look all right to me. Come on.'

'Thanks, Hector,' said Connie.

Bliss paused.

'What for?'

'For being ready.'

Bliss shrugged.

'Nothing. Boy Scout stuff. Are you fit?'

'Where to?'

'Anywhere, so long as it's away. If Sir Alec and Max are out there, they'll take some time to find that we're not coming out obligingly to have our necks broken. So we have a start.'

'Where are we going then? We can't keep going from pillar to post.'

'Just what I was thinking. Time perhaps for a shift of tactics.'

Connie puffed along beside him.

'So where to?'

'Ultimately, a telephone.'

'Why?'

'So that I can ring up Max and say "Yah! Boo! You can't catch me".'

Connie tripped and stifled a curse.

'I see,' she said. 'Ask a silly question . . . .'

'Something like that.'

*　　*　　*　　*　　*　　*

'Hallo, Pri? . . . . Yes, I'm sorry. It is a bit early, isn't it? . . . . Oh, we're getting on. Not far from journey's end . . . . Only a figure of speech . . . . Any news from your end? . . . . What? . . . . I don't believe it. In the school itself? . . . . Was anybody hurt? . . . . Did the Brigade say how it started? . . . . Mmm . . . . I could give them a few ideas . . . . Oh, never mind; I'll explain it all later . . . . But you must see how important it is to get action on this bastard . . . . Right. Good. I should bloody well think so . . . . And in France too? Because that's where . . . . Good . . . . So all we

have to do is sit under a hedge for two more days, eh? . .
. . It doesn't seem quite so easy from this end . . . . We'll
manage. Any news from Aunt Jane? . . . . My God! When?
. . . . What? . . . . Never! . . . . What does Dad say? . . . . Yes,
I'll bet . . . . Well, well, praise God for resourceful aunts,
I always say . . . . Yes, I'll tell her all right. It'll cheer her
up; she had a rough night . . . . Ch – um – indigestion. My
cooking, I expect . . . . Yes .. . . Oh, a day or so, I should
think, especially now that . . . . Yes . . . . All right . . . . 'Bye
– Oh, I say! . . . . Thanks, Pri. Thanks for everything. I love
you. Tell Parry and Mum and Dad. 'Bye.'

Bliss put down the 'phone and heaved a deep breath.
Stage One.

He picked up the 'phone again, dialled the number of
the Montpellier office of a newspaper, and asked for the
newsdesk. When a voice answered he put on a shocking
accent.

'Listen carefully. The terrorists who struck at Ste.
Sophie will strike again soon – near Carcassonne.'

He put down the receiver.
Stage Two.

Twenty-five kilometres down the road, Bliss and
Connie clambered out of a lorry and looked for an early-
opening café in the square.

Bliss ordered coffee and croissants.

It was early for the television to be on, but there was
a newspaper on a table round which sat a crowd of regulars in their blue overalls.

'D'you mind?' said Bliss.

'Carry on,' said one big man. 'We're just going.'

Connie was starving. She devoured the croissants
while Bliss thumbed through all the pages. At last he
tensed.

'Strewth!' he said. 'Listen to this.'

He lowered his head and read more intently.

Connie waited.

'Well?'

Bliss put down the paper.

'Policeman murdered in Pézenas – an inspector.'

Connie frowned.

'Pézenas. That's not far behind us.'

'Even closer behind where we were last night.'

Connie gasped.

'The fire.'

'Yes.'

'But you can't be sure.'

'Oh, yes I can. I haven't told you everything. There was another dead body found near the inspector. Shot. Big man. Name of Albert Beyer.'

'Albert!'

'Right. The inspector was strangled.'

Connie put down her empty cup.

'Poor man.'

'Yes. I suppose he was one of the first to try and throw off the shackles. Read about the fire at Ste. Sophie, and when Sir Alec turned up told him to go to Hell. They might have got something out of him about us, then told Albert to shut his mouth. Albert must have been careless for once.'

Bliss folded the newspaper.

'Well,' he said, 'at least it shortens the odds. Excuse me. I'm going to make another 'phone call.'

Two against two. A fair match. So be it.

Time for Stage Three.

'Hallo, Joseph? Hector here . . . . Hector . . . . '

Chapter Eleven

CONNIE HANDED DOWN the rucksacks, then Bliss helped her to jump. He walked to the front of the lorry and slapped the outside of the passenger door.

'*Bien! Merci beaucoup, Monsieur. Au revoir.*'

The driver let in his clutch.

'*Okay! Au revoir, Monsieur.*'

He rolled off in a cloud of brick dust.

Connie spluttered.

'Hector, you do pick them.'

'No, dear, they picked me – or rather you. That's a fetching tan you've got.'

'If you can see it for dust,' said Connie, trying to make herself presentable.

'Think yourself lucky the local industry is brick-making, not brewing beer. You'd be smelling like *Dirty Dick's* on Bank Holiday Monday.'

'Where's *Dirty Dick's*?'

'Between Liverpool Street Station and Petticoat Lane.'

Connie snorted.

'I might have guessed.'

She stood up.

'How do I look? I can't tell without a mirror.'

'Fine. Joseph will adore you.'

'How far is it now?'

'Not far. It's about midway between St. Martin de Villefort and St. Martin la Forêt.'

As they walked along, Bliss talked of happy holidays

with his family, and pointed out places of interest, or spots where memorable things had happened to them.

His infectious spirits made her forget her tiredness and hunger. A fresh wind had sprung up, which was a welcome relief from the many days of close heat.

It was only when they stopped for a rest that Connie realised how tired and hungry she was – and, now, how cold. She said so.

'Yes,' agreed Bliss, looking around at a greying evening sky. 'It's blowing up. Looks as if we're going to get a storm. They're quite common in these parts. Sudden cold – high wind – thunder and lightning – buckets of rain – and back to normal – all in a few hours sometimes. Never mind – not far now.' He smiled fondly. 'It was round about here that we used to start guessing what Sylvie would be dishing up for dinner.'

Connie pulled a jumper over her head.

'You're in the best spirits you've been since we started. What are you up to?'

'Nothing.'

'Hector, you're a rotten liar.'

Bliss took off his rucksack.

'Yes, that's what my family say. Come over and sit down. It's sheltered here. We can afford a few minutes.'

Connie sat down beside him.

Bliss offered some chocolate.

'Last bar. Make the most of it.'

'Thanks.'

'Now,' he said, with his mouth full, 'the Doctor wishes me to "reveal all". Very well. But I can't promise that she'll like it.'

'We didn't start this business because we liked it,' said Connie. 'So I don't suppose the ending will be all that enjoyable either.'

'Closer to the mark than you think,' said Bliss.

He broke off another piece of chocolate.

'I'm going to take them on.'

Connie stared.

'You can't be serious.'

'Never more serious in my life.'

'You're mad.'

'I don't think so. My decision, like all good command decisions, is based on a realistic appreciation of the situation. They're good at "appreciations" in the Army, in case you didn't know.'

'They also get themselves killed in the Army through foolhardy bravery. You're not in the Army now. Hector, be sensible.'

'I'm being very sensible. Hear me out. We know that the long arm of the law is now reaching out for Sir Alec, and, we hope, Max too. But we don't know how long they're going to take to catch him. He won't obligingly stand still for them.

'In that time there's no knowing what he can do. Last night's fire told us that. And his creatures have made two attempts on Alan's school, and one on the yacht. Whether they were serious attacks or mere demonstrations of power, I don't know, but we can't afford to be sanguine about it. How many more attempts will be made against us? How many times will we jump when we see little men in dark glasses at bus stations and wonder who they are?

'Sir Alec is on the run and he's desperate. He's even more dangerous than usual, as that poor police inspector found out at Pézenas.'

'He killed Albert for us.'

'Yes. That's another factor. It's now only two against two.'

'Me and you?'

'Oh, no! Me and Joseph.'

'Why not me?'

'Now *you* be sensible.'

'Why involve Joseph? I thought we were going there to hide.'

'We're not. We're going there to wait.'

'Yes – for Sir Alec to be arrested.'

'Or for Sir Alec to arrive.'

'What? How can he?'

'I invited him.'

'Hector, stop being clever. Explain.'

'Look. I don't think we can risk hanging around any more, waiting for Sir Alec to be taken out of circulation. Too many unpleasant things have happened. We won't be lucky every time.

'So I thought – right, stop running. Turn and face them. Take them on. Accept the challenge.'

'Challenge? What challenge?'

'I think Max has been challenging me since we started. I think Max worked out where we might go soon after we left. He knew about Joseph – I told him when I first arrived – and he'd had a letter from me at that address. He also has a near-photographic memory.'

'Because he remembers where you might go he is not issuing a challenge; he is simply taking a long shot.'

'True. But remember his statement to the police. He suggested road blocks and checkpoints in every direction except this one. He knew I'd read the paper; it was my only way of getting information. That or the telly. He was saying to me in effect, "We're watching the other ways out. Why not go west, to your friends?"

'When you saw those men at the bus station, and they didn't interfere, it confirmed it. We were being watched. Steered, if you like.'

'What about the fire?'

'That, I agree, was a bit different. They had a chance to clobber us there, either by burning or by catching us in the confusion when we ran out. They'd have been foolish not to try. When it failed, they fell back again on their previous methods.

'But it was getting harder. The inspector at Pézenas had proved that. Still, they were close. So, as I didn't want to continue jumping at shadows, I let him know that I accepted his challenge.'

'How did you do that?'

'I rang a newspaper, saying the terrorists who burned Ste. Sophie would strike again near Carcassonne. I guessed that Max would also be watching the news or reading the paper. Carcassonne is near enough to here. He'll know the terrorist message is false because he knows terrorists didn't burn Ste. Sophie. He'll put two and two together.'

'And come here?'

'Yes. I hope so.'

'You hope so! Is that why you're so damned cheerful?'

'It's a decision, Connie. It's an ending. No more running and wondering. Besides, it'll be on ground of my own choosing. The Duke of Wellington was a great believer in choosing his ground.'

'The Duke of Wellington happened to have several thousand troops with him. All you've got is an elderly French wine-grower who doesn't even know you're coming.'

'Oh, yes he does. I told him. He knows Max and Sir Alec are coming too. And don't run away with the idea that Joseph is some pigeon-chested, pot-bellied old wine-soak. He'd make two of me. And he's very tough indeed. He was in the Resistance during the war.'

'I see,' said Connie. 'So you're going to re-live the great days of the Liberation and round up Max the wicked Nazi and Alec Sherrif the fiendish international crook?'

Bliss put the last piece of chocolate into his mouth, screwed up the silver paper, and threw it into a bush.

'Something like that.'

'Where do I come into all this? And what about Joseph's wife and son? Have you considered them?'

'No. They're not my worry. Joseph will attend to that. He'll probably send them away; he has relatives in Carcassonne.

'You are my worry. I've told you all this because I want you to understand the issues. It could get a bit awkward in the next day or two.'

Connie looked sardonic.

'I suppose this is the gallant-officer-going-over-the-top bit, is it? Mustn't upset the little woman. Things could get "a bit awkward". What do I do now – kiss you on the cheek and say "bless you dear, and God save the Queen"?'

'It means,' said Bliss, 'that this is where you get off. You were not involved in the decision I took, so it is not fair you should be involved in the results of it. Joseph has arranged for you to stay with friends of his in St. Martin la Forêt.'

'Aren't you forgetting something, Hector? In fact, two things.'

'What?'

'Firstly, it was I who involved you at the outset. And when we decided to start the fire, I accepted what you said – that anything could happen. Well, I still stand by that.'

Bliss smiled.

'And secondly?'

'And secondly,' said Connie, 'the men you have so kindly invited to call are the men who blew my husband to pieces in a lift.'

She stood up, put on her rucksack, walked back to the roadway, and turned.

'Well? Are you coming?'

*   *   *   *   *   *

'I wonder where Bijou is.'

'Who's Bijou?'

'Joseph's dog. She's usually out from the shed like a shot out of a gun.'

Connie shivered.

'I'm cold. Now that we've stopped walking.'

The wind was becoming noisier. The sky was darker than usual for that hour of the evening.

Bliss banged again on the front door.

'Come on, Joseph,' he said, half to himself. 'Place is like the grave.'

At long last they heard footsteps in the stone passage. Joseph's massive frame filled the doorway. Because of a light behind him in the kitchen he looked even bigger.

He held out a hand.

'Hector! Come in.'

He turned to Connie and nodded.

'Good evening, Madame.'

'Good evening, Monsieur Gommard.'

289

Connie was so overawed that she almost ducked her head.

He went ahead of them towards the lounge.

Connie whispered in Bliss' ear as they shot the bolts.

'Is he always gruff like that?'

'He can be a bit moody sometimes. Pay no attention. He'll warm up after dinner.'

Connie shivered again, and not only from the cold.

'I hope I do too.'

Bliss was a yard or two behind Connie as she entered the lounge. He saw her stop suddenly, and knew from the set of her shoulders that something was wrong. He heard a noise behind him and turned round.

'No heroics, Mr. Bliss, I beg you.'

Max was standing in the kitchen doorway. His finger was already curled round the trigger. He motioned with the gun.

'If you would please follow Dr. Marshall, then we can all be together.'

In the midst of this crisis, Bliss found himself wondering how Max continued to look so well groomed. Three days of constant travel, excitement, crime, and changing fortunes, and he still looked like an advert for Austin Reed.

Max followed him into the lounge and shut the door.

Sir Alec Sherrif leapt to his feet from one of the old armchairs by the fire. Teeth flashed in the familiar smile. The dark eyes glowed. The customary gracious sweep with the hand. The short bow.

'Allow me to invite you both to sit down,' he said.

*　　*　　*　　*　　*　　*

It was an odd sound. If it was possible for a voice to be

290

both soft and rasping, thought Bliss, that was it. Another comparison that came to him was – like a joint moving stiffly and slowly after long damage or inactivity. Which was roughly what it was, really

The deliberation and lack of volume added to the menace. Bliss and Connie knew that both Sir Alec and Max were perfectly capable of carrying out any threat they uttered.

To the fear was added revulsion – for Bliss, at any rate. He had not thought out the full implications of inviting them here. Looking at them – at Max, lounging and smoking in one of the fireside armchairs; at Sir Alec, who had now moved to a hard wooden chair near the door – and looking too at the familiar features of the room – the old photographs and the rickety television stand and the dog hairs and the open piano – Bliss felt their very presence to be a sort of desecration.

Nor had he reckoned with Joseph being so easily overpowered. Now that he was vanquished, they had dismissed him from their mind. They had not even invited him to sit down. He stood by the table, his massive hands hanging in front of him, like some ancient piece of sculpture.

Connie sat bolt upright in the other armchair, her hands in her lap.

Max leaned forward and held out a bottle.

'Wine, Madame? It is Monsieur Gommard's own produce. A trifle bucolic, perhaps, but refreshing nonetheless. No? Perhaps yourself, Mr. Bliss. Ah – ever the practical man, I see. One cannot attend to administrative details on a dry throat, can one?'

Why the cat and mouse, thought Bliss, and then remembered. Of course – Max was enjoying it. No doubt

Sir Alec too. This was what they had been looking forward to – part of it anyway.

He had no doubt what the other part would be.

'There remains only the small matter of your disposal,' said Sir Alec, as if reading Bliss' thoughts.

'Let Dr. Marshall go,' said Bliss. 'I did the burning, not her. She just ran because she was afraid.'

Alec Sherrif shook his head and smiled.

'A feeble, last-ditch effort, Mr. Bliss, barely worthy even of Bulldog Drummond. Besides, a man of your education should be aware that revenge is not negotiable.'

That was it, then. It all depended on Joseph now.

Max looked at Joseph.

'You,' he said. 'How could one dispose of two bodies here?'

Joseph frowned.

'If Monsieur will speak French?'

Max repeated his question in that language.

Joseph shrugged.

'Not a great matter, if properly approached.'

Max looked at Sir Alec, who nodded. He turned back to Joseph.

'Sit down at the table.'

Joseph obeyed, and sat facing Sir Alec.

Max took an envelope out of his inside pocket, selected a packet of notes, and tossed it on to the table. Joseph's eyes lit up.

Bliss felt his muscles begin to tighten. What's Joseph up to? What does he want me to do?

Joseph took off the elastic band and slowly counted, licking his finger every so often.

'Well?' said Max, when he had finished.

'Disposal is easy. There remains the matter of

concealment, and of dealing with police inquiries, if any.'

He placed a huge hand either side of the pile and waited.

Max tossed another bundle, which Joseph counted equally laboriously. He was impervious to the nerve-grinding silence in the room. Outside, the wind rose. Droplets of rain hit the window.

Bliss felt his first twinge of disquiet.

'A franc is a franc.' How often had he heard Joseph say it? To pay off the loan on the new machinery; to buy a new lorry; to lend money to daughter Monique for new en-suite bathrooms in their Normandy hotel – money in the hand, and no questions asked.

Nobody knew that he and Connie were there. He had deliberately not told Pri where he was going and what he hoped to do. God! It seemed such a pathetic plan now. They would simply disappear off the face of the earth.

Bliss pulled hard on the reins of his imagination.

Don't be stupid – this was Joseph Gommard, his friend of nearly forty years.

And yet there was – there always had been – a dimension to Joseph that he had never fathomed. Joseph had always had the capacity to create unease.

'I will do it.'

'Joseph!'

The big man turned slowly to Bliss.

'You English,' he said. 'You never learn from history. You only live in it. Give me one good reason why I should risk death to help you out of trouble which you have brought upon yourself.' He flung out a hand in Connie's direction. 'And all, it seems, because of a woman. Not even a young one.'

Bliss felt his anger rising.

293

'I should have thought,' said Joseph, 'that you had learned your lesson from the first one.'

Bliss could have struck him.

'And now,' continued Joseph, 'you descend upon me and expect me to be grateful enough to help you. Grateful for the Liberation, after forty years. We must forget your insularity; we must pat your football thugs on the head; we must allow your farmers to bury us in English meat; we must smile as Margaret Thatcher tries to take over the Common Market – all because you "liberated" us forty years ago – freed us from the Germans and handed us over to our patriots, who celebrated with more shootings and hangings.'

My God! He's going to do it. He's really going to do it.

Joseph stuffed the money inside his shirt, lit a cigarette, and turned to Sir Alec.

'You want me to show you where? Or do you wish to see for yourself? By yourself?'

Bliss leapt to his feet.

'You bastard! You shifty, mercenary bastard!'

'Sit down, Mr. Bliss, or I shall shoot Dr. Marshall here and now.'

There was a loud click.

Bliss sat down again.

Alec Sherrif rose, still keeping his own gun trained on Bliss.

'Stay at the table, both of you. Dr. Marshall, you also remain seated. I shall go and see for myself. I don't want you breaking my neck outside in the dark, my friend, do I?'

'And lose his money?' sneered Bliss. 'Hardly.'

Joseph shrugged, leaned on the table, and poured himself some wine.

'Out of the yard,' he said. 'Turn left and up to the track for seventy to a hundred metres. You will come to the first well. They come at regular intervals thereafter. You can either help me fill them in or I'll do it all when you've gone – if you make it worth my while.'

'Don't you use them for the vines?' said Max.

'Not any more. We have a more modern system.'

'Be able to pay for it now, won't you?' said Bliss.

Alec Sherrif went to the door.

'Watch them,' he said to Max.

'There is a coat behind the kitchen door,' said Joseph. 'The rain is getting heavier.'

In the silence after he had gone, Joseph puffed his cigarette and sipped his wine. Connie looked at Bliss, who asked Max if they could sit together.

He gave a leisurely approval.

'A tender, final scene? Of course. You should have been a writer, Mr. Bliss.'

Another silence was broken only by the clink of bottle on glass.

Then Joseph said something.

Max looked startled, but replied.

A conversation began, but not in French or English. Bliss guessed it was Arabic. He remembered that Joseph had done some military training in Algeria, and that Max dealt with Dolly's 'string of wogs' at Ste. Sophie.

Joseph barely moved at the table save to puff at his cigarette, but Max showed unusual interest, even suppressed excitement.

They switched back to French when they heard Sir Alec returning.

He took off the old coat and shook it.

'All right,' he said to Max. 'It will do.'

Connie clutched Bliss' hand.

Bliss tried a desperate ploy.

'You know you're insane, don't you? Mad as a hatter.'

To his surprise, Alec Sherrif laughed.

'I'm afraid you will have to do better than that, Mr. Bliss. I am not insane, nor will you provoke me by suggesting that I am. You can not spin out your final moments by inducing me to gloat. Gloating comes more easily to Max. My taste is for much lengthier revenge, and if that is not readily available, an immediate dispatch of one's victim is usually preferable. It does at least have the merits of speed and efficiency.'

Max stood up and motioned them both to their feet.

'I'm sorry, Con,' said Bliss.

A soft look came into Connie's eyes.

'That's what David used to call me.'

Bliss didn't know what to say. He gestured awkwardly.

'I'm sorry.'

Connie's eyes glowed.

'I'm not. Bless you.'

Joseph Gommard cleared his throat.

'Wouldn't it be better to kill them beside the wells? I don't fancy carrying bodies in this rain. I don't know if you do. You could take them out one at a time just as easily.'

'What an excellent suggestion,' said Max.

The capped teeth flashed in Bliss' direction.

'Then we can point out the spot to Mr. Bliss as we pass.'

There was a distant rumble of thunder.

Alec Sherrif sat down, and wiped some of the wet from his face. He got out his handkerchief and mopped his hands.

'Take her first. You? Go with Max and help him.'

Joseph offered Max the wet overcoat.

Alec Sherrif trained his revolver straight at Bliss. Max had his gun pressed right into Connie's back.

There seemed nothing for it but to show as much dignity as possible. Funny how you feel emotions that you never expect to feel when you imagine such scenes.

'Goodbye, Con.'

Connie managed a little nod, before Max pushed her out of the room. Joseph followed without a word.

Bliss heard them shut the front door.

Alec Sherrif watched him.

'In case you are measuring the distance between us, Mr. Bliss, let me inform you that I am an excellent shot with both pistol and rifle. You would be dead before you could reach an upright position.'

There was a crack of thunder. Bliss jumped.

'Do not strain to hear, Mr. Bliss. I doubt very much whether you would hear a gunshot at this distance and in this storm. I'm afraid you must regard Dr. Marshall as already dead.'

'Like Aline and Dolly.'

Alec Sherrif shrugged.

'If that is how you care to see it.'

Bliss spat.

Alec Sherrif laughed.

'If you are hoping to induce in me a sense of shame, Mr. Bliss, let me save you further effort by saying that you are wasting your time.

'You Englishmen are constantly paralysed and emasculated by your precious sense of fair play. It is the one serious sign of decadence in an otherwise admirable national character.'

Bliss saw no point in arguing at this stage. Alec Sherrif warmed to his theme, simply as a means of filling the time.

'You show the greatest will to power since the Romans; you build the biggest empire the world has seen; you produce an entire educational system to train young men to run that empire; you vindicate all that power by winning two world wars.

'And then you proceed to give your empire away, and dismantle half your educational system in favour of alleged equality. If your socialist opposition ever get into office again, it is only a matter of time before you dismantle the other half. You beat your breasts and tell all your old colonies that you regret having exploited them, and offer to pour millions into their bumbling national governments to show how sorry you are. Power certainly corrupted you. Unlike the Romans, though, whose corruption took the form of moral degradation, yours took the form of moral rectitude. Ruthlessness, single-mindedness, the will to win and dominate – all these are now suspect. You are a nation of weaklings, and I despise weaklings.'

Bliss could see that he was enjoying himself, though not so much because he liked his position of superiority. Rather that he was relishing the use of his vocal chords.

'Was Aline a weakling?'

Alec Sherrif looked genuinely surprised.

'Good Heavens, no! She was a worthy adversary who fought me tooth and nail for over a decade. It was she who provided me with the two greatest shocks of my life. One took my voice away; the other brought it back. I shall miss her.'

'Yet you killed her.'

Alec Sherrif waved casually.

'A momentary lapse of self-control – under severe provocation, you must admit. I did not have the time or the opportunity to devise an appropriate means of regular vengeance.'

'You enjoy revenge, don't you?'

'Enormously. It is one of the few gratifying emotions that in my opinion has not been studied to anything like sufficient depth.

'Most people think that revenge is a matter of instant, heated reprisal. A minority claim that it is a dish to be taken cold. I go further; I maintain that it is an elixir to be savoured constantly. It refreshes and raises the spirit and is a spur to further action.'

'Then why don't you devise a lengthier torture for us?' asked Bliss. 'Why execute us immediately?'

'Because you are beneath my respect, Mr. Bliss. You are not worthy adversaries, like Aline, who stood up and fought me all those years.'

'So we are to be brushed aside – like Dolly.'

Alec Sherrif shook his head in amusement.

'There you go again, Mr. Bliss. Another feature of your national weakness is your tiresome chivalry. Where you acquired this sense of gallantry towards women I cannot imagine. If yours had been a Catholic country I would have blamed the excessive devotion to the Virgin Mary. As it is, you make heroines out of the most domineering, overbearing females – Florence Nightingale, Emmeline Pankhurst, Nancy Astor. You may have noticed that the French had a different way of treating the only virago in their history: they burnt her.

'One look – one glance – at even the insect world would have told you that females can be every bit as predatory as males. It is a fallacy that men chase women. I speak from wide experience. Take it from me: *they* come after *me*. Once they have caught me, of course, they must take what is coming to them.'

He saw the sneer on Bliss' lips.

'I assure you I speak from fact, Mr. Bliss, not vanity. I can name hundreds of women to prove my point.'

'Hundreds?'

Bliss repeated the figure in amazement before he could control himself.

Alec Sherrif nodded.

'Oh, yes. A capricious deity has endowed me with an unusual body odour. To put it crudely, they like the way I smell. Some of the effects, I have noticed, can be quite startling. Of course, I have no doubt that financial inducements have also contributed to the interest of many, though may I hasten to add that I can reasonably claim to have built up a competent technique in various other departments of courtship. But there!'

He made a dismissive gesture.

'Women are cheap. Mothers are expendable. It is the children who are immortality.'

Bliss stared. That monstrous prospect, that horrifying possibility, which he had persistently refused to face, now reared in reality before him and would not be denied.

The front door was flung open and crashed against the passage wall.

They heard footsteps rushing down the passage. And Joseph's voice.

'No, Monsieur. I beg you. Please.'

Joseph burst into the room, his jaw dropping in dread.

'Monsieur, I appeal to you.'

'What is it?' said Alec Sherrif, not taking his eyes off Bliss.

'He is coming in an instant, Monsieur. Please, tell him. Look, I give you back your money. Take it, Monsieur.'

Joseph fell to his knees beside Alec Sherrif's chair. He groped inside his shirt, pulled out the two wads of notes, and held them forward.

Bliss noticed that the backs of his hands were bloody.

The backs!

'Please, Monsieur! I am a poor man but I want to live like anyone else. I will bury them for you, Monsieur. By myself. Nobody will ever know.'

Joseph began sobbing. Raindrops ran down from his matted hair across his forehead – over the tidemark made by the near-constant presence of his cap on his head.

'Please, Monsieur – by the Holy Virgin, Monsieur. I beg you.'

He clutched at a sleeve.

Alec Sherrif stood up and tried to shake him off.

Bliss dived.

Alec Sherrif tried to turn back to aim the gun, but Joseph's huge bloodstained fist took him full in the groin.

As he doubled up, Joseph grabbed the gun hand, and broke the arm across his knee.

Sherrif screamed, and Bliss seized him from behind as the gun clattered to the floor.

Joseph produced some rope, tied him hand and foot, and then tied him to the wooden chair.

The face was contorted with pain; the eyes blazed. When he heard Joseph bring Connie into the room he turned his head and fixed on her a look of such fury that she physically recoiled.

Joseph settled her tenderly into a chair. She was

sobbing, trembling, and soaking wet. Bliss knelt in front of her and held her hands.

Joseph pulled some serviettes out of a sideboard drawer and tossed them over. Bliss wiped Connie's face, arms, and hands. Rain drummed on the window.

'Upstairs,' said Joseph. 'In the bedroom. One of Sylvie's sweaters.'

When Bliss returned, Alec Sherrif was lying on the floor, chair and all. Blood ran from his mouth.

'What happened?' said Bliss.

'He moved,' said Joseph.

He righted the chair, and made sure its occupant was securely held on it.

'Don't worry; he won't do it again.'

'My God, Joseph, you had me fooled.'

'That was the idea. Your rage had to be genuine. They were too clever to be taken in by bluff.'

'And when you counted the money.'

'They had to see me take the bribe. If I had refused it, they would have respected me. That was no use. I wanted them despising me. In the end they wrote me off. It was going to be only a matter of time before one of them killed me when it was all over, so he did not suspect when I rushed in and said Max was after me.'

'It was only when you started speaking Arabic to Max that I began to wonder. Even then I dared not hope.'

Joseph nodded.

'I had to separate them and get one outside, and I had to find a way of catching Max's interest.'

'What did you say?'

'I had noticed that Max was in fear of him.'

Bliss amazed himself by thinking suddenly of Dolly. Dear Dolly. She had spotted that very early on. God! And she thought she was 'not much of a girl'.

Joseph gestured towards Alec Sherrif, who was alternately glaring in rage and grimacing in pain.

'I offered Max a way of removing him. To remove a source of fear, to prove oneself superior, to kill without fear of reprisal – the temptation was too much for a man like Max. So I was able to get him outside – if only by a cruel trick.'

Joseph looked apologetically towards Connie.

'I am very sorry, Madame, but it was a difficult situation. I could think of no other way.'

Connie nodded, keeping her eyes down. Her body was still shaking.

'It wasn't till I saw your hands,' said Bliss. 'There was blood on the backs. If you had picked up a wounded body the blood would have been on the palms.'

Joseph nodded and rubbed his knuckles reflectively.

'I'm afraid Max did settle one or two debts on earth before being sent where he belongs.'

'Where is he?'

Joseph lit a cigarette, keeping the gun in his other hand trained on Alec Sherrif.

'One step nearer to Hell.'

He lit a second cigarette for Connie, who accepted it gratefully with trembling hands.

'He never recognised you then?' said Bliss.

'He barely knew me. But even if he had known me better, I think he was too busy despising me. It is easier, on the other hand, to remember those whom one hates.'

Connie raised her head.

'What does Joseph mean?'

Bliss explained.

'D'you remember Max's war record – how he blotted

his copy book and was packed off to occupation duty in southern France? Well, it was here.'

'I never thought the chance would present itself, Madame, but, thanks to Hector, after forty years, it did.'

'Is that soldier down a well too?' said Bliss. 'You know – the one who dropped the grenades?'

Joseph frowned for a moment, then raised his eyebrows.

'Oh, him? Yes. He's down there. We put him down with the man he'd killed. With all the pieces. We shone a torch down so that he could see. Then we dropped dummy grenades. Asked him to guess when the real one was coming. After twenty minutes he was off his head. So we buried him.'

Connie shuddered.

'Well?' said Joseph.

Bliss licked his lips.

'Yes?'

Alec Sherrif looked keenly from one to the other.

Flashes of lightning lit up the paintwork on the window. Streams of water ran down the panes. One great crash sounded almost overhead.

Joseph pulled Max's gun from his trouser pocket and laid it on the table.

'Here you are.'

Bliss walked to the table. One or two smears of blood were on the barrel. So Joseph had hit him with that too.

Bliss turned to him.

'Now that we're in control, wouldn't it be better to ring the police?'

'We could have done that before they arrived,' said Joseph. 'We chose to do it this way.'

Bliss looked at the smeared black metal.

'It's like execution,' he said.

'It's not *like* execution,' said Joseph. 'It *is* execution.'

Bliss put his hand towards the steel as if it were leprous.

'You see? He can't do it.'

Alec Sherrif's voice was hoarse. 'He's half a man – he can't do it. He's just seen it done and he still can't do it!'

Bliss looked at Joseph.

'I am an executioner,' said Joseph, 'not a murderer. Debts to me have been paid. It is your debt that awaits payment. This man owes me nothing.'

'Nothing?' said Bliss. 'He's an enemy to all society. He's evil.'

'Then kill him,' said Joseph.

Alec Sherrif twisted round to face Connie.

'This is the man you have chosen to share your fate. See him now. He cannot look me in the eye. Nor will he be able to look you in the eye, Dr. Marshall. He will slide round the truth and rationalise it and talk of law and righteousness. He will shelter behind a rampart of empty moralising.

'He will also attempt to protect you from what he considers unwelcome truth. But I shall pay you a greater compliment than that. Whether I go to prison or to my grave, I shall leave you the possessor of truth that you can carry to your own grave.'

'Shut up!' shouted Bliss.

'What colour is Ruth's hair?'

The voice was struggling now against increasing congestion.

Connie looked puzzled.

'What colour is it!'

'Dark,' she said, in spite of herself.

'Dark,' repeated Sherrif. 'And your Mr. Bliss had a daughter – with dark hair. Yes, Mr. Bliss?'

He wriggled round to look at him, then wriggled back.

'And did Mr. Sherman Foster show you a photograph of his beloved daughter?'

Connie's eyes began to widen in horror.

'You idiots!' said Sherrif, rattling the legs of the chair in his excitement. 'Did you think all those precious adoptions by Max were pure chance, the accidental result of circumstance?'

Connie had risen to her feet.

'Ah, so you begin to appreciate,' said Sherrif. 'But then you are a highly intelligent woman whose services were invaluable to me. But never fear; I shall find another. And another. Just as I shall find other Dolly Vartans – Dolly Vartans who will be flattered to bear my children. To share my immortality.'

Connie could not find words.

'Speechless, eh?' said Sherrif. 'I know the feeling. To have emotions so pent up that you could go mad. With me of course there was always the chance of recovery. To you, no such release will come; the knowledge will never fade. You can never unlearn it. You see? It is as I told Mr. Bliss – revenge is a great art. You carry a hideous fact to your grave, Dr. Marshall, and the more I can make you hate me, the more hideous the fact becomes. The more evil I become in your eyes, the more potent the poisonous fact in your mind. And the greater my gratification.'

Connie put her hands over her ears and sat down again, rocking in anguish.

'Get him out of here!'

Bliss rushed forward, cut the ropes holding Sherrif to the chair, and bundled him to the door. Joseph prudently

306

hobbled him so that he could not run, grabbed something off the table, and thrust Max's pistol into Bliss' hand.

The storm was at its height. Trees bent in the wind, and rain lashed them like whips.

Oblivious of the pain in his arm, ignoring the rain, slipping and stumbling, Alec Sherrif kept up a mindless monologue; he seemed afraid that if he once stopped talking, his voice would go away and never return.

'Alan would have the best, the very best. He would start at the beginning – in the prep. school. Then public school and private tutor. Always the best. By the time he reached university he would have the English manner, the ease. I had to work for everything; I had to prove things all the time. "Oh, yes, Alec Sherrif," they'd say. "Yes – a fine effort – for a foreigner" when they meant "pretty bright for a wog".

'Alan will grow up at ease in this decadent world. He will have total acceptance as of right. Then I shall place in his hands the means of domination. My legacy will be strength, reputation, connections, and a family network all over the world. An unstoppable combination of blood, money, and power.'

They reached the gate and turned up the track towards the wells.

The rasping, crazed monologue continued.

'For me, no single blinding climax of revenge. Alan can choose his method, his time, his place – an arms deal here, a drugs operation there, a crime syndicate somewhere else. He can place whatever germs he wishes into Britain's bloodstream in whatever place he chooses. Together we can watch the limbs weaken and the body atrophy. We can hasten or delay the process as the whim takes us. And they will never know . . . . it is the fact of

307

power, not the facade that is the true intoxicant . . . . to prove to the world the truth of the decadence I have witnessed over the years . . . . '

Joseph knocked him down, picked him up half-winded, and dragged him the rest of the way.

When they stood by the stonework at last, Joseph turned to Bliss.

'Right. Now!'

Bliss held his right arm loose at his side. Hundreds of splashes leapt up over his shoes where rain thumped into puddles.

'For God's sake, man!' shouted Joseph over the thunder.

'It is taking a life,' said Bliss.

'Is it useful? Is it any good?'

'No.'

'Then do it again.'

'Again?'

'You took Sarah's. What is the difference? There you pressed a switch. Here you pull a trigger. Father and daughter – do it.'

'Do it, Hector.'

Bliss whirled round.

Connie was standing behind him, her hair dark with rain.

Bliss looked at the gun.

'To be judge and jury.'

'What do you want?' said Joseph, his face streaming. 'A Wild West duel – "may the best man win"?'

'He would lose,' said Alec Sherrif, struggling for breath. 'It would take an Alec Sherrif to destroy an Alec Sherrif. You break my system, but you do not break me. I shall build again. Even if you take my son, I shall have another.

I have the world to choose from. Next time perhaps a true blood son to mould to my image. Or a true daughter – eh, Dr. Marshall?'

Even in the dark the eyes glowed like fire.

Connie snatched the gun from Bliss' hand and pointed it.

'No, Connie! He is trying to make you do it.'

Bliss reached out, grasped her hand, and grappled.

'He is trying to make you the killer of Ruth's father!'

The report was masked by a huge clap of thunder. Bliss thought at first that he had prevented her. Then he saw the body writhing in the mud, the throat and chest a mass of blood. The eyes still stared; the mouth worked without noise.

Connie stood back in horror, the gun hanging at her side.

Joseph pushed his own weapon into Bliss' hand.

'Do you want her to carry it all? Finish him!'

Bliss looked down at the twisted face and contorted body, the arms still held by ropes. Hideous gagging noises came from the open throat. Lightning flashes showed up red streaks in the leaping puddles.

Bliss leaned down, pointed, and fired once.

'Thank God for that!' said Joseph. Bliss knew that he did not refer to Sherrif's death but to his executioner.

Connie turned away, collapsed to her knees, and was sick.

'Quick,' said Joseph. 'In with him.'

The body was neither large nor heavy.

Afterwards they stood still. The thunder was weakening. Bliss held his face up to the dark sky, letting the pouring rain run over him.

Connie struggled to her feet, walked to the edge of the

crumbling well wall, and threw in the gun. Bliss dropped in his own. Joseph fished inside his shirt, took out the two wads of notes, and threw them down.

'Blood money,' he said.

He looked round.

'Come, Hector, my friend. You and I can do what is necessary in the morning.'

Bliss put his arm round Connie.

As they began to walk back to the house, a last flicker of lightning made something gleam in the mud. Bliss saw it and stooped.

He picked it up, walked back to the well, and threw it in.

'What was it?' said Connie.

'A cufflink. A gold cufflink.'

Epilogue

'IS THAT YOU, Armand?'

'Yes.'

'We are in here. You are early.'

Armand Sainval went down the passage and into his kitchen. He presented his wife with a huge bunch of flowers, and then kissed her.

He turned to where his daughter sat drawing at the table. He lifted her up bodily, folded her in his arms, and held her tight.

'Armand – what is it?'

'Nothing, *chérie*. It is just that today I feel very, very happy.'

He went out whistling, leaving his wife and daughter gazing in amazement at each other.

Upstairs, he took his old sweater and trousers out of the wardrobe. He stood in front of the mirror and began to unbutton his jacket.

He paused for a moment and looked at his reflection.

What a joy – what an unspeakable joy – to be proud of his uniform once more.

* * * * * *

Joseph Gommard walked inside the *Café de la Gare* and banged on the bar counter.

'Hey! Jacques! Come on. Let's have some service.'

Jacques appeared, looking for trouble. His face cleared when he saw Joseph. They shook hands.

'Bring us one of my bottles on the *terrasse*,' said Joseph. 'The white.'

Jacques came and poured the wine himself.

'It must be a special occasion,' he said, 'for you to be drinking white wine.'

'It is,' said Joseph, as he passed the glasses round to Connie, Aunt Jane, and Ruth. 'We are saying hallo and goodbye. *Voilà*, Sylvie. Raymond. And you, Hector, my friend. Join us, Jacques. If you have the face to, after what you charge for my wine.' He winked at Bliss. 'His mark-up is scandalous.'

Jacques just made the bottle stretch to eight glasses.

Joseph gestured towards him.

'Jacques is a very old friend of mine from wartime days,' he explained to Connie. 'We have seen some times, eh, Jacques?'

He held up the wine to the light.

' "St. Martin-les-Puits." Here is the future.' He extended his glass towards Ruth. 'And you, *ma petite*, are also the future.'

Ruth blushed.

Joseph stood up.

'We drink to old ghosts laid, old debts paid, new friends made. Let the past remain buried deep, thought on from time to time, but not dwelt on. Let us draw strength from the trials we have shared, and let us draw joy from having kept faith with each other. *Santé!*'

When he sat down, Connie leaned over and kissed him.

Bliss saw how happy she was and squeezed Aunt Jane's hand.

'Genius, Aunt Jane – sheer genius.'

Aunt Jane waved her glass.

'Elementary, my dear Watson.'

It had taken Aunt Jane about three minutes to snap Connie out of her blinding depression.

Bliss had tried pleading, logic, bullying, everything.

'He was a liar, Connie. He was deliberately spreading poison before he died. He admitted it.'

'But he's put the idea there.'

'I have to live with it too,' said Bliss.

Connie looked at him.

'All right,' said Bliss. 'I know – Sarah's dead and Ruth isn't. I always come up against this, don't I?'

'Stuff and nonsense, Connie,' said Aunt Jane, when she heard about it. 'Where's your intelligence? Answer me this. What is your blood group?'

' "O",' said Connie. 'Why?'

'And David's?'

' "O", as it happens. What is the point of this?'

Aunt Jane waved in annoyance.

'Just answer. Now tell me, what is Ruth's?'

' "O" as well. But that means nothing. "O" is the commonest group.'

'As I am well aware,' said Aunt Jane. 'It will therefore come as no surprise to you to know that both Hector and Joy are also group "O". Sarah's, however, was group "A". So if that awful man is telling the truth about Sarah, he is therefore group "A" himself, and cannot be Ruth's father. If he is telling a lie about Sarah, he is almost certainly telling a lie about Ruth.'

'It is still not conclusive.'

'I can make it conclusive, but only by referring to unpleasant details.'

Connie became watchful.

'Go on.'

'Hector had blood on his clothes. You know whose it was. On my recommendation, he had a sample of it analysed. Never mind how; he did. He has a most resourceful brother. Back came the answer – as I suggested – group "A".'

'Why didn't Hector tell me this before?'

'He didn't want to upset you by referring to that dreadful night. I'm afraid Hector's finer feelings often get in the way of his common sense.'

'I've noticed.'

'I, on the other hand,' said Aunt Jane, 'have no such scruples. Hector is not only bad at telling lies; he's even poor sometimes at telling the truth. You might not have believed him. You would have accused him of lying to save your peace of mind, and that could have led to no end of trouble.'

Connie hesitated.

'You see,' said Aunt Jane, 'I have no axe to grind. I'm not in love with you.'

'A brilliant performance,' said Bliss afterwards.

'You should have seen me on the yacht,' said Aunt Jane. 'Academy Award stuff. And both,' she added, 'in a very good cause.'

The band began to play in the station square. A light breeze flapped the bunting that hung from the half-finished hospital. Small children ran about clutching ice-cream cones.

'Can we go and have a closer look, Mummy?'

Connie stood up.

'Please excuse us, Joseph.'

'Can Mr. Bliss come too?'

Bliss looked at his watch.

'The train's due soon. Excuse us, Joseph. Tell them to

put another bottle of "St. Martin" on the ice. I'll be back soon.'

Half-way across the square he stopped, came back, and picked up a parcel.

'Nearly forgot. Better make that two bottles, by the way.'

Joseph grinned.

'With pleasure. It's all good for trade.'

'No doubts about Joseph?' said Connie, as they walked away again.

'Not now,' said Bliss. 'For the first time he's treating me like an equal. I feel that I've somehow graduated.'

They watched Ruth run on ahead.

'Doesn't it occur to you, though, that Joseph nursed that grievance against Max for all those years? Isn't it a bit like Sir Alec's long-term grudge against England?'

'Does it trouble you?'

'A bit.'

'You think we're only justified because we won?'

'Something like that.'

'I can't answer for us,' said Bliss. 'All I know is – I can live with myself. I'm not always the best of company, but I can just live with myself. So I don't intend to justify myself. But I can, as it happens, justify Joseph.'

'How?'

'I think there is a difference between vengeance and justice. That poor soldier they put down the well – that was vengeance. But it was also wartime; if they hadn't killed him that way, they'd have killed him another. Max was different.'

'Why? Because he gave the first order?'

Bliss looked thoughtfully at her.

'Of course, you don't know. I'd forgotten. Come with me.'

He grabbed her hand.

'Where are we going?'

'Not far. Back in a couple of minutes.'

Connie told Ruth and followed Bliss.

As they went along, Bliss explained.

'Max was not the officer who ordered the grenades. Joseph and his friend Jacques bumped him off soon after the incident of the well. Max was the replacement commander. He was here at the time of D-Day and the Liberation – what that band is banging on about right now.'

'What happened?'

'Shortly after D-Day, the Resistance naturally began operations on a huge scale – ambushes, blowing things up, everything you can think of. The Germans in many cases could only respond with reprisals – against the civilian population. Here.'

They stopped in front of a simple stone column on a concrete plinth. Small wreaths and posies decorated the foot of it.

'Read what it says,' said Bliss.

Connie bent down.

'*Etienne Gommard, 16   Fusillés par les allemands*
Pierre Gommard, 17   26 juin, 1944'

'That was not war. These were civilians, boys. This was murder. I think Joseph would argue then that Max's death was not long-warped vengeance but long-overdue justice.'

Ruth ran towards them when they returned.

'What's the time?'

Bliss looked at his watch.

'Getting on. Pop and look at the timetable, love, and check on the train, will you?'

Bliss held Connie's hand as they walked across the station square. The band was still blaring martial music. They stopped for a while to listen.

Bliss cleared his throat to speak. Connie forestalled him.

'Don't say it, Hector. Please.'

'Why not?'

'It's – it's just too soon. I can't explain. Just – don't spoil it.'

Bliss shrugged.

'Come on, then. Let's go and meet the train.'

Ruth came to meet them.

'Five minutes,' she said.

Connie watched Bliss pace up and down. Ruth went to walk with him.

Connie thought of something else Aunt Jane had said when Hector was not there.

'You must not let that terrible man poison your life. God knows, there has been enough evil in the past. Don't let it spill over into the future as well.'

'The knowledge was put there, Aunt Jane. I can't make it go away, even after what you said.'

'Of course not, you silly girl. But there is other knowledge there too, which you are ignoring.'

'Such as?'

'Such as – that Hector loves you, and is prepared to be a father to Ruth. If he can face it – after Sarah – I think you should be able to as well. He barely knows the child, and you brought her up. Have you no confidence in your own abilities?'

'Suppose it comes out later on?'

'Suppose, suppose! Who cares? Suppose she runs away with a transvestite Lebanese drug-pusher? Suppose she gets polio? Suppose she's bitten by a mad dog? You will still stand by her and do your best, won't you? Hector's prepared to. He stood beside Sarah.'

Connie looked glum.

'Mmm.'

Aunt Jane put a hand on her arm.

'Look, my dear, I may be an interfering old woman. I may or may not have told you a story to make you feel better about the future. Perhaps I was wrong – I don't know. Perhaps I should really have told you that there is no certainty about the future. Whether that man was telling lies or not doesn't matter. You want Ruth to grow up fine and strong and good, but you also want her to grow up with a mind of her own. If later on she chooses evil instead of good, that's just too bad. You will have done your best. You are no better and no worse off than any blood parent. However, don't worry; she won't. Just enjoy her.'

Connie went to where Bliss and Ruth were chatting together. She put a hand through his arm.

'Nervous?' she said.

'Yes,' said Bliss. 'Wouldn't you be?'

'I presume that's it,' said Connie, nodding at the parcel under his other arm.

'Yes. Nearly forgot. After all the trouble I had getting it here too.'

The train drew in at last. Handshakes and hugs and introductions.

'Thanks for everything, Parry.'

Paris flashed his broadest smile.

'Glad of the break. Pri would have come too, but there is a big case on. Joan hadn't got the heart to come swanning down here while he's sweating in court. Thelma's got the kids. I tell you, both the girls are dying to meet Connie.'

He stood back. Bliss fixed his full attention on the small figure behind him.

'Hallo, Alan. I expect they've explained about me. I've – er – I've got something for you. From Aline.'

THE END